The Lady and the Thief

THE LADY AND THE THIEF

The Duke's Men Romance

Kate Moore

The Lady and the Thief
Copyright© 2024 Kate Moore
Tule Publishing First Printing, June 2024

The Tule Publishing, Inc.

ALL RIGHTS RESERVED

First Publication by Tule Publishing 2024

Cover design by Erin Dameron-Hill

No part of this book may be used or reproduced in any manner whatsoever without written permission except in the case of brief quotations embodied in critical articles and reviews.

This is a work of fiction. Names, characters, places, and incidents are products of the author's imagination or are used fictitiously. Any resemblance to actual events, locales, organizations, or persons, living or dead, is entirely coincidental.

AI was not used to create any part of this book and no part of this book may be used for generative training.

ISBN: 978-1-962707-14-5

Dedication

To my favorite story lovers—Sebastian, Elizabeth, and Andrew

"If the sky falls, we shall all catch larks."

PROLOGUE

From the archives of London's newspapers, an account of the destruction of the Houses of Parliament by fire on October 16, 1834.

> We mentioned in our last the alarming fire which between the hours of six and seven on Thursday evening, burst out from one of the apartments connected with the House of Lords, and spreading with fearful rapidity, soon consumed the houses both of lords and commons....
>
> In future tables of chronological events, the terrible destruction occasioned by the fire which broke out last evening, will stand out in startling effect... The interior of the House of Lords was filled with one vast flame, casting its lurid glare far over the horizon—lighting up the broken clouds above, which were driven on before a strong westerly gale—spreading over the silent Thames a vast sheet of crimson, that seemed to smother the feeble rays of the rising moon—bringing out the stately and majestic towers of the abbey in strong relief against the deep blue western sky... The gable end of the former, the last relic of the chapel of St. Stephen, with its beautiful Gothic window, stood up between us and the glowing furnace of fire in strong and beautiful outline. Whilst at intervals, as the smoke varied in its motion, other por-

tions of Gothic architecture, oriel windows, turrets, and towers, broke on the view; all within them was feeding the devouring element.

By half-past seven o'clock the engines were brought to play upon the building both from the river and the land side, but the flames had by this time acquired such a predominance, that the quantity of water thrown upon them produced no visible effect, and in less than an hour from the time at which the flames first appeared the entire roof of the House of Lords had fallen in.

The firemen now abandoned all hopes of saving any part of this portion of the building, and their attention and efforts were from this time wholly directed towards the House of Commons, and to the preservation of that venerable structure, Westminster Hall. It was unfortunate that the tide was out, and the water in the river very low. A floating engine from Woolwich played from the river with much effect, but arrived late in the night.

The pickpockets were busy; but the mighty multitude behaved well, and even decorously.

Westminster Hall is saved.

CHAPTER ONE

London, April 1835

LARK DUCKED INTO a shadowy by-street off the Strand. A narrow slit of fading blue to the west where the street rejoined the main thoroughfare told him the shops would not close for an hour or more. He fingered the ring in his pocket. He had expected the ring to trigger a memory of his mother, but the experiment failed. Now, as he had promised, he was to meet his former partner, Rook, at the meeting place Rook chose.

Babylon Street, as infamous for the display of erotic prints in its shop windows as for the grime on its cobbles, was a street where the clumsiest of pickpockets could do a prig. Even coppers stopped to stare at print shop windows, the target of all the proper souls of London's Anti-Vice Society. As Lark slipped into a doorway to wait for Rook, his gaze caught on a chunk of clear ethereal-blue sky, where no sky should be, on the dirty stones in front of Number 36.

For a moment, it seemed to his disoriented senses as if London's unusual spell of dry weather had cracked the sky like an old plaster ceiling, and a piece of it had fallen into the street. He grabbed the door frame where he stood, anchoring himself against a sudden tide of other memories, not the one he sought. He glanced up at the jagged line of gables and chimney pots, half-expecting to see a gaping black hole in the sky above them. The days when he and Rook and all of the lost boys, Robin, Finch, Raven, Swallow, and Jay, had roamed the rooftops of London under the sky with Boy, their leader, were long gone. Lark and Rook had stayed firmly on the ground for years, never speaking of old days or old friends. Even now when Lark had ended their partnership, Rook kept their original suite of rooms, and the charwoman Lark had hired to clean for them. For Rook, London offered an endless supply of gulls, unwary or distracted enough to give up the contents of their pockets. But Lark had investments now and money in Hammersley's Bank, and a new set of rooms not far from Regent's Park.

Memory was a teasing jade. When Lark worked to summon her and question her about the secret of his birth, she fled. Now she came on strong. Lark shook off the unwanted recollections of his old companions. Ten years had passed since he'd left them behind. What appeared to be a piece of sky was merely a woman in a fashionable blue dress. In Babylon Street that dress made her a mark.

The mark stretched out one feminine gloved hand over the display of dusty books in front of Number 36. A bag in rich blue velvet dangled from her wrist on thin gold cords. From the tautness of the cords, Lark put the bag's weight at two pounds. The lady had come prepared to shop, and the titles on the sagging shelf above the pavement appeared to engross her. Lark should warn her that she was tempting fate. Rook made a pass behind her, close enough to brush against her skirts. She never broke her trance-like concentration. Rook would pass again. He glanced at Lark for a signal, which Lark refused to give. He was there to persuade Rook to quit the game and take up some legitimate enterprise.

Lark looked up and down the street, assessing the scene. Recent plans to tear the street down had come to nothing. From the north end a one-horse cab approached, forcing pedestrians to keep to the pavement under the gabled projections of the old houses. Today the usual mix of London's citizens passed by, tradesmen and gentlemen, ladies and drabs. People who knew the neighborhood used the by-street to go about their business more quickly than the crowded Strand permitted. Other persons, the ones Rook watched for, came into the street drawn by its reputation for radical politics and erotic prints. The mark remained absorbed in her book. No doubt Rook pegged her as an easy prig.

Lark had his doubts. In the past, his job had been to read the mark and signal a yes or no to Rook. He gave the woman a more thorough scrutiny. The vivid freshness of her appearance in the grimy street was a mystery. She was more fit for Regent Street than for her sordid surroundings. Her gown of figured blue silk had the nipped waist and full skirts of the current fashion. A short dove-colored cape covered her from shoulder to waist. A plain close-fitting bonnet concealed her face, and made it impossible to guess her age. His mind rapidly calculated the sums she must have paid for fabric and dressmaker, shoes, and petticoats. Unlike the other women in the street, she appeared to be alone. He didn't like it. Going unaccompanied to one of London's most infamous streets spoke of bold independence.

A sign above Number 36 read SCHOOL BOOKS. Lark

wondered whether the lady's eyes had widened as she read the actual titles of the volumes on that hanging shelf. He knew them well. *The Adventures* of *Lady Lovesport* and *The Lustful Turk* were the tamest titles of the lot. She tipped a book free of its neighbors and held it open in one palm. With the movement of her arm, the heavy purse slid into the crook of her elbow. That bag bothered Lark. The bend in her arm would make Rook's job harder, but the temptation was great, especially as the lady's concentration on her book was deep. With her free hand she turned the pages.

Lark glanced up and down the street again. Nothing looked amiss. He did not see any other fellows on the game. A girl passed with a tray of flowers on her head, and a barefoot boy teased a dog with a stick. The blue of the mark's dress and the memories she stirred were reason enough to warn Rook off. Lark caught Rook's eye and shook his head.

But Rook went into his act anyway. Rook saw only a pigeon, and pigeons were made to be plucked. Coming along the pavement from the north, he pulled a bottle from his patched greasy coat, took a swig, and lurched forward. His boots, caked in river muck gave off a noxious stench that made people swerve into the street to avoid him. This time when he reached the mark, he slammed into her with his left shoulder, spinning her round. She dropped the book with a startled cry, stumbling back against the hanging shelves and flinging out a hand to catch hold of something. The purse slid down to her wrist. Rook snagged it and staggered on, bent low to the ground, dropping his bottle.

The dropped bottle was Lark's old cue to enter the scene.

He stepped out of the doorway and strode forward. "Miss, may I help? You look ..." His voice faltered as he caught sight of her face. Nothing had prepared him for the effect of large, startled dark eyes above cheeks of pearl and roses.

Her dark glance flicked his way and swung back to Rook's retreating figure. Her expression changed. She righted herself and reached under her short cape.

"Miss?" Lark needed to draw her attention to him. "Has something overset you?"

"No, thank you, I've got this." From under her cape, she drew out a small pistol and pointed it toward Rook. Lark stared at the short-barreled gun, his thoughts scattering like dry leaves in a breeze. It was a Toby, a muff pistol with silver and gold chasings, expensive like everything about the mark. He'd seen such a gun in a shop on Snow Hill, but never in a lady's hand.

"Stop, thief!" She leveled the barrel at Rook with a steady hand. "I'll shoot," she cried, cocking the firing pin with her thumb.

Lark stepped into her line of sight as the approaching cab pulled up beside him. The rumble of iron wheels on cobbles filled his ears. Her finger squeezed the trigger. A hot searing pain bloomed on his right side, and he pressed a gloved hand to his ribs. He had been right to distrust the lay. The lady was not the mark she appeared to be.

"Oh dear." The woman, not much more than a girl really, lowered the gun. Lark doubted that she was a day over twenty. Her eyes were the deep brown of Turkish coffee, he thought irrelevantly. "How bad is it?" she asked. "Did the bullet lodge? Are you bleeding much?"

"Hard to tell," he said. It cost him a sharp twinge to

speak. "What were you thinking?"

"I might ask you the same. I meant to shoot the thief, not you." She tucked the pistol away under her cape, and stepped forward. "Why did you come between us?"

"To be of assistance. I could have ..." He couldn't feel blood, just the burning sensation in his side, the sting of burned powder in his nose, and an unaccountable wobbliness in his legs.

"Chased him? I doubt it. I'm sure he's disappeared across the Strand by now." Her eyes had a look of disappointment. Something she wanted had eluded her.

A sudden spurt of anger heated him. He suspected that the heavy purse had been a decoy, and he didn't know whether he was angrier at her or at Rook. "Are you mad?" he demanded. "What lady fires a pistol in a public street? Even the Peelers don't shoot a man."

She shot him a glare. "I was assured the police never ventured into this neighborhood."

"One block from the Strand?"

She shrugged. "I came prepared. Never mind. Let me see what's happened to you." She stepped right up to him and gently lifted his hand away from his side. He caught the fragrance of her, something fresh and floral.

"You are bleeding," she said. Her eyes were earnest now, full of concern.

Lark suddenly knew what verse-writing saps meant about drowning in a pair of eyes.

"I know someone who can help."

"A good tailor, I hope. You've likely ruined my favorite coat."

"A surgeon. Let me take you to him. That's my cab, you

see."

He had the oddest feeling that he had been played, that she had seen Rook coming and laid a trap. He couldn't think clearly, and he had no way to reach Rook. He did want a surgeon, and no questions asked. The only sawbones in this neighborhood had shaking hands and wiped them on his filthy linen. Lark should play out the scene. He couldn't help Rook now. Rook would wonder where he'd got to, but he'd explain later. "Don't you want your book?"

"*The Spanish Brothers?*" She bent down, scooped it from the pavement, and piled it back on the shelf. "No. I don't need it anymore. Will you tell me your name?"

"Lark...in," he said. "Edward Larkin." It was the name he planned to use in his new life, if his old life didn't do him in first.

She nodded. "Vivian Bradish."

IN THE CAB, Viv subdued her billowing skirts and stripped off her gloves. She brushed aside the edges of her cape, and twisted to see her companion, a bit startled at his nearness on the narrow seat, so close the scent of his shaving soap reached her, and his coat's unmistakable tang of London smoke. She was grateful that he'd tipped his head back against the squabs and closed his eyes. His fine, full mouth was pinched. With his eyes closed, he looked young, almost boyish. She doubted he was thirty.

"We'll be there in no time," she told him. "May I see the wound?"

"Are you a doctor?" he snapped.

"I've done my share of nursing." She supposed he was justified in sounding cross, as the cab jolted over the cobbles. Any distraction she could offer might help. "Do you have a clean handkerchief?"

"In my pocket." He didn't move, and his arrogant profile gave no indication which pocket he meant. Now that she could observe him more carefully, she noted the richness of his brown tweed coat with its velvet collar. His black silk tie was perfectly tied and held in place by a single gold stickpin. His waistcoat was an old gold silk jacquard, and his linen was dazzling. With one hand he clung to his hat, with his other hand he pressed his side where her bullet had grazed him. She hoped it was no more than a small groove in his flesh, but the ball might have hit a rib. Her Toby pistol was a lady's gun, meant to dissuade would-be robbers, but at a distance of mere yards, it packed a punch.

If he did not have the sense to apply a handkerchief to his wound, she would have to do it. She dipped her hand into the outer pocket of his coat. Her fingers closed not around linen, but around a ring. She pulled it out and held it in her palm. The stone was a square-cut garnet, framed by two rows of tiny pearls, set in a gold band. It was a lady's ring, and for a minute she could not imagine what it was doing there.

She became conscious of his gaze on her and lifted her chin. His deep-set eyes were startlingly blue.

"You've never seen a ring before?" he asked.

"I beg your pardon," she said. "Were you about to propose marriage?"

He laughed and immediately groaned. "Do ladies always think of marriage when they see a ring?"

Up behind them on his perch, the driver turned the cab west into the traffic of the Strand. Viv dropped her gaze. She wasn't going to admit past folly. Two years had passed since she'd been a green girl in a Bath ballroom, dazzled by a gentleman's attentions. "I only meant that if there is a lady waiting for your addresses, we should get a message to her so that she doesn't worry."

"You think I was about to propose in a shabby street full of dirty books?"

"Oh." She looked up again. She had stung him somehow. There was a curl to his lips and a tone of offended pride in his voice. She stuffed the ring back in his pocket and stared out over the horse's head. He meant to be a disagreeable patient. She resolved to let him.

The cab rattled along, bumping her leg against his, and jostling them shoulder to shoulder, every move stirring awareness of his lean, taut body. She balled her hands into fists in her lap. He didn't want her help.

"I have the ring because the lady ... ended our betrothal." He rushed the words a little, offering more than she'd asked. He leaned his head against the squabs again just as the cab stopped in the bottleneck of the Temple Bar. Over the centuries the monumental white stone structure with its single narrow arch for horse-drawn vehicles had become a traffic stopper. There was talk of tearing it down. Around them, drivers of every sort cursed each other to no avail.

"We're not moving, so you'd better let me see to that wound."

She didn't wait for a reply, but opened the front of his coat. A bit of fine lawn cloth peeked from an inside pocket. She plucked it out and laid it in her lap. He plainly had a taste for expensive things. Gently she lifted his hand from his side, uncovering a singed black hole in his waistcoat. Around it, blood had stained the silk in streaks, like storm-reddened clouds at dawn.

"Why were you there?" she asked him. "It was oddly fortuitous, was it not?"

"If you call getting shot fortuitous."

She ignored the sarcasm, unhooked the fob of his watch, and went to work on the buttons of his waistcoat until she could fold it open. The same black mark marred his shirt, and blood had plastered the sheer linen to his skin in a fist-sized blotch. The wound would need to be cleaned and dusted with basilicum powder. With her fingertips she peeled away the stained patch of shirt. A slight tremor shook him, and he inhaled sharply.

"What I can't work out is why you stepped in the way?"

"I couldn't let you shoot some poor wretch in the back."

"I aimed only to wound." She tugged at his shirt to free it from his trousers. His body arched briefly and froze. She halted.

"And you never miss? Lots of practice shooting fellows?" He spoke through gritted teeth.

"What makes you think the man was a poor wretch? Did you see him?"

"Who else would set upon a lady in broad daylight in a London street?"

"I expected the low ruffian. He was just what I imagined

a pickpocket would be. Except for the stink." She managed to free the long tail of his shirt.

"You imagined a ruffian stinking of beer and gin?"

"Oh, that would be a cliché. This fellow reeked of something much worse. But you ... you just appeared, you know, completely out of character with the place." Viv gathered the ends of his shirt in her hands. She had been falling backward, reaching for something to catch hold of when she heard him speak in a voice fit for a Mayfair drawing room. It had turned her attention from the fleeing purse snatcher.

"I was on my way to Lincoln's Inn on business. You're the one who was out of place, staring at those titles. Don't you have any female ..."

The cab lurched into motion. Viv pressed the folded handkerchief against his side. Her fingers brushed his skin, sticky with blood and pebbled with a chill. He sucked a breath through his teeth. She placed his hand back over the wound to hold the handkerchief and tied the ends of his shirt in a knot. He might look a little odd, but her arrangements would hold the wound until they arrived at Henrietta Street.

"*Decency?* Is that the word you're looking for? I have no use for it." She settled back in her seat. "I suppose you are one of those men who think women must be sheltered and coddled their whole lives as if we had no right to walk the streets?"

"You don't mean that you were *walking the streets*," he said. "And, if you're so keen on an unaccompanied stroll, there are a thousand other streets to choose."

"Why should women not freely go where men freely go?"

"Because they'll be treated as doxies ... or pigeons."

"Wait. You think we women are helpless."

"I don't think it. I saw it. You were falling backward, and a bundle of rags, and probably lice, was running away with what? Your purse?"

"It doesn't matter." Things hadn't gone exactly as she'd planned, but there was no need to tell him the true contents of that purse. He was already annoyed by her shooting him.

"I think it does. You looked quite disappointed to lose that purse."

Somehow, he'd got the upper hand in the argument again. "Fine, if you must know, I was waiting for a story to happen. I collect them. A different story for each street. That's what London is—a book of a thousand stories. Your pickpocket was my story. He'd already passed me once."

"You were trying to lure the pickpocket to you?" He sounded incredulous. "You wanted him to snatch your purse? Are you cork-brained?"

"I did not want him to take my purse. Well, maybe I did, but only because I wanted to talk to him. A pickpocket must know London, and he must be a keen observer of his fellow man, don't you think?"

"The way a stray dog is a keen observer of crumbs. A pickpocket sees his fellow men, as you put it, as gulls."

"You are too harsh. I'm curious. I want to know London as it really is not merely its polite spaces."

"Babylon Street is definitely not a polite space for a woman to be in."

She twisted to confront him directly, and poked him in the chest. He pressed back against the side of the cab. "Well, is it any better a space for a man? Why didn't the pickpocket target you? You are a no less a prize, a fine gentleman with a watch."

"I was not standing idle with my head in a book."

"Hah," she said. "Next I suppose you'll accuse women of being overcome by fiction."

The cab halted in front of the house on Henrietta Street, and Viv reached for her purse, which wasn't there. She clasped her hands in her lap. Again, her deception came back to bite her. Shooting Mr. Larkin over the few pebbles she'd weighted her purse with to lure the pickpocket was most inconvenient. She could hardly pull up her skirts to reach her concealed stash. She looked up at the house. Its neat stone exterior gave no indication of who might be standing ready to answer the door. She stiffened her spine.

"Let me guess," he said, leaning to speak in her ear. "You just realized that it might be awkward to bring a bleeding stranger into your family's drawing room."

"Not at all." She hopped down from the cab and turned to grin up at him. "But you'll have to pay the driver, as my purse was pinched."

CHAPTER TWO

THE MOMENT HE entered the house, Lark noted an unsettled feeling in the air. Hurried footsteps and anxious voices rustled around them. He tried to focus on the layout of the rooms. The street door opened into a hall with creamy walls and a floor of black-and-white tiles as if London had neither mud nor muck. To his right, he could see the base of a fine staircase. He had a momentary sense, powerful in its immediacy, of being in such an entry before.

He shook it off. He had to keep his wits about him. It was only that the design of the house was a common one, similar to the design of Dav's mother's house on Hill Street where their gang had first lived when they left the rooftops behind. Lark had to remember that Dav, their boy leader, was no more. Dav's grandfather, the old duke was dead, and Dav was now the Duke of Wenlocke, not a street urchin. The grinder Dav had hired to teach the gang to read, the girl who'd stolen Dav from them, she would be his duchess. Lark could slip up here if he let memories of his old life take over. He shook off the swarm of them and fixed his gaze on a straight-legged table with a silver tray full of cards. He had to act as if he were the man he meant to be, a gentleman who left his calling card in silver trays every day.

He let a staring footman take his hat and gloves, although it was against his nature to give any possession of his into another man's hands. Moments earlier, in the cab, Vivian Bradish had reached into his pockets, held his ring and his handkerchief, and undone his waistcoat buttons. Her touch was dangerous. It made him momentarily weak as if he had been fitted with leg irons. He gritted his teeth against the weakness now. If he had to bolt, he could run for it, abandon the hat and gloves. He would go straight through the house. He didn't know the neighborhood, but he knew there would be a door at the back of the hall to a patch of garden with a path through it to a mew. He reined in the direction of his thoughts. That was old thinking from his days on the game with Rook. He was a gentleman now.

He straightened his shoulders with only a twinge in his side. He'd come to turn a minor catastrophe to his advantage. An hour in Vivian Bradish's company had brought him to the edge of posh London. She had gone looking for her thousand stories. He would follow her to find one story, his own. First, he'd get her sawbones to stitch him up. Presumably a man who tended to patients in this neighborhood was neither filthy, nor a drunk. Lark steadied himself. His old days and old ways were over. The place wasn't the Bow Street magistrate's hall, and Lark wasn't facing a lagging, just a female who showed no disposition to involve the authorities. When his head cleared, he would have to think about why. He suspected that heavy purse of hers was the reason.

Miss Bradish handed her cape, hat, and gloves to a fluttering maid, who seemed to be her ally.

"'urry, miss, they'll be 'ere soon," the girl said.

"Is Lady M very bad?"

"In a taking. Says 'er 'eart is racing like a Derby 'orse."

"Oh dear, I must go to her." Viv turned to Lark, looking directly at him and speaking.

He saw her lips move. His brain said she was offering an explanation, but he missed half the words. He was seeing her again, not in the dingy street, but in her proper surroundings. The smooth, close-fitting bodice of the blue silk gown defined her breasts and ribs and narrow waist above the flaring skirts. A mad thought occurred to him that his hands could span that waist.

He wrenched his gaze away.

"Thomas has gone for Doctor Newberry, Mr. Larkin. This is Jenny. She will bring you to the dining room. You must drink a cup of tea, I think, while you wait for the doctor." She hurried off in a whirl of skirts.

"Mr. Larkin, sir, follow me," Jenny said. She led him from the foyer into a hall and opened the door into a dimly lit, pale blue room. A dining table occupied the center. A crystal chandelier hung overhead. Silver candelabra gleamed on polished mahogany. The last of the day's light faded outside the curtained windows. He caught a glimpse of himself in the mirror above the hearth, surprised at his gentlemanly appearance.

"Who is Newberry?"

"My lady's doctor, sir. Lady Melforth's a poor invalid these days, and these cousins of 'ers fret 'er dreadfully."

"She's not Miss Bradish's mother?"

"Not at all, sir. Lady Melforth is a very great lady. They call 'er *the Traveling Viscountess* on account of her guidebooks. Miss Bradish is 'er companion and helper."

He turned from the mirror. He liked that. Vivian Bradish was a hired companion, not a titled miss. The richness of her garments was borrowed finery. She might have a cushy situation with a wealthy employer, but Lady Melforth probably knew nothing of Miss Bradish's reckless forays into London's streets. Maybe Lark had it wrong about that purse. It was simply the threat to her employment situation that explained the momentary desperation in her eyes. She depended on her situation and did not want the folly of trying to make the acquaintance of a pickpocket exposed to her employer. Lark thought he could regain the upper hand in their exchanges.

Jenny dropped him a curtsy and bustled off with a promise to bring him some refreshment. The door behind her remained slightly ajar. Lark positioned himself to bolt if necessary. He could hear but not see the comings and goings in the hall. He gathered that the expected cousins were the source of the unease. His wound burned, and his mouth felt dry. The promised tea might help. A clock chimed the hour, and he thought of Rook. Rook would return to their old digs, shed his reeking disguise, hide the captured purse, and go in search of food. He was always hungry, a leftover from their boyhood. Once he ate, though, he'd start to wonder where Lark was.

The front knocker sounded, and a heavier, more stately tread crossed the hall. The door opened, and a deep, male voice greeted the newcomers with cool politeness. Lark guessed the plummy voice belonged to a butler. There were more footsteps, maybe those of a footman, and the rustle of coats being shed."

"Thank you, Haxton. How is our dear cousin today?" asked a female voice.

"As well as can be expected, ma'am. You know she never complains when Miss Bradish is with her."

"Of course."

"I'll let her know you've arrived." The stately footsteps trailed off. Lark judged that the butler had headed for the stairs. His words suggested that Miss Bradish had another ally besides the maid Jenny. For a moment there was silence in the hall, then the female voice came again.

"Haxton presumes, Arthur, I know he does. He will not be butler here, when we inherit this house."

"You must be patient, my dear Mrs. Stryde," answered a smooth male voice.

"How can I be, Mr. Stryde? Your cousin may die any day. She doesn't fool me with that foot of hers. She's ill. And when she goes, that clever, artful girl will be at hand to take advantage!"

"We haven't seen the will," said the reasonable voice.

"But we cannot afford to discover at the reading, Mr. Stryde, that your cousin Aurora has written out our dear boy, or reduced his rightful inheritance, in favor of a chit who has used her wiles to ingratiate herself into this household. We agreed that she must go."

"Yes, but how to dislodge her from her position, that's the question."

"We must discredit her."

"How do you propose to do that?"

"*Vice*, Mr. Stryde. We must discover the hidden vice in

her. She has low connections, I'm sure of it. The servants say she goes out alone."

Footsteps returned, and Lark heard the butler Haxton invite the visitors up. So, Miss Bradish had enemies among her employer's relations. Her trip to Babylon Street seemed doubly foolhardy in light of the Strydes' undeclared campaign to have her sacked.

The hall grew quiet except for the clock. After an interval, another knock sounded at the front door, and someone was admitted.

"Doctor!" There was surprise in the butler's voice. "I was unaware that my lady sent for you."

"She didn't. Apparently, you've got some fellow on the premises with a gunshot wound."

"I beg your pardon."

"Don't worry, Haxton. I'll find him."

Lark moved away from the dining room door an instant before it opened. The man who entered was like no sawbones Lark knew, young and smooth-cheeked, with a head of thick brown curls over a wide brow and a pair of sharp hazel eyes. The doctor appeared equally surprised to discover Lark as his patient.

"Hah," the man said. He set a leather bag on the dining table. "I suppose you tried to make violent love to our Viv and she was having none of it."

Lark did not miss the man's casual proprietary claim to Miss Bradish. "Actually, I stepped between her, and her intended victim, a common pickpocket." He thought he'd managed that smoothly enough in the voice he'd first learned to use as a boy at Dav's mother's house.

"Best let me see then." The doctor snapped into a professional manner, lighting the candles on the table and pulling from his bag a leather strap with a single magnifying lens suspended from it. This he placed around his brow, positioned so that he could look through the glass. He directed Lark to stand within the candles' light and lift his shirt to reveal the wound.

For a few moments the doctor peered at it through his glass. "Not many gunshot wounds in this neighborhood," he said.

Lark recognized the probe. The man was wondering where Lark had encountered Miss Bradish. "How does it look?"

The doctor straightened and lifted the examining lens away from his eye. "Like raw meat in a Smithfield butcher's stall. It's about two inches long. The skin at the edges is flayed and powder-singed. The bullet isn't in you, apparently, and no ribs show. You're lucky."

"Can you treat it?"

"Handily, but let's move to where I can have more light. I need you lying down. I'll clean it, cut away the powder, and stitch you up. Infection's the biggest risk. Wait here. Jenny will fetch you when I'm ready." The doctor opened the door and stepped back into the hall.

Lark eased his shirt down over the wound. The doctor considered him a rival, which meant Lark had been accepted as a gentleman. Rook would laugh when Lark told the tale later. Lark should have no objection to the doctor's proprietary claim to Miss Bradish. Lark knew the rules. In the country, one didn't fish in another man's stream. In town, one didn't run a lay on another man's street. This was the doctor's street. It was plain that as Lady Melforth's physician, Newberry knew both the house and its inhabitants well. But Lark found that he disliked the clean, young sawbones, and particularly disliked the man's use of the phrase—*Our Viv.*

Jenny showed up with the tea, and he drank it down. Then a footman came and led him to a much larger ground floor apartment with tall windows overlooking the street. In a pinch, he supposed he could escape through a window if he needed to, especially if the matter of paying the doctor's fee should prove awkward. He had no idea how such fees were handled by a doctor like Newberry. At the dispensary where Lark had taken Rook to treat a cough one winter, a patient paid his sixpence for two minutes of treatment and a preparation of rhubarb powder.

The room was a far cry from any place Lark had met a doctor before. Its walls were a rich dark green, divided by panels of red and gold fabric up to the tall ceiling. There was a white stone hearth in which a fire burned with little regard for the price of coal. In the center of the room, a sheet had been draped over a bench. Next to it stood a low table with the doctor's instruments, a basin and ewer, and another branch of candles. When the doctor returned, Lark submitted to orders, lying on his side and letting the doctor position his limbs and his garments, exposing the wound and surrounding it with a layer of towels. Once again, Newberry fixed the leather strap and viewing lens around his head.

"This won't take long, but it will sting. Do you require some laudanum?"

"No." Lark gritted his teeth.

"Suit yourself. Try to relax your limbs if you can."

Lark doubted that was possible. A sharp scent hit his nostrils. He felt the press of a warm wet cloth against the wound. Then the stinging started, and the doctor began to chat.

"You know you're likely to end up in one of her tales."

"Her tales?" Lark remembered. She'd said something about every street having a story, but he couldn't hold onto the thought while something with sharp teeth nibbled at his side.

"The stories she tells Lady Melforth to amuse her. They're scribblers, the pair of them."

"Oh." Lark sucked in a breath and held it.

"She'll give you a fictional name. You'll be a Mr. Wickersham or a Mr. Windle."

Newberry was stitching him up and dismissing him at the same time, telling Lark that he was an episode in the girl's life, an anecdote told to amuse her employer and then forgotten. It shouldn't matter. It shouldn't bother him, but it did, more than the probing and scraping at his side. It was the thing he'd been fighting his whole life, the opinion of the world that he, Lark, was nobody, a man without a family or a proper name, a face in the crowd.

"You'll do," the doctor said. He pulled the towels away, and turned to the basin. "Too bad about that waistcoat, though."

Lark righted himself. He couldn't see it, but he felt the plaster bandage stuck to his side. He stood cautiously and began to put his clothes to rights, thinking about the fee. "Thank you."

"Don't mention it. Anything to help Viv out of a scrape." The doctor washed his hands and wrapped his implements in one of the towels. "Get your valet to change the dressing tomorrow. Keep the thing clean. In about a fortnight, the sutures will dissolve. They'll itch some. Here's the bullet, by the way. It lodged in your coat." The doctor held the spent ball between his thumb and forefinger.

Lark extended a hand, and the doctor dropped the bullet into his palm.

CHAPTER THREE

THE MINUTE DOCTOR Newberry entered the upper drawing room, Viv relaxed the rigid smile she had in place for the Strydes. Their daily visit was most ill-timed today. Viv sat within reach of Lady Melforth's papers and spectacles while from across the drawing room Mrs. Stryde gave one of her scolds.

"Dear Aurora, you will never really recover health without the strictest regimen of abstinence from all stimulants, and avoidance of rich foods."

At any moment Aurora was likely to snap and send her visitors downstairs.

The doctor flashed Viv a grin that told her he was on her side. He knew the danger she faced. As active members of the London Anti-Vice Society, the Strydes must not discover Mr. Larkin below. They would use his presence as a reason to discharge Viv, and just now when Lady Melforth was at such a low ebb, she might not resist her cousins' tactics. Viv could be sacked before she and Lady Melforth finished their London guidebook for women.

Newberry crossed the room, going straight to Lady Melforth, inquiring in his warm, direct way about her symptoms.

"Oh, Doctor," she said. "I've had such flutterings and

tremblings today." Lady Melforth lay swathed in a lace wrapper against the cushions of a pale Aubusson sofa, her injured foot elevated on a peach velvet ottoman. Partly, the lacy wrapper and querulous complaints were an act Lady Melforth put on for the cousins, but Viv knew her employer was genuinely ill. For weeks now, maybe longer, Viv had been handling all of the lady's correspondence and all of the manuscript pages of the guide and making weekly visits to Dodsley, their publisher.

"We'll put you to rights, ma'am, Miss Bradish, Jenny, and I. Tell me what you've taken today for your distress." The doctor pulled up a chair beside Lady Melforth, and taking her hand, felt for her pulse. After a silent moment, he said, "Let me send Viv downstairs to fix a soothing draft for you." He winked at Viv.

She grinned back at him and hurried from the room. Newberry might enjoy the awkwardness of Viv's situation, but he was willing to help. She could count on him to support Lady Melforth for a few minutes while Viv made sure Mr. Larkin was on his way.

Viv wished the Strydes were not so dogged in their attentions to her employer. Their daily visits appeared as concern for Lady Melforth's health, but Viv was certain it was the lady's fortune that mattered most to her persistent visitors. Viv did not know the details of her ladyship's will, but Mr. Stryde, as Lady Melforth's nearest male relative, would inherit the bulk of her estate. Each of the Stryde's visits caused Lady Melforth to fret a good deal about being fair to people she didn't much like. *Why must they be so disagreeable?* she would ask. The fretting made Lady Melforth uncomfortable at night, unable to sleep, her heart racing.

At the base of the stairs, Viv met her ladyship's youngest footman, Thomas. She sent him to Mrs. Brandle the cook with instructions to prepare the doctor's usual soothing draft. Then she squared her shoulders, and turned to the dining room. A word from Haxton stopped her.

"I believe the visitor is in the drawing room, miss."

Viv corrected course. "He is still here then?"

Haxton nodded. "Jenny has removed all signs of the doctor's treatment from the drawing room."

An odd little bud of relief sprouted in Viv. She could count on Haxton and Jenny. Of course, her relief had nothing to do with seeing Mr. Larkin once more. She opened the door to the green drawing room and found him standing at the window looking down into the darkening street, his profile sharp-edged against the blackness outside. His presence added something sensual to the room with its straight perpendicular lines. It was a momentary impression. As he turned her way, she saw that he was his orderly self again, neck cloth, waistcoat, and coat in place so that no one would suspect him of having sustained a wound.

"You've been tended to, I see," she said.

"I have." He watched her cross the room. "Thanks to your Doctor Newberry."

"The bullet did not lodge in your side?"

He held out his hand, and uncurled his fingers, revealing the spent ball in his palm. "It caught in my coat."

"Oh." It was no bigger than her thumbnail, so small a thing out of which to make a connection. It occurred to her that he would have expenses. "I must apologize to you again for any ... inconvenience I've caused. You will let me know your tailor's charges."

She would dip into the monthly sum she sent her sisters if his tailor charged heavily for the damaged clothes. Each sister was to help the next to a new beginning in London. Pippa, at fifteen, was already dreaming of the pleasure gardens and balloon ascensions she would see when her turn came.

Mr. Larkin looked at the ball in his hand, not at her. "Your doctor friend told me I might treat this as a souvenir." The word *souvenir* felt like a dismissal, as if he were already relegating her to the past, to his store of memories. And he seemed to have a wrong idea of her relationship with Newberry.

"Will you make a story of me?" he asked abruptly.

"A story?" It was true, but he had that wrong, too. Surely, there was something more to their meeting, some fated element that made it inevitable and necessary to each of them.

"The doctor said it's what you do, tell stories to amuse your employer." His gaze rose to challenge her, the blue intense and bitter. "Every street has a story, you said. So, am I to be the poor sap you shot in the street?"

"Yes, I might tell Lady Melforth a story about meeting you, but no, you will not be a poor sap, as you put it. You'll be another man who thinks women cannot fend for themselves in our great city, a man who thinks we ought to stick to safe pathways."

He moved then, coming toward her, stopping just short of the wide circle of her skirts. "What do you know of this city? You have money in your purse."

She gave a short laugh, conscious of the awkward truth that her purse had been full of pebbles. "Had," she recovered. "What's money got to do with it?"

"Without it, without Lady Melforth, you'd find London a far different city. You'd know it better."

"What?" He trivialized her stories. He doubted her ability to know the city.

"Your enemies would use your trip to Babylon Street against you."

"You speak... plainly. I do not have enemies."

His gaze didn't waver. "You do. I heard them in the hall. Your employer's cousins. Who are they?"

"Oh, the Strydes. They're members of the Anti-Vice Society." She wondered how he'd learned of their enmity in the hour he'd been in Lady Melforth's house.

"They'd like to see you lose your position."

"They said as much? You heard them?" She had suspected them of scheming against her for some time.

He nodded. "They did."

"Well, you needn't be concerned for my position. I'll not be driven away by them."

"You could shoot them."

"Don't be daft. I only—"

"Shoot strangers?"

"I will simply stay until Lady Melforth no longer needs me."

"And then?"

She tried to penetrate his gaze. The whole conversation was going wrong. She didn't understand why he was challenging her, trying to throw her off-balance. She folded her hands together. "I'm not without resources. I will find another employer. Besides when our book is ..."

"Is that what you want? To be employed, at the beck and call of some grand lady? I thought you wanted to be ... an independent woman."

"I beg your pardon. We...you and I are hardly acquainted. You know nothing about me."

At the sound of voices on the stairs, among them Haxton's, indignant and affronted, she froze. Mr. Larkin apparently caught the sound and shot her a questioning gaze.

"The Strydes. Oh no! They're coming. They mustn't find you here." She glanced around. "Move. Crouch behind that sofa."

With the same quickness with which he stepped between her and the pickpocket, Mr. Larkin dropped to one knee in front of her. She started, her skirts swaying with her movement, the blue silk lapping at his booted foot. The door opened behind her.

Mr. Larkin took her left hand in his and slowly slid the garnet ring into place on her ring finger, looking up at her.

Behind her Mrs. Stryde gasped as Viv looked down, meeting Mr. Larkin's gaze. In spite of the pose of ardent worship, it was not love she saw in his eyes, but a challenge, a dare. Maybe he did understand her, after all.

She gave a nod, unable to speak.

"Miss Bradish," he said in a loud, clear voice. "You have made me the happiest of men."

Mr. Larkin rose, still in possession of her hand and turned her to face the others. The hand in Viv's was steady.

She had no idea what Mr. Larkin would make of the Strydes, but she sensed that he had their measure. Mrs. Stryde leaned toward them like a dog straining against its lead.

"And who are you, young man?"

"Good evening, Mrs. Stryde, Mr. Stryde. Though we've not met, Miss Bradish has mentioned you to me. I beg your pardon." He turned and gave Viv such a besotted smile that she wondered if he was an actor in a London theater, maybe the Camberwell, a theater known for its showy performances.

"Our pardon?" Mrs. Stryde was tall, thin, and severe in the lines of her face, and rigid in her bearing in spite of dark curls over her ears and layers of flounce on the sleeves of her Nile-green gown. Mr. Stryde's blue eyes were small behind his round spectacles. His jaw bristled with straw-colored whiskers, like the whiskers of a fox, and his person was as comfortably padded as a velvet cushion.

"Yes, your pardon. I admit to seizing the occasion of your visit to Lady Melforth to have a word with my... betrothed."

"Your betrothed?"

"Only today. It was mere luck that I called at a time when Miss Bradish could step away from her duties, however briefly, for as you must know, she is devoted to her ladyship."

Viv did her best to maintain her composure. She could not look at him. He was remarkably adept at making statements that were true, but far from illuminating. He was, perhaps, too good at it.

"But how can this be? How can you have met Miss Bradish when…?"

"In the most ordinary way. Over a book."

Mrs. Stryde shook her head. "A lady's companion may not enter into a clandestine acquaintance with a gentleman. To do so violates the rules of her employment, and indeed, of decent feminine conduct."

"Ah, but there has been nothing clandestine about our acquaintance. As a lady, Miss Bradish knows what's due her station and her family." He turned to Viv again. "Will you permit me to explain how we met, my love?" he asked. One of his dark brows quirked upward.

Viv nodded. She had no idea how she managed to keep her countenance. The part he played and asked her to play grew riskier by the minute.

"Miss Bradish had been looking for a particular book for… some time. *The Spanish Brothers.* Do you know the novel?"

"A rubbishy novel? Full of folly and vice? Of course not. What does a novel have to do with this… intrusion into Lady Melforth's house?"

"As the usual booksellers failed her, Miss Bradish was forced to apply to … collectors."

"And?"

"My employer is a known collector of rare books." He spoke as if his words perfectly explained the situation, but Viv could see the Strydes' baffled expressions. She admired his coolness in spinning a fiction out of the merest details of their meeting. He offered crumbs of information and never a direct answer to Mrs. Stryde's questions. He'd altered his voice to make it a bit more pompous.

"Your employer?"

"Yes, among my ... other duties ... I see to the cataloguing of certain collections. Naturally, it fell to my lot to deal with Miss Bradish's inquiry. You cannot blame me for being curious about a lady whose bookish interests match my own."

"Bookish?" Mrs. Stryde stared as if Viv had sprouted a second head. Viv managed a faint smile.

"See here, fellow," said Mr. Stryde. "You're giving us a bit of a runaround. Who is this employer of yours?"

The drawing room door opened again, and Newberry entered. He glanced at Viv's hand in Mr. Larkin's, and frowned, turning a cold stare on Mr. Larkin.

"The duke does not wish his name bandied about in conversation. However, he was happy to make Miss Bradish a present of the book she sought." At that, Viv could not help giving her accomplice a quick reproving glance. *Where did a duke fit in the story?* He gave a careless shrug. "And thus, we met."

"A duke? What duke?" demanded Mrs. Stryde. "Who are your people, young man?"

Viv felt Mr. Larkin's hold tighten on her hand, but he merely said, "My people are old Londoners."

"Well, Mr. whoever you are ... a man without fortune or connections, how are we to believe you have ties to the peerage?"

Viv stiffened. She did not know why Mr. Larkin had brought a duke into the story, but Newberry could easily sink them. He might not know the full details of how Mr. Larkin had come to be in Lady Melforth's red-and-green drawing room, but he knew enough to cast doubt on any pretensions the gentleman might have to such lofty connections.

Newberry turned a skeptical gaze on Mr. Larkin, as if daring him to produce a duke.

"If you must know, it has been my privilege to spend a number of years in the Duke of Wenlocke's household."

Viv tried to look very much at ease with the revelation. Mrs. Stryde gave a good imitation of a landed fish gasping on the shore. Her husband took her by the arm to offer his support. Newberry shook his head. Viv had to act. It was necessary to remove Mr. Larkin from the line of fire before he said anything more outrageous and before the Strydes recovered their full faculties.

"Pray do excuse us," she said. "We must share our happy news with Lady Melforth. Haxton will see you out." She gave a tug on Mr. Larkin's hand, and headed for the door.

She did not slow her steps until they reached the landing above. There, she halted, conscious of a mad jumble of feelings, gratitude for the way he'd faced the Strydes, admiration for his quick wit, and vexation for how he'd complicated her situation with the charade of a betrothal. She turned to him and released his hand. It was one thing to deceive the Strydes about the nature of their connection, but she did not want to conceal the truth from Lady Melforth, who had been her benefactor, friend, and mentor for the best part of a year.

"What?" he asked.

"I don't want to … lie to Lady Melforth."

"You think I lied to the Strydes?" His sharp blue gaze

challenged hers.

"Not lied, but omitted … certain details. And a duke? You had to bring a duke into it? Do you really catalogue the Duke of Wenlocke's collections?"

He gave a careless shrug, and winced. "I've known him for many years."

"Why did you do it, anyway? Propose to me?"

"I couldn't let you get sacked for helping me."

"But I shot you."

"Do you want to give your employer the pickpocket and pistol shot version of our betrothal?" Now he looked amused.

"Ooh, when you put it that way, I don't see how it can be done. What am I to say—that I went husband-hunting with a gun and bagged you?"

"Tell her whatever convenient fiction you like, but if you don't want to be sacked…"

"Very well," she said. "We met over a book and are betrothed and will remain so until—"

"—you decide we no longer suit." His gaze didn't waver.

Viv shook her head. "Until Lady Melforth and I finish writing our guide."

"Your what?"

"Our *Lady's Guide to Walking in London*."

CHAPTER FOUR

THE FIRST THING that struck Lark about Lady Aurora Melforth was the keenness of her gray gaze. The second was the shaking of her right hand where it lay on the arm of her couch, as if the hand had a will of its own separate from her ladyship's intentions. She caught his glance and moved the hand, arranging the folds of her wrapper. The shaking stopped. She was a long, thin woman with an abundance of wavy red hair loosely coiled around her head and a nose that descended from her brow like a buttress jutting out of a wall.

"Those insinuating Strydes think that because my foot is broken, my brain is not working. Have you sent them packing, Viv?"

Viv left Lark's side and went to adjust her ladyship's cushions. "Haxton is seeing them out, ma'am."

"Thank goodness. Their Anti-Vice tirades are tiresome beyond endurance. And who is this gentleman?"

Viv glanced at him. "I ... we ... He is my betrothed, Mr. Edward Larkin."

"What?" Lady Melforth's startled gaze met Lark's, but she spoke to Viv. "He's not one of your beauxs from Bath. How did you meet?"

"Ma'am, if you'll permit me to explain," Lark ventured. "No blame attaches to Miss Bradish."

"That's for me to decide young man," she snapped.

"Oh, Lady Melforth, you must thank Mr. Larkin. He's the one who routed the Strydes."

"Routed them?" Lady Melforth's gaze turned curious. "And how did he accomplish that?"

"It turns out that Mr. Larkin is acquainted with the Duke of Wenlocke." Viv Bradish gave him a challenging look, daring him to stick to his story in front of the viscountess.

"I lived in the duke's household for many years, ma'am," he said.

"You know her grace then?" Lady Melforth's voice grew wistful.

"I do."

For a moment Lady Melforth looked a little lost. "I knew her parents in Italy years ago before the French came. Ah, well, those times are gone. Who are your people? What are your prospects?"

"My people are old Londoners, ma'am. I bank with Hammersley's."

For a moment her ladyship was silent, whether because of the decidedness of his reply or because she knew Hammersley's. At last, she said, "You must not expect to marry any time soon, young man. Miss Bradish is quite necessary to my comfort."

"And you have your guide to finish. I understand, ma'am. We have made no immediate plans. It is enough that I may call her mine." He felt Viv's glance, and knew she would take him to task for that remark.

"Very well, you may go. I must talk with Miss Bradish now."

LARK STEPPED INTO the street and turned away from the house, moving east. The sky was black, the gas lamps lit, making pools of yellow light at intervals along the street and casting shadows across the stone facades of the houses. He refused Haxton's offer of her ladyship's carriage. He wanted to avoid unnecessary questions about where he lived, but he felt a little lightheaded, and walking pulled at the wound in his side. His own rooms were close by, but to reach Rook and find out how his old partner had fared in the event, he'd have to find a cab soon.

He'd gone but a short way when a man fell into step beside him. It was the doctor.

"Acquainted with dukes, are you?" Newberry asked.

"Just the one."

"I doubt it. Whoever you are, you're no duke's secretary. And you never met Vivian Bradish over a book."

"No? The title is *The Spanish Brothers*."

The doctor snorted. "Nevertheless, my money says you're out to ruin our Viv."

Lark gritted his teeth. He really didn't like that *our*. "Since when is a proposal of marriage likely to ruin a lady?"

"Since when does a lady shoot her betrothed? I give you fair warning, Mr. Larkin, if that is your name, I mean to find out why she shot you and expose you for the scoundrel you are."

Lark halted and faced the doctor. If they put gloves on and stepped into a ring, Lark had no doubt he could take the man. Another memory surfaced with the idea, a day at

Daventry Hall when all of Dav's lost boy gang had taken turns sparring on a patch of lawn behind the house. "Expose me if you think there's something to expose, but don't injure Miss Bradish. You do not want to see her dismissed from Lady Melforth's employ, I think."

"Don't think I can't manage to expose you without harming our Viv."

"Perhaps you can, Doctor, but remember she's *my* Viv now, not yours." Lark began walking again. He felt absurdly satisfied to lay claim to Vivian Bradish. The doctor didn't move. Now, if Lark could only make it to the nearest cab stand without passing out.

THE CAB DROPPED Lark on Holborn at the top of Chancery Lane. From there he headed south, threading his way through dark turnings to the forgotten little court where he and Rook had shared rooms until the great October fire at Westminster Palace.

Lark let himself in to the once elegant house, divided long before Lark was born into separate dwellings for as many as fifty souls. Suddenly weak-kneed, he leaned heavily on the stair rail to pull himself up to their old rooms, now Rook's domain. Wide stairs turned upward around a central well that by day let in hazy light. By night, the stairs were quite black, except for faint rays emitted from under and around doors that no longer fit snugly in their jambs. Lark could find his way as much by smell as by sight, by gin and ale, and fish and tar, and the fragrances of several occupations on the lower end of the wage scale. The smells seemed to mock him for the part of a gentleman that he'd been playing. Vivian Bradish might be a hired companion, but her genteel dependence on a rich lady, still left her many strata above Lark in the layers of London society.

It was quiet on the stairs. Few of Rook's neighbors were at home as they had occupations better suited to darkness than daylight. Lark heard only the occasional muffled quarrel as he passed up the two flights and around the landing to the rooms at the front of the house overlooking the sad little court. Rook's reeking boots covered in river muck sat in a tin tub outside their door. Rook hated to risk having his boots pinched, but their charwoman, Alice Povey, refused to have the boots inside.

In the common room when Lark entered, other smells reminded him that he'd left posh London far behind. The remains of Rook's dinner, a fried bloater, a jacket potato, and ale, mingled with the scent of burned bread. In Lady Melforth's house, no coarse kitchen smells reached the main rooms. The fragrant tea Lark drank in her dining room faced no competition from humbler scents.

"Where'd ye get to?" Rook grumbled from a chair by the fire. He held a long fork with a smoking hunk of bread on the end near the glowing coals.

"Henrietta Street."

"Wot? Where? How'd ye end up there?" Rook had long abandoned the effort of speaking the way Daventry taught them.

"She shot me." Lark wanted a bed and his old one would do. He wanted to shed his coat, tie, and ruined waistcoat.

His wound burned, and his skin itched around the edges of the sticking plaster.

"Who?"

"The mark. She had a Toby under that cape of hers." He wondered what she had done with the gun.

"A barker? Did she twig you?" Rook sat up straight, giving Lark a closer took.

"No. She was aiming for you. I got in the way."

"Where'd she hit ye?"

"Right side. Can you help me out of my coat? The sawbones told me to have my *valet* change the dressing for me."

"Valet. 'e thinks ye have a valet? You fooled 'em proper, did ye?"

"They think I'm Edward Larkin, a fine gentleman." Lark grinned.

Rook snorted. "The more fool them, and I'm no valet, no servant neither."

"Just help. I don't want to undo the sawbones's handiwork."

Rook put aside the smoking piece of bread and pushed up out of his chair. Lark extended the arm on his unwounded side, and Rook pulled the sleeve until Lark could shrug out of his coat. At fifteen, when they'd left Daventry Hall, they'd been about the same size. Now at seven and twenty, Rook was a good four inches taller than Lark and much broader. He had a pleasant open face, which he concealed as much as possible behind a dark beard and heavy moustache.

Rook whistled at the sight of the bloodied waistcoat. "Why'd ye go t' 'enrietta Street for a sawbones? Why not go t' the casual ward?"

Lark did not want to explain his dislike for dirt and drunkenness. In Rook's part of London, a man was hardly a man if he didn't have beer on his breath and grime under his nails. Lark's preference for soap and clean linens was an ironic holdover from their time with Daventry. He was having entirely too many thoughts of that time lately. Maybe the memories had clouded his judgment.

"The mark took me. I wanted to see what I could get out of... the adventure." He needed to turn Rook's thoughts elsewhere. "How much did you get from her purse?"

"Naught. She's a minx. Had stones in 'er bag is all. The bag might fetch somethin', but ye won't be payin' fer new threads with stones."

Lark laughed. It was as he'd suspected. She had used the weighted bag as a decoy and kept her money elsewhere.

"Ye can laugh?" Rook protested. "I call it a bloody cheat. That skirt is dangerous."

Lark nodded. Rook was right. The woman was dangerous, but the balance had shifted in his understanding of their situation. The wrong of shooting him far outweighed the wrong of taking a false purse. No wonder she had been willing to take him to her own fancy sawbones for medical help.

"She offered to pay my tailor," he said. His tailor was E. Isaacson Brothers, the ready-made retailers with their fashion guides and their huge gas-lit shop front, or the used clothes shops on Monmouth Street. If a man read the bankruptcy listings, and headed for Monmouth Street in their wake, he could dress fashionably on the cheap in London. Anything saved on tailoring bills could be invested.

"Ye mean ye turned 'er up sweet?"

Lark didn't answer. He had thought to make a story of it, to have a laugh at how he'd pulled the wool over the eyes of some toffs, but now he wanted the adventure with Vivian Bradish to be his alone, not a shared thing. He concentrated on removing his bloodied waistcoat and shirt. A sudden chill shook him, and he clamped his jaw shut. He might spend the night with Rook for old times' sake.

"So, is she old or young? Pretty or plain?"

"Young, pretty." But dangerous. If her guidebook taught other women to go boldly about London, prepared to meet danger with courage and a weapon, his old profession would disappear.

"Yer sure she didn't twig ye?"

"She didn't. I'm going to see her again." He was starting to shake all over, and he could feel his knees going slack. He needed a room, a bed.

"Why? She's above yer touch, ain't she?"

"Doing her a favor." He turned away and crossed the room. It was one half of some ancient lady's drawing room, bare now of the amenities that had once graced it, no rugs, no sconces on the wall, no paintings, no fine furnishings.

"Wot's in it then? Yer not thinking of turning cracksman, are ye? Pinching her silver?"

"Don't be daft. We should take a holiday is all." He said *we*, as if they were still partners.

"'oliday?"

"No clicks." Lark shrugged. He had been trying to persuade Rook to quit since the fire. Now the problem of Rook had become urgent. Lark needed time to see what would come of his arrangement with Vivian Bradish.

"Are ye bosky?"

He wasn't drunk. He just felt crazy as if he'd climbed into one of Mr. Green's famous hot air balloons and taken off skyward with no tethers to hold him back. "Tired."

"Wot 're ye not telling me?" Rook asked. "If we don't do clicks, 'ow do we eat?"

"We'll eat. Don't worry. Just hold off until ... these stitches come out." He pushed open the door to his old room. Rook had changed nothing as if he had expected Lark's return to their old life. The room had once been a lady's boudoir. Now it had a bed, a chair, a makeshift wardrobe, and a trunk bolted to the floor and securely locked. Lark could make it to the bed. He knew he could.

Rook came up behind him. "Wot's wrong w' ye? We do clicks. You and me. Ye've been taking a bleedin' holiday since the fire. Ye can't keep on like 'at. Wot'll I do?"

"Just a bit more holiday," Lark said. He reached the bed and pulled back the coverlet. Old and worn as it was, he needed its warmth. He let himself sink down on the bed, and pulled the cover up around him and fell back onto the mattress. He could barely see Rook standing puzzled in the doorway.

"I don't need a bleedin' 'oliday," Rook said.

CHAPTER FIVE

A CARRIAGE AT the door of Lady Melforth's Henrietta Street house confirmed what Lark had feared from the moment he woke—that Viv meant to avoid seeing him again. He readied himself to play the smitten fiancé and rang the bell.

Haxton admitted him to the house with muted cordiality just as Viv came down the stairs. She wore another silk, a vivid plaid of deep blues and reds and threads of gold. Her wide skirts rustled like a wave foaming up a rocky shore. The short dove-colored cape covered her torso. A bit of lace encircled her throat. A chocolate-colored bonnet and tan leather gloves dangled from the hand that wore his garnet ring. He saw no sign of the pistol.

"I see I haven't kept you waiting," he said to her. "Where are we off to today?"

"Oh," she said, checking her steps. "The duke has given you another holiday?"

"In honor of our betrothal and to help you with your work."

"What an accommodating employer!" She resumed her descent.

"Only because of my long service to him."

At the foot of the stairs, she turned to don her bonnet

and gloves, and he couldn't look away. He supposed it was the novelty of feminine action that held his gaze, the settling of the silk bonnet on the smooth crown of her head, the angle of the bow under her chin, the tugging on of gloves. He and Rook had lived a male existence, except for Alice Povey, their charwoman, and Lark had never stopped to watch stout, blunt-spoken Alice make adjustments to her appearance.

At dawn, he had awakened with his throat dry and his whole side sore and aching. He had managed with difficulty to clothe his stiff limbs in his ruined gear and leave before Rook stirred. At Isaacson's Fashion Emporium, Ezra, the proprietor's son, admitted him through the back door and helped him purchase a new shirt, waistcoat, and coat. Lark would be willing to wager on Ezra's talent for valeting against any gentleman's gentleman in the city. His last stop before Lady Melforth's had been at Number 36 Babylon Street, where he'd purchased *The Spanish Brothers*, a novel in the two-shilling series from Nelson's Royal Library.

When Viv turned back to him, he handed her the book. "The duke wanted you to have this," he said.

Her gloved hands closed around the green cloth binding and gold lettering. She glanced at the title and shot him a swift look that said she would not be taken in by his acting the part of her betrothed. Lark might feel as though he'd been run over by a drayman's cart, but at the challenge in her eyes, a swift undercurrent of excitement coursed through him. He wanted to spar with her all day.

Haxton opened the door. Outside, the coachman greeted Viv, and Lark stepped forward to let down the carriage steps, aware as he did so that perhaps a true gentleman might have left such a task to the servant. He let the doubt go. He would have to be his own sort of gentleman and brazen it out.

"Where are we going?" he asked, sitting opposite her, his first time in a well-appointed private carriage for some time. The blue velvet of the squabs stirred another faint memory.

"To old St. Pancras Church to visit a grave," she said.

"Ah," he said. "No need for your pistol if your quarry is already dead." The carriage lurched into motion, and he couldn't repress a groan.

"How is your wound?" she asked. "Shouldn't you keep to your lodging?"

"And miss your next exploit? Whose grave are we going to visit?"

"Mary Godwin's." She said the name with a bit of reverence and the apparent expectation that he would know of whom she spoke, but the name meant nothing to him, except a chance that he might falter in his role and expose his ignorance.

"You're not an admirer of Mrs. Godwin?" she asked.

"One day you're seeking pickpockets and the next day, a dead woman's grave? Pardon me if I don't see the connection."

"Not any dead woman, a gifted writer who refused to be limited by the usual constraints men impose on us."

"Ah. Were you following in her footsteps when you visited Babylon Street and shot a helpful stranger?"

She gave him a stunned look. "Yes, how did you... Well, she never shot anyone that I know of, but she broke boundaries, and our guide encourages women to do the same. That's our theme, you see."

"No matter the risk? Does your guide advise ladies to carry a pistol?"

"We're back to that, are we? You think women incapable of defending themselves." He liked to see the lively sparkle in those dark eyes as she met his challenge.

"I think a sensible ... person avoids near encounters with ruffians. Shouldn't a visitor's guide for ladies steer them away from unsavory neighborhoods?"

"Should women be limited to certain streets and shops?"

"Only if they want to keep their purses."

She looked away, and he thought he detected a slight blush on her cheek. He wondered if she'd admit to the contents of that purse. But she came back at him with another challenge. "Do your mother or your sisters never complain about being told where they might and might not go in London?"

For a moment he had no answer. He had not yet given his fictional Mr. Larkin a family.

To hear the words *your mother* unsettled him when he had been thinking about his mother ever since the fire, trying to revive elusive wisps of memory that would yield some clue to her fate, her absence in his life. The one sure memory he had was of her beringed fingers turning the pages of a book as she read to him.

The carriage, well-sprung and comfortably padded as it was, rattled over some uneven ground, jarring the wound in his side. He flinched, and the fleeting sense of memory returned more strongly. He had ridden in such a carriage with his mother.

"What? What did I say?" Viv asked, stretching out a hand.

He froze, waiting for her touch, but she withdrew her hand. "Nothing. I have no sisters. My mother is ...gone."

"I beg your pardon." She folded her hands in her lap and dropped her gaze.

"No need to apologize. You could not know." Her ready sympathy undid him. He turned to the window. He needed a story, and he was quite used to making one up in the moment, taking his cue from the mark. Already, he'd told this girl truths about himself. He needed to be more careful.

He made himself concentrate on their direction and the distance traveled. He figured they'd gone nearly a mile before she again lifted her gaze to meet his, her expression earnest.

"I've been thinking. My blunder about your mother only shows the weakness of our charade. Were we truly betrothed, we would know more of each other's ... histories."

The carriage slowed and made a turn. Through the window Lark could see a green expanse unlike his usual London haunts. "Do you expect Lady Melforth to unmask us?"

Viv shook her head. "She's clever, you know, but her illness makes her less likely to worry over inconsistencies in our story."

"The Strydes, on the other hand ..." he said. *And*, he thought, *the good doctor*.

Viv grinned at him. "The Strydes would delight in discrediting you and seeing me gone. If they meet your duke, they will question him."

He laughed. "The duke is definitely not a member of the Anti-Vice Society, but let them try to reach him."

THE LADY AND THE THIEF

She gave him a puzzled look.

"Don't worry, you can tell me all about your family, and I'll tell you about mine."

"After we visit the church. You won't mind if I wander and take notes. This is a working visit for me."

"To find your story of the day?"

"Just so."

The carriage halted, and Lark opened the door and let down the steps. They had stopped in a lane above a green embankment with a river flowing below and some boys lounging with fishing poles on its banks. He paused to get his bearings. They'd gone east and north, somewhere near Camden Town, he thought. On a rise above them stood the old church, the east section of its roof crumbling, surrounded by leaning headstones crowded near one another like a throng pressing to enter a narrow gate.

Viv put her hand in his and descended, a small act of customary feminine dependence on a man. Her feet on the ground, she let go at once and headed down a path toward the church tower. "I'll be a while. Wander as you like."

"You didn't mention that the place is in ruins," he called after her.

"It's picturesque," she said. She stopped to read a lichen-darkened headstone, reaching into her reticule for a moleskin notebook and a pencil.

He turned the other way, along the south side of the old church. At the moment, her keen enthusiasm for discovery grated on him. Maybe it was their conversation in the carriage, but at the graveyard gate, the old sense of abandonment had come over him, and he needed to clear his head. He had no idea how long he could keep the false betrothal going, but he meant to make the most of it. In her company he would explore that part of London he had so far avoided. He could name no wrong his mother had done him, except the wrong of being absent. He tried to shake off that reflection, winding his way among headstones with faint names, obscured by time and mossy growth, no clearer than his old resentments.

A slight breeze stirred the leaves of the trees beyond the graveyard's boundary, the air fresh after the stink of the city's streets. At the end of a row of larger monuments, he halted, surprised to come upon an open grave. The smell of newly turned earth assaulted his senses and a chill passed over him. He stared into the dark pit of the unfilled grave. He had not thought of his mother as dead. By his calculation she would be a woman in her fifties, younger than Alice Povey or Lady Melforth. It struck him now, facing that emptiness, that he was unjust to blame her. Maybe her absence had not been a desertion, but something else entirely. Maybe she had not chosen to leave him, but lay in a grave somewhere in London. He shuddered and lifted his gaze, but the sight that met his eyes did not help. Beyond the tended and marked graves, at the very edge of the cemetery, were low mounds over which a few blades of vegetation had sprouted, the sort of graves that drew the Resurrection men to their work.

He turned back, looking for Viv, and when he didn't see her, his heart gave an odd skip. Then he spotted Lady Melforth's carriage outside the church gate. Viv had not deserted him. He picked up his pace, striding the main path to the west. There she stood in the far corner in front of a large square monument surmounted with a moss-covered capstone, her skirts vivid with color and life. She was scribbling away in her notebook, and he couldn't wait to spar with her again.

"You found the lady's grave, I see," he said, coming to stand beside her.

"I did." She kept up her jotting in the little notebook.

He read the inscription on the monument.

MARY WOLLSTONECRAFT GODWIN

AUTHOR OF A VINDICATION OF THE RIGHTS
OF WOMAN

He noted the years of her birth and death. "How did she die? Do you know?" he asked.

"Of a complication after giving birth to her daughter Mary, the writer, Mary Shelley." He must have looked blank because she added, "*Frankenstein?*"

"So, you'll turn her mother's grave into a tourist attraction?"

She turned to him, bristling at once. It was easy to provoke her. "Not at all. More like a place of pilgrimage, for women to be inspired. Being a man, you may not have noticed how few of our London monuments celebrate women, as if we were an invisible thread in the city's history."

He made an effort to keep his expression bland.

Then she laughed. "You," she said, "are having me on." And she gave him a more penetrating glance. "Is your wound troubling you?"

He started to deny it and changed his mind. Better that she thought him weak in body than in the head. "A little," he said.

"Then let's get you off your feet." She tucked her pencil and notebook into her bag.

"You found your story of the day?"

She nodded. "Now to find somewhere nearby where a lady might refresh herself."

"There's a tavern across the way." He pointed to a two-storied building in the old half-timber style with a rather large sign reading THE ADAM AND EVE.

"I'll tell Tim Coachman to bring the carriage round."

FROM THE BRIGHTNESS of midday, they stepped into a dark, low-ceilinged chamber smelling of ale, beef, and smoke. Lark instinctively turned for the taproom when the host, with a white apron tied around his middle, came to greet them.

"Private room for you and yer lady, sir?" the man asked. "We have a fine ordinary, if I say so meself," he added.

Lark halted, abruptly, and Viv slammed into him, jarring his side. He sucked in a breath, waiting for the sharp pain to subside.

"Idiot," she said. "You're hurting."

Lark turned to the landlord. "Yes, to the room and the ordinary, and coffee, if you will." He hoped he'd covered his mistake. He'd been about to blunder into the common taproom because he'd forgotten the role he was playing.

Viv thought The Adam and Eve's upstairs dining parlor, quaintly pleasing. The old-fashioned room had butter-colored walls above a dark oak wainscot and a bow window that looked back across the green toward St. Pancras church. A large round table in the center of the room was set for two, and a small fire burned in the grate. If the ordinary was at all edible, she would make a note of the tavern in her account of the day.

Mr. Larkin immediately took up a position at the window facing the old churchyard.

Viv put down her bag and removed her bonnet, cape, and gloves with quick efficiency. They'd had little more than a day's acquaintance and already she understood that he was stubborn and determined to conceal his injury. She had been trying to judge his mood since he'd met her at the Wollstonecraft grave. Something had sobered him, though perhaps it was only the wound in his side. He was dressed with the same unobtrusive elegance as before with just a hint of flash in the burgundy silk waistcoat he wore. Her Mr. Larkin did like his finery.

"How is your wound?"

He turned that blue gaze on her. "It smarts some," he said.

"Let me look, then. Just to be sure you've not undone the doctor's work."

"The doctor's work?" He quirked one dark brow.

She reached for his waistcoat buttons, and their hands met. The contact jolted her. Her gaze locked with his, until the intensity of it made her pull back. He really was a difficult patient.

"You must not suppose that I make a habit of undressing gentlemen," she said.

"Just the ones you've shot, or the ones to whom you're betrothed?" He continued unbuttoning the waistcoat.

"Well, you wouldn't need nursing at all, had you not insisted on following me about London. I hardly need a protector. I've been managing on my own for months."

He spread the edges of the waistcoat and tugged the lawn shirt free of his trousers, turning to present his side for her inspection. "All the more reason for me to worry as you seem indifferent to your safety."

Viv peered at the place he'd bared in the folds of white lawn, where smooth, pale skin covered the ridge of his ribs. He was neatly made, his flesh taut and spare, nothing like the feminine softness she was used to seeing. She concentrated on the wound. His valet had not changed the dressing, and the edges of the plaster curled up around the place she'd shot him. She took a step closer, nerving herself to touch him. There was no sign of redness or swelling. With her fingertips she smoothed the plaster back into place, pressing against warm flesh and solid bone. She did not think he breathed. She needed him talking, sparring with her. She stepped back. "I suspect you worry more about the proprieties."

"That, too, but a man can't be indifferent to the safety of his betrothed."

"You like saying that word, don't you?"

"Does it bother you?"

"For a man who passed his newly returned ring from one woman to another on the same afternoon, you seem remarkably attached to the idea of our...connection."

"Merely doing my duty."

"You needn't worry. I am perfectly capable of protecting myself from danger."

"It's the danger to the gentlemen of London, I fear. You see I've worn burgundy today." He waited until she met his gaze. "I'm sure this waistcoat can handle bloodstains."

"You are absurd. I'm not going to shoot you again. The danger is that our betrothal will be exposed as a sham. The Strydes delight in bringing people down. Scandal is their...meat." She stepped back to let him restore his clothes to rights. "What we need is a signal between us."

"A signal?" He turned away.

For a moment the only sound in the room was cloth sliding against cloth. Viv swallowed, suddenly conscious of the intimacy of those little rustlings. She liked how he was constructed, how the easy elegance of his clothes revealed his form. She had not been embarrassed to examine his wound. Nursing, after all, was a woman's province. Only now did she feel she had overstepped some boundary. She dragged her mind back to the problem of a signal. "More like a code, a word you can say, or I can say, when the other is getting us into dangerous conversational waters."

"What do you mean?" He turned back to her, his hands working the waistcoat's tiny buttons.

Viv's gaze narrowed to his hands. Her brain took a little nap. She had hardly slept, trying to see a way out of their sham betrothal. Now she could not remember why it had seemed so important. When her brain woke again, he was watching her, and she remembered what she had been about to say.

"We need a signal for moments like the one when you produced your duke, like a parlor conjurer pulling a dove out of an empty hat. Shouldn't I, as your betrothed, know about the duke, who, according to your account, provided me with a copy of *The Spanish Brothers*?"

"Ah, good point." He looked anything but worried. "You'd best tell me your story, then. Leave nothing out."

"As you should tell yours to me."

"Ladies first."

Viv meant to resist him, to make him tell his story, but the landlord returned with a waiter. A little bustle ensued of setting covered dishes on the table and pouring drinks. The ordinary was a baked sole with roasted potatoes and a green pea soup. The mingled scents of still-warm loaves and freshly brewed coffee filled the little room. When the inn people withdrew, they ate in silence until Viv decided she must start the conversation.

"Very well. I'll go first, though there's little to tell. My father died at Waterloo on the day I was born. He was Lieutenant Richard Bradish of the 95th, and he died defending La Haye Sainte. Needless to say, his family found a living girl-child a poor substitute for a dead hero. My mother kept to her mourning couch at my grandparents' estate until obliged to seek sympathy for her style of grieving elsewhere. We changed house often until she met an invalided navy man, Captain Frank Pennington. They married, settled in Weymouth, and quickly produced my four half-sisters. As making a low income go a long way is not my mother's greatest strength, my sisters and I have become...resourceful."

She watched his face for signs of judgment or pity, but he seemed to regard his fish with more interest than her story.

"What are your sisters' names?" he asked.

It was not what she expected. "Pippa, Charlotte, Anne, and Eliza. Anne and Eliza are twins."

"And how did you come to be in Lady Melforth's employ?"

"Nearly two years ago, my aunt Louisa, my father's youngest sister, took me to stay in Bath for a time as her companion. We met Lady Melforth, who had returned to England for medical treatment for her injured foot. At first, she thought the waters at Bath might serve, but soon found she required a London physician. Her relations, the Strydes, insisted that she hire a companion, and she asked my aunt if she could spare me, and I was hired. I consider myself most fortunate."

He put down his fork and took a swallow of coffee, as if he'd not been listening at all.

"Waterloo."

"Waterloo?" She didn't follow.

"That must be our signal." He lay his napkin on the table.

"What? We're supposed to bring up Waterloo whenever there's a risk of exposure? How are we to do that?"

"Simple. Suppose Mrs. Stryde wants to know something about your impression of the duke and you feel trapped."

"Yes?"

"You say *the duke collects Waterloo prin*ts, and I take over. Or suppose I'm confused as to which of your four sisters, Pippa or Charlotte, is keener about playing the pianoforte, and I ask—"

"—is Pippa the musician or the mad historian, always going on about Waterloo?"

He grinned at her, his eyes full of merriment. He was enjoying their situation. He was not the one who might be exposed and sacked. "It'll work, won't it?"

At that moment the landlord returned to ask whether they required anything else. Mr. Larkin rose instantly and excused himself to deal with the bill. As he stepped through the door, the landlady appeared to show Viv to the necessary, and she collected her things. It was all done in the most gentlemanly of ways, but he had not told her his story. Viv knew she'd been outmaneuvered.

CHAPTER SIX

Lark held his breath as Lady Melforth's carriage rocked to a stop. Somewhere between the old church with its crowded graveyard, and Henrietta Street's row of fine town houses for the living, Viv had fallen asleep, gently collapsing against Lark's side. He made no move to wake her. Yet another elusive memory teased at him. He'd fallen asleep in such a coach once.

Outside their coach on Henrietta Street, vehicles rattled by with harness jingling, voices cried out wares for sale, footsteps echoed from the flagstones. Viv's chin rested above his heart, a tiny point of contact in contrast to the dull ache of his wound. He breathed in the faint flowery scent of her. The rise and fall of her breast made him acutely aware of its softness, covered in layers of silk and linen, whalebone and twill, yet soft and yielding.

He had lain with women, brief couplings with accomplished professionals. The book stalls of Babylon Street offered guides to dozens of London establishments, their services, and their prices. Lark had been twenty, perhaps, when he and Rook, flush from a run of rich takings, had tried one of the most celebrated houses. The experience had been a cheat. The rooms, tricked out to seem exotic and luxurious, were an invitation to a man to lose himself in fantasy. But Lark knew a fraud when he met one. After all, he was one, a gentleman thief. Rook simply shrugged off any trappings of the act. He preferred a girl he knew in the neighborhood. Liza was quick, silent, and glad of an extra coin for her children. She offered Lark the same bargain. Lark declined out of loyalty to Rook, but he suspected himself of fastidiousness, of liking clean linen and fine wool, and wanting something more.

He had not considered a carriage as a likely place for carnal embrace, but now the thought intruded with a kind of insistence. And not any carriage, this one, with its elegant padded interior and its blue velvet curtains that could be drawn over the windows separating those inside from the ordinary life of London on the pavement. Within two days, Vivian Bradish had slipped into that blank space in his mind occupied by the ideal lover he could vaguely imagine. She annoyed him, and stirred him in equal parts. He was getting into a predicament from which he did not know how to extract himself. He was certain that, for all her boldness, she knew nothing of the things that a girl like Liza knew. He glanced at her moleskin notebook full of jottings lying on the seat, peeking out from under her billowing skirts. He wanted to see inside the little notebook. Did she understand anything of the city?

Against his side, she stirred and drew in a deeper breath.

"We're here," he said. He slid his arm up the cushions, breaking contact with her shoulders.

She lifted her head and straightened. "Oh, you let me fall asleep."

"It's warm, and soft as a baby's pram in here. Put you

right out."

She cast him a doubtful glance. Her dark eyes still had the faraway look of sleep. "You agreed to tell me your life story."

"I did. You yawned prodigiously."

"What is the hour?" Her cheek, rosy with heat, bore the slanting imprint of his coat lapel. Lark guessed that Haxton or the young footman would open the door, but he knew she should not be seen by her employer with that mark on her cheek.

"Near four."

With an abrupt start she came back fully to her senses. "Oh dear. Have we been sitting here long?"

"Just arrived."

"I must go in." She twisted, reaching for her bonnet and bag.

"Wait, you're still waking up." He didn't move. "Make sure you…look…presentable."

"Presentable?" Her gaze flew to his.

"You look…a little…"

"What?"

"Warm." He hoped she did not detect the note of carnal interest in his voice.

"Do I?" She touched her cheek. "This is your fault. You deliberately set out to…to lull me, like some nursemaid putting a child to bed. And I don't know your story."

"Ask me for it again tomorrow."

"Tomorrow!" She frowned. "You can't accompany me everywhere."

"Can't I?"

"Don't be difficult. I have a job to do, as you must." Her skirts rustled with a sudden burst of movement. She scooted forward, and looked pointedly at his legs stretched across the space between the benches. He dropped his hand to the seat behind her and gave the little notebook a push toward the back of the bench.

"I really must go to Lady Melforth."

He pulled his legs out of her way and turned the door handle. "Go."

She lurched past him, bent awkwardly, her skirts a froth of silk in the narrow space. Her hand came down to grasp his knee.

He drew a sharp breath at the contact. "Steady," he said.

"I'm sorry." She moved her hand to the door. "I forgot your wound."

"Go," he said again through gritted teeth, unreasonably stirred by that hand on his knee.

Lady Melforth's door opened and the footman hurried down the steps to help Viv. She accepted his hand and descended. "How is Lady M?" she asked him.

"She needs you, miss," he said.

Lark stuck his head out of the carriage door. "Tomorrow," he said.

She gave him one last exasperated glance. "You're impossible," she said, and turned away.

He watched the door close behind her and stepped down to the pavement. He thanked the coachman, waved the man off, and headed for his own neighborhood, the little moleskin book, tucked inside his waistcoat.

IN THE UPPER drawing room, Viv found Lady Melforth drowning in a sea of silk cushions on the Aubusson sofa. The drapes were drawn. The air was close and heavy with the medicinal scents of vinegar and tisane, signs of one of her ladyship's headaches.

"Oh dear." Viv crossed to the windows to let in light and air. "You've had a dreadful day, I take it."

"Why did you stay away so long? I expected you hours ago. I could have died, you know, alone here, unable to reach the bell."

"I'm sorry. I thought the Strydes were with you."

"Well, I suppose there are some things worse even than being seized and fitted for one's coffin."

"No one is fitting you for a coffin yet. Let me fix those cushions and you won't feel so low. Can you lean forward?" For a few minutes, Viv arranged and fluffed pillows to give Lady Melforth's back more support. She righted her ladyship's sagging coiffure and rang the bell for Jenny to take away the old teacup and the vinegar-soaked cloth and bring one of her ladyship's cordials.

When all had been done to make her ladyship more comfortable, Viv drew a chair near her employer and settled. "What would you like to hear first?" she asked. It was their usual practice for Viv to tell some story of the day and to read her notes, letting Lady Melforth pass judgment on how to shape the material, where to start and what to emphasize. Viv marveled at her ladyship's way of spotting the details that gave a scene vivid life. Later Viv would make revisions.

She reached for her notebook and realized she didn't have it.

The thought left her momentarily confused. She always had her notebook with her, but she couldn't remember bringing it into the house. She had simply needed to get out of that carriage, away from Mr. Larkin. In a flash she saw her awkward stumbling over his knees and hurried rush to the door. With effort, she could picture her bonnet and bag on the hall table, and her flushed face in the mirror, but not the notebook. She must have left it on the bench of the carriage. She drew in a calming breath. Tim Coachman would no doubt find it and return it to the house.

Lady Melforth sipped the cordial.

"The Strydes suspect your young man of being a *swell*, you know."

"You don't think him one, do you?"

"In my day we called them *dandies*. The thing is…what could I tell the Strydes? I really should know who his people are and where he got his education. You know how Eustacia can go on with her Anti-Vice blather about the decadence of London's youth. You mustn't leave me at such a disadvantage." Lady Melforth's right hand began to tremble.

"I hardly think he's either a *swell* or a *dandy*. He seems to care more about clean linen and good cloth, than fashion excess." Viv didn't know why she was defending him, but she hadn't seen any personal vanity in him.

"Apparently he reads novels." One of Lady Melforth's red brows quirked upward. "*The Spanish Brothers?*"

Viv recalled the book she'd left in the hall. "You won't fault him for that, will you?"

"The point is, Viv, I thought you'd got over the folly of

being in love, in Bath, before I hired you. Yet, here you are again. I suppose he made sheep's eyes at you and flowery speeches." Her ladyship put down the cordial and subdued her shaking right hand.

"Not at all." Viv thought Mr. Larkin would be much easier to manage if he were the sort to make speeches. As it was, he was quick and he distracted her, as he had from the first when he stepped between her and the fleeing pickpocket. Until today, she'd never forgot her notebook.

"But if you marry him, can you be sure he will let you write? For you must write, Viv. I've not spent my time on you to have you throw away my good instruction so you can pin nappies around babies' bottoms and haggle with servants over your husband's comforts."

Trust Lady Melforth to reduce marriage to its spirit-killing demands. Viv was quite sure that her ladyship had never pinned a nappy on a bottom. Viv wanted to say that she would not be marrying Mr. Larkin, so there was no need to worry, but for the moment the charade must be preserved. "Shall I have the lawyers put it in the settlement papers—Mr. Larkin's wife must have a desk and a private corner and be permitted to write no fewer than a thousand words a day?"

"Yes. But, Viv, it's not just his income you must be sure of. Or his willingness to have a scribbling wife. As a writer, you must be seen to be a lady, the granddaughter of an earl. I dare say, half of the secret of my writing success is not in the word *traveling*, but in the word *viscountess*. If you must marry, you must marry well. What are this man's origins?"

"I haven't checked the peerage for his family, but ..."

"Invite him for tea tomorrow evening. I must question him."

"Tomorrow? Surely there's no rush for you to…know him better. We promised not to marry before the guidebook is done."

Again, Viv experienced a bit of confusion. Lady Melforth seemed to think that Viv was going to need a husband after all, on whose income and rank in society Viv would depend and not on her work as a writer. But the point of their guide was for Viv to make her way in the world by her own abilities, by fearlessness and skill with words. With the publication of the guide, Viv was to have her own money and not depend on Mr. Larkin or any man.

She did not want Lady Melforth questioning her betrothed too closely. Mr. Larkin had the careless air of a man who did not need to *grub for money*. That was the phrase. Viv knew she would always need to grub for it with ink stains on her fingers and precious notebooks filled with her observations. But if he had an employer, even a generous one like the Duke of Wenlocke, he could not have a large income. His income was something about him she had not yet considered, like his direction, which she did not know. She had the impression that he no longer lived with the duke, so she had no sure way to send him an invitation for tea. He did say he would see her on the morrow, but could she count on his coming? What if the duke required him for some reason? "Oh Waterloo," she said. She was going to need the signal he'd invented.

"Waterloo? My girl, are you woolgathering?"

"Not at all, ma'am. I'm sure Mr. Larkin will be delighted

to join us for tea. Now, let me tell you about Mary Godwin's grave."

"I see you don't have your notebook. You've not lost it, have you? It's not like you to be careless with our work. No rivals must ever get hold of our material."

"I'm sorry. We were so late returning, I rushed in. I left it in the carriage. Tim Coachman will bring it in, I'm sure."

"Ah, well, Godwin's grave can wait until you have your notes. I'm tired. Help me up to bed, will you?"

"Of course, ma'am."

An hour later Viv sent Thomas, her favorite footman, to ask Tim Coachman if her notebook had turned up. The two men returned to the house together to assure her that they'd both searched the carriage thoroughly and the notebook was not there.

"But it must be," Viv insisted to the two sober-faced men, "I put it..." Realization stopped her. She knew where it was, well, she didn't know where it was, but she knew who had it. "Thank you both for looking."

ROOK WAS OUT when Lark turned up at the old place. He put a meat pie and a pint pot of ale on the ancient vanity in his old room, lit a lamp, and withdrew the little notebook from his inner pocket. Taking the notebook had been an impulse. Walking to Rook's with the little moleskin pad pressed to his good side while each step pulled at his stitches, he had rapidly passed from being curious about her writing to needing to see it for himself. Now he saw the notebook as a dilemma. He tossed it onto the vanity into the circle of lamp light.

He turned to the makeshift wardrobe he had long ago created out of a pair of old doors and some green damask bed hangings from a bankruptcy sale. He shed coat and waistcoat, discarded his silk tie, and gingerly pulled his shirt away from the wound in his side. A bit of blood now marked the shirt. He pulled it off and draped it over the cabinet that formerly held his shaving things. For a moment he regarded the blood-marked plaster on his ribs. It would have to be changed, and he had no valet to do the changing. He hoped he could persuade Rook to do it, but what he wanted was for Viv to change it. She seemed to have no hesitation about examining the wound or even about touching him. He would just need a story to explain his dependence on her help rather than a valet's.

A sudden chill shook him, and he reached into the wardrobe. His hand brushed the black velvet coat Dav had worn as their leader, the coat he had discarded when he returned to his family and true name. That day, the day Lark and Rook had set out for London, Lark had picked up the fallen coat and donned it. He slipped it on now. Though the hem was in tatters, the silky lining warmed him.

He settled in the chair at the vanity and took a pull from the ale pot, ready to consider the problem of the little notebook. There was no question that he would return it to her. Nor was there a question of when. He would return it first thing in the morning.

She would be angry that he had taken it. The little notebook mattered to her, unlike the purse of pebbles she'd lost in their first encounter. He wondered whether she would confess the trick to him. She apparently had no need of ready money in Lady Melforth's household, but she wanted money, he was sure of that. The story she told, revealed half-sisters and a mother who did not manage well on a low income.

He put aside the ale and took up the notebook. It fit neatly in his hands. In taking it, he had planned to read it, at least those parts where she might have written about him. He wanted to know whether the doctor was right, that Lark was a mere anecdote in her tales of London, a bit of passing street life. He wanted to know if the book was dangerous and whether reading it would put ladies on their guard against pickpockets. He wanted to know whether she knew anything of the city as he knew it. He wanted to know if she wrote in a fine lady's delicate hand, or in quick jottings that matched her rapidity of thought. He held the book to his nose and thumbed the edge, letting the leaves fan his face as if they would release her secrets. *Oh, he wanted to read it.*

The problem was that if he read it, he would satisfy his curiosity, but violate her trust. Taking the notebook was one thing, but reading it, he knew, would be a worse offense. As it was, he had no idea whether he could distract her from her anger when he returned it. But he must. He might be daft to keep their charade going, but he meant to try. She declared herself at odds with the ideal of female respectability, a woman who fired a pistol at a fleeing assailant. She was the opposite of a mark, curious and confident, and bold. He'd grant her that, but she was no Liza. Whatever desires he'd had while Viv nestled against him in the carriage, she fell into that lofty category of respectable women known as ladies.

Not that he wanted her to be Liza, but he wanted her to be susceptible to him, and not in the way that the usual female mark was. He never had carnal thoughts about a mark. Most of them didn't see him at all. They saw his clothes, heard his posh accent, and accepted that he was a gentleman, a man to lean on in a moment of distress when the city proved to be too much for them. Later when such a woman spoke to a copper, she would describe the kind gentleman who helped her. She wouldn't remember his appearance or the name he gave her.

The city did not seem to overwhelm Viv, but to thrill her, and she would not forget his name, still his heart was in no danger. He was having a lark, playing a game in her company. With her he could stroll those regions of London he had not yet searched. And what he needed was for her to change the bandage without suspecting his real circumstances. That meant he had to come up with a story for her. He could cover the bit about his education, but he needed to invent some sort of family. How lofty a family, that was the question. He broke the still-warm pie in half. He thought he'd allow himself a maiden aunt, of modest means, but generous in nature. She'd live a retired life in a country village, perhaps Somerton, and from time to time she'd send her nephew a gift.

The door opened behind him. Rook was not one for knocking. "You going to eat that pie?"

"I am."

"I did a click today."

Lark spun around, immediately regretting the action, as a sharp pain jabbed at him. "Where?"

"There was some ceremony, ribbon-cutting thing, at a digging. I bagged a gold turnip watch. Sold it, too." He jingled some coins in the pocket of his ragged jacket.

"In Hoxton?" They never fenced anything in their own neighborhood.

"I can do clicks without you, you know. Most dippers do."

"What if you'd been twigged? How would I get you out?"

Rook shrugged. "Sure yer going to eat that pie?"

"I'm sure."

Rook shrugged again and turned away.

Lark bit into the pie and caught the crumbs before they landed on Viv's notebook.

He knew what he wanted, what everything around him could deny him. He wanted Viv to read the notebook to him.

CHAPTER SEVEN

THE DAY PROMISED to be warm, and Lark found no fire lit in Lady Melforth's green drawing room. He set his package down and stood in front of the hearth to wait for Viv. The clock on the mantel ticked a very few measured ticks before she burst into the room.

"Where is it?" She crossed to him in a rustle of lavender skirts, her dark eyes flashing with indignation. Her gaze narrowed to the package he'd laid on the round table at the end of the sofa. "What have you done with it?"

"Good morning, Viv." Lark patted his side where an inner pocket of his brown wool coat held the little book, willing her to come closer. "It's here."

"You took it." She halted, facing him, dark eyes ablaze with anger, skirts rocking from her movement, stirring the air, bringing him the faint flowery scent he already recognized as hers.

"You left it in the coach. I kept it safe."

She cast a puzzled glance at the brown paper package. "What's this then?"

"Fresh plasters and linen. Will you do me the favor?"

"Your valet didn't change the dressing?"

"He's squeamish about blood."

Her expression turned skeptical. "You should dismiss him."

"*He* didn't shoot me."

She looked at him then, taking in the plain brown coat, the red and gold swirls of his waistcoat, and the deeper chocolate silk of his tie with its diamond pattern of reds and blues. As a rule, he played down any flash in his attire, but her scrutiny went beyond the hasty appraisal he was used to.

"Fair enough," she said, "but I need my notebook back."

"Today?"

"Of course, today."

"If the tide is right, I thought we could take a boat up the river to picnic."

"A boat? Up the river?" She looked away. "I have work to do."

He caught an odd note of unease in her voice. "We could look at the ruins of Parliament. Did you see the fire?"

She turned back to him, her curiosity plainly piqued. "I wasn't in London then. Did you see it?"

"From the bridge." Rook had had easy pickings that October night as crowds of Londoners gawked at the monstrous flames consuming the Palace of Westminster. But for Lark, the fire had been the deciding moment. He'd left his old life behind that night. "Help me change the plaster, and we'll be on our way." He shed his coat and laid it over the sofa arm.

Her skeptical gaze returned to him. "You're distracting me again. Why should we go up the river to see the ruins?"

"The best view is from the river. And you don't know London at all if you don't know the river." The trick with Viv, he'd discovered, was to keep going until she stopped him. He worked the buttons of his waistcoat until the sides hung open and drew the little book from his pocket.

She snatched it and clasped it to her chest. Her eyes closed briefly, then flew open again. "Did you read it?"

"Would you let me?"

"My writing is private."

"Maybe it's merely...dull."

"Dull?"

"And earnest—full of graves and grimy streets. Don't ladies want to read about the pleasures of London?"

"Pleasures?"

"Picnics, parks, gardens, shops?"

"I haven't... *We* haven't ignored those things. One of our walks is through a park."

It was his turn to look skeptical. "I'll wager you've never been to one of Mr. Green's balloon ascensions at Vauxhall."

"No, but...ladies may stroll in the parks without any special guidance."

"Because you went to Babylon Street to find your pickpocket, you think pickpockets don't go to parks? Don't go where ladies carrying purses go?" He watched to see whether she'd blush again over his reference to that purse.

"Is that what pickpockets see? Walking purses rather than women?"

That was a question he'd best not answer. "I thought your plan was to publish your guide to the world?"

"When it's been revised and edited." She slid the little book into a pocket of her skirts.

"So, someone will read it?"

"Yes, but not..."

"Not a man you might have written about?"

"If I did write about you, none of your acquaintance

would recognize the portrait."

"Still a man might not want to appear ridiculous in one of your stories like a figure in a print shop window." He removed his waistcoat and laid it on top of his coat. His shirt had been pristine when he'd put it on, now he feared there would be a spot of blood from the unchanged plaster. His sham courtship was proving costly.

"You're bleeding, and yet you worry about the sort of figure you'll make in a guidebook for ladies?"

"A man has his reputation."

"Really, men think that we women are the helpless ones. Let me send for some water and towels." She strode to ring the bell pull, and the ever-prompt Jenny appeared and was duly sent off, wide-eyed, to retrieve the needed items.

Lark pulled the ends of his shirt from his trousers, conscious that Viv's gaze had come back to him. He didn't want her thinking about his useless valet. "You don't feel an obligation to those you portray in these accounts?"

"What obligation should I feel?" She turned away and opened the package, laying out the linen and plasters with brisk efficiency.

He had a moment to doubt the wisdom of letting an angry woman change his bandage. "Shouldn't you ask permission of your subjects?"

"London is my subject. My stories are...illustrations of...of the types one meets."

A knock on the door signaled Jenny's return. She set towels and a water basin on the table. "Should I stay, miss?" she asked, looking at Lark with his shirt hanging out.

"No thank you, Jenny. I'm just changing Mr. Larkin's

bandage. Could you ask Mrs. Brandle to make a small picnic for us?"

Jenny bobbed a curtsy, and retreated.

"Am I a type?" Lark asked.

"I don't know. Yet. Show me your side."

He turned and lifted his shirt, fixing his gaze on the window. From her silence he knew at once what she was seeing. The unchanged bandage was ugly. There came a ripple of water in the bowl and a whisper of muslin. Viv's skirts brushed his legs in the same instant that she pressed a warm, wet towel to his side. He stiffened in response, and she put a steadying hand to his waist. His heart lurched, and he sucked in a breath.

"What do I know of you after all?" she asked. "I suspect that for all your lofty connections to a duke, you are, in fact, an actor, capable of playing a part at a moment's notice—helpful gentleman, rejected suitor, ardent lover—whatever the moment calls for."

She was dangerously observant and very near, though not as close as he wanted her to be. He stood in an intoxicating little cloud of her presence, as disorienting as a thick fog. Under the flowery fragrance was another slight thread of a scent, warm and elusive, woven into the layers of fresh silk and linen, that was simply *her*. "Why an actor?"

"You could have been coming from Wych Street or Drury Lane when we met."

She was obviously in no fog. Her thinking was clear and analytic, her memory precise. He didn't like it. "You only think that because you fell asleep during my thrilling life story."

"Thrilling, is it?"

"And full of pathos."

"Tell me, then."

"On our picnic. In your story, did you give me a name?"

"You're curious, are you?"

He was. The name she'd given him would tell him something about how she saw him. "I didn't read the notebook, Viv. I'd rather have you read it to me."

"It's just notes." She removed the damp cloth from his side.

"I could make helpful suggestions."

"I have Lady Melforth for that, thank you."

"But Lady Melforth wasn't there. On Babylon Street."

She looked up, and their gazes met. A flicker of interest appeared in her eyes. He knew he'd got her thinking. She did want to share her writing.

"I'm going to pull away the old plaster now," she said.

Lark just had time to grip the edge of the mantel when she tore the plaster off. For a moment, his head swam, at the mercy of sensations, cold air against stinging skin, and above all, the firm press of her hand at his waist. She turned away to discard the old plaster. Then her fingers pressed lightly around the aching place in the middle of the sting, and her voice came again. He thought he detected a quiver in it, as if she were not as detached as she appeared to be. "The stitches are holding. You can thank Dr. Newberry for that."

Lark did not want to thank Dr. Newberry.

"The bleeding's not bad, but you are a little bruised around the wound." Her fingertips traced a circle on his skin setting it tingling. Again, she dipped a cloth into the basin.

"Do you really think you can manage a boat ride?"

"If you wrap the new plaster securely."

"Very well."

He forgot time as he gave himself up to her ministrations, her hands smoothing the plaster in place and winding the strip of linen around his middle. Her elusive scent wound around him, too. Her garments whispered with her movements.

Then she stepped away, as if she'd been wholly unmoved by their nearness. "You'll do," she said. "Let me collect my things, and we'll be off."

"Wait," he said. "Did you give me a name in your notes?"

"A name?"

"Newberry said you give your subjects a name." Lark thought she blushed.

"You have to tell me your story, remember."

"On our picnic."

"Oh, very well. Winkworth," she said and slipped through the drawing door.

"*Winkworth?*" he called after her.

CHAPTER EIGHT

VIV STARED AT the stone steps leading down from the water gate to a cluster of open skiffs bobbing on the dull sage surface of the river. The wooden hulls knocked together with the restless movement of wavelets lapping the shingle. Gulls cried overhead. Memories stirred fixing her in place on the first stair. As she reached out a hand to keep her balance, Mr. Larkin called up to her.

"Don't touch that wall, Viv. Mind your skirts don't brush it either."

She glanced at the vivid reeking band of green along the boards beside her and pulled her skirts close. She'd not been on the river since she'd come to London, but the stink was familiar. She was trying to place where she'd smelled it when Mr. Larkin gripped her elbow, steadying her as she descended.

At the river's edge pebbles crunched under her sturdy half-boots, and a rough young waterman, red-bearded and muscled, a billowing white shirt rolled up over his strong arms, offered a hand to lift her into his skiff. She stepped in and stiffened against the rocking under her feet, an instant reminder of being on one of her stepfather's unsettling sailing expeditions.

Captain Frank Pennington had a side business of helping

gentlemen move their pleasure boats from Weymouth to other harbors along the southern coast. Occasionally he'd *borrow* one of those boats to take his girls out for a sail, usually after a quarrel with their mother. *Where's my navy?* he'd yell. They were expected to leave their work unfinished over their mother's objections, don jackets and caps, and line up for his inspection. He'd be his most charming self, leading them from their lodgings along the Strand past the statue of the old king to the long inlet lined with masts and gleaming decks. There he'd pick out some gentleman's grand pleasure boat. *Who's for the Indies?* he'd cry. *Who's for the Americas?*

They'd head out to sea until the shore was a faint distant line, and she and her sisters were wet and shivering, their gloved hands frozen to lines or winch handles. In time, Viv realized that her unease on these adventures sprang not from the roughness of the waves or the darkness of the waters, but from the theft and the threat that her stepfather would not turn back, as if he were saying to their mother that he could charm her daughters away from her. Viv's relief was always profound when he'd order them to come about. *Is it tea time?* he'd ask.

"Viv?" Mr. Larkin called her back to the present. "Bend your knees, or you'll topple over."

She did as he said. She didn't want to think about her stepfather or what it meant that her sisters were still subject to his whims and that until the guide was published, she had so little to send them. Then she remembered the smell. The pickpocket had smelled like the river. She would add that detail to her notes later.

Mr. Larkin lifted their picnic basket and a rug into the little boat and stepped in beside her. She had agreed to his river expedition in order to get a story, two stories—his and the one about the great fire. She had to admit he'd made her curious, and the writer in her knew the value of a firsthand account of such an event.

"You owe me a story," she said, sitting down on the forward bench.

"First, the ruins." He settled beside her, leaning close, speaking into the gap between her bonnet and her cheek, a warm puff of breath that made her shiver. "Then, the picnic."

The waterman pushed them off the shore and leapt in, taking his position in the stern of the little boat, and sliding his oars into locks. With a few pulls he turned the sharp nose of the skiff westward up the river, and with a few more dips of the oars, the incoming tide took them. The river boiled along, swift and swirling, its somber surface broken into jagged points of slate flashing in the sun. A breeze rushed over them, and the great city all but disappeared behind a fringe of shabby, sagging buildings along the water's edge. It was a new perspective. Viv reached for her notebook and pencil, but the chop on the water made notetaking impossible.

Dozens of vessels rode the current, from low, heavy barges strung together to single-masted boats with slanting sails, crisscrossing the river against the tide, and steam packets crammed with passengers, their paddlewheels churning and their tall stacks belching smoke.

Their waterman hailed the crew of a long string of barges

rippling through the water. A conversation followed of which Viv understood hardly a word, but in a minute a competition had begun as their skiff raced the line of barges bearing down on one of the great round arches of Westminster Bridge. The bridge loomed over them as the boats converged on the narrow opening. They were nearly neck and neck with the heavy barge so close that Viv thought their near oar must touch the barge's side. The bridge opening was clearly too narrow for both the fat barges and their skiff. They were doomed unless their waterman backed off. Instead, he gave a great pull on the port oar. The wooden skiff would be crushed against the stones.

Mr. Larkin wrapped an arm around her shoulders and pulled her close. "Hang on," he said.

Abruptly, the nose of the skiff dipped and the river sucked them down until they glided into the blackness under the bridge and shot through the other side into the flash of ripples well ahead of the barge. Viv sat stunned, clinging to Mr. Larkin, which was madness.

"You knew that would happen, didn't you?"

"It's a trick the watermen have," he said. "Where the river's flow narrows, the water speeds up and gives a lighter vessel the advantage over the heavier one."

A trick. Viv's heart returned to its regular beat. She shook off Mr. Larkin's hold. It was the very thing she and Lady Melforth wanted to warn their unsuspecting readers of, whether writing of boatmen or hackney drivers, or any of the dozens of men who offered to help the unsuspecting female traveler navigate the great city.

The waterman turned their skiff toward the river's north

bank. At once the ruins of the burned palace appeared. The waters below the ruins made a calm pool beyond the reach of the current and the chop of the main channel. Viv took up her pencil and put it down at once. It was necessary simply to look at the ruined palace.

She had not anticipated the melancholy of the scene. Blue and gold streaks alternated on the water's smooth surface reflecting both sky and ruins. Though it was six months since the fire, a smell of damp ash filled the air. Roofless and backless, the saffron stone walls faced the river with light streaming through the ancient tracery of the central arch. Other windows stared, empty black holes. The trees along the bank, as tall as the buildings themselves, stood blasted and withered like mourners, as if no spring would ever come to them again.

"You saw the fire?" she asked.

"From the bridge," he said. Like her he seemed sobered by the scene.

"Tell me what you saw." She bent her head to the little notebook.

Next to her on the bench, Mr. Larkin began to speak. "Black smoke was billowing when I arrived a little after sunset. Flames had burst some of the windows, streaming out in great orange tongues."

"Where was the fire brigade?"

"Not on the river, the tide was low, so fire boats could not get near, nor could they fill their hoses. There was a great crowd on the bridge, but you couldn't hear anyone speak over the roar of the fire." He gestured to the span behind them. "You could feel the heat. Ash blew over the crowd, and showers of embers lit the sky. The flames turned the river orange. The moon was full and—"

Viv stopped her notetaking to give Mr. Larkin a glance. "And?"

"Red...like a...a wound in the sky."

The words surprised her. His face in profile revealed little, but she thought the fire had affected him, changed him in some way. It was loss he described.

He recovered his usual easy manner and went on. "Not long after I arrived, there was a tremendous blast. The roof collapsed, and the fire exploded heavenward in a great ball. There was no stopping it after that. Everyone knew the palace was gone."

"What was the mood of the crowd?"

"Some were glad of it, but most were sobered. London is stone and brick. It's solid and real." He paused. "A man's city is not supposed to go up in flame and smoke."

She closed up her notebook and simply watched him. It was plain that the ruins held some personal meaning for him. "What happened next?" she asked.

He turned back to her with a rueful laugh, as if he'd been the object of a joke.

"What?"

"With the palace gone, the call came to save the hall next door. I answered. I joined a crew manning pumps on a fire engine. We were at it for hours, but we did save the hall." He pointed.

"That's it? That's all you have to say about an epic battle with flames?"

"I ruined a good set of clothes."

They were more alike than she'd thought. Though he was not telling her what amused him about manning a fire engine pump, it was plain that London was his place, his home, and that he had been shaken in some way by the destruction of a major institution.

"Do you think Parliament will rebuild?" She tucked her notebook away.

"Grander than ever," he said. He turned to their waterman with instructions.

THEY WENT UP the river a little way and crossed to the south bank where a grassy knoll rose above the marshy shore. Their waterman beached the boat and handed Viv out onto a wooden plank that stretched across the mud to drier ground. Lark followed carrying their rug and picnic basket. They climbed the knoll and found a spot to spread the rug. Lark stretched out on his good side and let Viv unpack their basket. Her mood had been sobered by the ruins or the boat ride. He couldn't decide which, but he hoped the picnic would restore her spirit.

"You wanted my story," he said. Best to tell her while she was distracted by the items in their basket.

"Yes." She removed a green lacquer tray from the top of the basket and began setting items on it.

"It's easy to tell. I was orphaned young. Wenlocke, who takes an interest in orphans, saw to my education, and kept my one relative, an aunt on my mother's side, apprised of my progress. From time to time, she generously supplies my needs."

Her hands paused in setting out a covered dish. "Really, that's your story?"

"You see. No wonder you fell asleep the first time I told it." He reached out a hand to lift the lid on the dish, but she stopped him with a hand over his.

"You said your story was *thrilling* and full of *pathos*."

"Are you not moved that I was orphaned young?" He pressed a hand over his heart.

She pulled a jar of lemonade and two glasses from the basket. "Where does this aunt of yours live?"

"Somerton." It was a question he'd prepared for.

"Where are your parents buried?"

"They were lost at sea, so I've no grave to visit."

"You were an only child?"

"I was."

"And did you go to school somewhere? Where the masters beat you and denied you enough to eat?" She arched a brow.

"Not at all. I was privately tutored in Wenlocke's house with other boys like me." That, at least, was not a fiction. He should have anticipated that she would keep probing. Now he'd have to remember the answers he gave. "Are you going to let me see what's in that dish?"

"Cold meats," she said. "This aunt from Somerton did not take you into her household?"

"She's elderly," he said. "What elderly maiden takes on a boy?"

"You do know that your story is not going to help much tonight when Lady Melforth asks questions over tea."

"Tea?"

"Lady Melforth insists that she get to know you."

As long as she did not ask the obvious question, the one for which he had not yet formulated an answer, the question of how a random orphan came to the notice of a duke. "I shall regard too many questions as impertinent. Shall we eat?"

"Hah," she said. "Great ladies feel quite entitled to know the business of the young gentlemen betrothed to members of their household."

"Then I shall have to charm her."

Her expression sobered at once. He pushed himself into an upright sitting position. "What? You don't want me to charm her? You don't trust charm?"

"I don't." She lifted the lid on the covered dish. "Chicken?"

AT THE FASHIONABLE hour of nine, Haxton showed Lark into the upper drawing room where Lady Melforth held court. She had left her couch and cushions for a high-backed gold velvet armchair with a crown of elaborate gilt woodwork. The chair's gold filigree gleamed in the light of a dozen wax candles in tall silver candelabra above the stone mantel.

Her ladyship's red hair was piled high above her imperious countenance, and one thick curl coiled artfully down over her right shoulder. Heavy black lace on a moss-colored silk gown spilled over her wrists on the arms of the chair.

Her injured foot lay on a small padded velvet stool. Her posture was erect, her alert eye poised to detect a visitor's every misstep. Lark noted the bit of vanity in that one curl. He did not see any tremor in her ladyship's hand.

He made his bow as Haxton announced him. He had dressed in black dinner wear, as if he'd just left his club or perhaps the duke's house and not his modest bachelor's quarters. Straightening, he risked a brief glance at Viv, stiffly upright and obviously uneasy in a low chair to her ladyship's right. He nodded. She looked at her hands clasped in her lap. He had not thought his remark about charming Lady Melforth would offend Viv so deeply.

She wore a wool gown the color of ripe plums, her hair up, no jewelry except for pearl bobs in her ears. The low chair, the dark gown, the occasion, he didn't know what had subdued her spirits. If he could get close to her, he would lean into that exposed curve between her shoulder and the pearl-studded tip of one ear and whisper a challenge to make her eyes flash.

He gathered that he was to face Lady Melforth's inquisition on his own.

"Mr. Larkin." Lady Melforth tapped the arm of her chair. "I must take you to task for this engagement you've entered into. You really should have sought my permission to pay your addresses to a lady of Miss Bradish's standing."

"Forgive me, ma'am. Necessity prompted me to act in haste." Lark crossed the rich carpet, stopping only when he stood where her ladyship was obliged to look up at him.

"Necessity?"

"Your relations, ma'am, the Strydes, were at hand, and

from what Miss Bradish has told me, I feared that they might mistake my intentions toward her."

Lady Melforth cast him a reproachful glance. "I don't like this going behind my back. I should have been warned, you know, that an engagement was imminent."

"Again, ma'am, I beg your pardon. Miss Bradish and I could hardly be more open with the Strydes so often here."

"Yes, well. Do sit down, Mr. Larkin. I cannot be looking up at you like this." She waved a lace-draped hand toward a shield-backed chair in the opposite corner.

Lark concealed a smile and drew the chair into a position where Lady Melforth could look down her nose at him.

"You do know Miss Bradish has no fortune of her own," her ladyship continued.

"I do."

"And you must not be misled by her position in my house. You must not rely on anything from me."

Lark looked at Viv again, at the low chair and the plum dress, and returned his gaze to Lady Melforth. His jaw tightened. There was no mistaking Viv's position. She might not be Jenny or one of the footmen, but she was subject to her ladyship's whims. His position as her false fiancé gave him no right to protest that she deserved better.

"I do not, ma'am. If anything, I prize Miss Bradish the more for her independence from borrowed prospects." It was a daring thing to say, and he wondered if he'd gone too far. He waited in silence while the coals on the fire hissed and a clock on the mantel made the faintest of ticks.

"You're very sure of yourself, young man. Who are your people?"

"Miss Bradish hasn't told you?"

"Only that you were orphaned about the time of my father's death at *Waterloo*," Viv said.

Lark caught the warning. "You mustn't blame Viv, ma'am. There's little to tell. I've an aunt in Somerton, and no other relations that I'm aware of."

"A very inadequate account, young man, but you are an only son."

"I am."

"So, what property is there?"

"Investments. Through Hammersley's Bank. My aunt's Somerton property will come to me in time, I suppose." Lark was warming to his convenient fictional aunt.

"You are very sanguine about your prospects. Do you expect anything from the duke?"

"No, ma'am."

"He has not offered to buy you a commission or to give you a living in his gift?"

"Nothing of the sort would suit me, ma'am."

"Well, Miss Bradish cannot live on nothing."

"Nor will she have to." Again, Lark's jaw tightened.

"Still this engagement remains most inconvenient. There must be no delay in the publication of our guidebook."

"There won't be, ma'am. What may I do to assist Miss Bradish?"

"Viv, what do you do tomorrow?"

The door opened, admitting Haxton followed by a young footman in green velvet livery burdened with a particularly large silver tea tray, and Dr. Newberry. As the footman set his tray on the table next to Viv, Newberry, in a brown coat and careless black silk tie, strode toward Lady Melforth, perfectly at ease.

Lark saw that he had erred in dressing formally.

"Newberry." Her ladyship stretched out a hand. "What brings you to us tonight?"

Newberry took the offered hand and held it in his. "I hope I'm not intruding, ma'am. My rounds brought me into the neighborhood, and I thought I'd look in to see how you all were doing."

"You see we are well and entertaining Viv's...Mr. Larkin. Have you met?"

"We have." Newberry gave Lark an amused scrutiny. "What's the occasion, man? A state dinner? Dining with your duke?"

"Just dinner with school friends at their club." Lark's club was a cook shop on Baker Street where they were quite surprised to see him in evening wear.

Newberry returned his gaze to Lady Melforth, turning her hand palm up in his and feeling her wrist.

"Newberry, I tell you I'm well," she protested, withdrawing her hand. "Tell me about your other cases."

He laughed, and began telling her about an evening call on a gouty retired admiral.

Lark rose and crossed to Viv as she arranged the cups and saucers on the silver tray. With his back to the others, he said, "You seem quiet tonight. Worried?"

"I should be, shouldn't I? You like flirting with danger." She held a slotted spoon over a blue-and-white porcelain cup and began pouring.

"We're well-matched, then. You like courting risk."

"I like writing a book with Lady Melforth." She gave him a measuring glance. "This charade will never work. I don't even know how you take your tea."

"We won't be exposed over tea," he said. "Where do you go tomorrow?"

She stirred sugar into the cup she had poured. "No need for you to accompany me. I can manage on my own, thank you. Will you take this to her ladyship?"

He nodded, accepting the cup. "Should I worry about the safety of other unsuspecting gentlemen you might shoot?"

Her eyes flashed, and he lost himself briefly. From behind him came Lady Melforth's voice. "How is her grace?"

He tore his gaze away from Viv.

"Why, well, ma'am." Lark really had no idea, but he could not imagine that anything had befallen the Duchess of Wenlocke with Dav, that is the duke, at her side. "Your tea."

Lady Melforth took the cup. Her voice turned wistful. "She was just a young girl when I met her, pretty spoken, fond of her ponies. Her family often called upon her to speak with English visitors, before the French came, of course."

"You met her on your travels then?" Lark meant to turn the conversation away from dangerous territory.

"Yes. I was writing my first guide, my *Letters from Florence, Rome, and Naples*."

"It's your practice, then, ma'am, to write your guides about cities?"

"What else! The English traveler seeks the best elements of a culture—its art and history, its markets, and its architectural glories. All these things are to be found in the great cities."

"And this is the method you've taught Miss Bradish?"

Lady Melforth glanced at Viv, as if she'd remembered her protégé's presence. "Well, they are *my* methods, of course, but I'm sure in time Miss Bradish will...profit from my tutelage."

"No doubt of it," Newberry chimed in. He took a cup of tea and set it on the mantel, leaning casually against the stone and grinning at Viv.

"Why London?" Lark persisted. "Surely every Englishman of means knows London, and there are dozens of pocket guides to the city."

"Ah, but my—*this*—book is for women, for the new woman of this new age."

"The woman who is free to go anywhere in London? Without a companion?" Lark pressed. "That's where Viv comes into it?"

The teacup rattled in Lady Melforth's hands.

"Your tea, Mr. Larkin," Viv said, calling his attention to her. He turned and took the cup she offered him.

Lady Melforth continued. "We women should be able to choose our companions, and not be saddled with nursemaids or chaperones. It's absurd that a woman of sense must have a ninny at her side to be considered respectable." Lady Melforth put down her cup and crossed her hands in her lap, burying the offending hand under the steadier one.

Newberry straightened away from the mantel. "We mustn't tire her ladyship, Larkin."

Lark returned his untouched cup to Viv, turned, and bowed to Lady Melforth. "Good evening, ma'am." He followed Newberry to the door.

"Wait, Mr. Larkin," Lady Melforth called, "one more thing. Have you placed an announcement in the papers?"

Lark glanced at Viv. "We agreed to tell our news to Viv's family first."

"Hmph." Lady Melforth waved a dismissive hand. "They, of course, can do nothing for her. Much wiser to introduce her to your duke."

"A good thought, ma'am."

"And soon. The Strydes will wonder at it when they see no announcement in the papers. Trust me, young man, charm of manner will have no effect upon Mrs. Stryde."

Lark bowed again. The footman opened the door, and Lark and Newberry descended the stairs in silence, accepted their coats and hats from Haxton, and stepped out into the night. Lark took a deep breath. The evening was not a complete disaster. He'd gained ground with Lady Melforth, but seemed to have lost it with Viv.

"How are those stitches?" Newberry asked.

"I hardly notice them. You did your work well."

"Where did you say you had dinner?" Newberry asked.

"With school friends."

"And what school was that?"

"In my aunt's part of the country, Newberry, it's common for boys to be schooled together by a local grinder. I regard those boys as my *school* friends."

"You always have an answer, don't you? One day, I suspect, you won't. Good night." Newberry strode off.

CHAPTER NINE

IN THE MORNING, Lark met Viv in front of Lady Melforth's house. London stood gray and solid under a pale blue sky except where a few fearless blades of grass had sprung up between the paving stones. The prolonged spell without rain had dried the usual muck of the streets, and passing vehicles stirred up dust. "No carriage?" he asked. "Where are we off to today then?"

"Shopping." She pulled on her gloves. "No woman is at home in a city until she knows where to find the things she needs for her household or her work."

Lark thought that only Viv would mention work in that way, as something a woman would inevitably have. They were a short walk from three great shopping streets. "What things did you have in mind?"

"Everything from linens to pressed paper," she said. "So, if you have any manly objection to choosing textures and patterns, you may leave me to it." She set off toward Cavendish Square.

As they passed the plain brick St. Peter's Church, he let her outpace him. He admired the tilt of her chocolate silk hat above the intertwined coils of her hair, and the set of her dove-colored cape on her shoulders. Today, printed blue cotton skirts rustled with her quick stride. She was everything neat and contained. In a vivid flash he saw her at her dressing table that dark, honey-colored hair spilling down, hair pins scattered on the carpet, a silk wrapper loose around her. He corrected the vision at once. Viv's pins would be in a little porcelain dish. The blue silk wrapper would be properly tied at her waist.

He guessed that in her head she was leagues ahead of him, peering in shop windows, opening doors, examining goods for sale. "Your method is wrong, you know," he said.

She glanced back at him without slowing. "My method? What do you mean wrong?"

"If you always have an objective on your walks, how will you discover anything?"

She halted and turned, a look of strained patience on her face. He knew that look. He was sure that his own face wore it when he explained some obvious point that Rook refused to understand. "You enjoy provoking me, don't you?" she said.

He shrugged. It was a new pleasure, an unexpected one. He couldn't deny it.

"Do you have another method to suggest?" she asked.

"I do." He caught up with her, and they started walking again, until she turned the corner at Holles Street. Abruptly, she stopped and whacked him with her bag, which, he noted, was not weighted with stones.

He laughed. "Do you want to hear my method?"

"Tell me."

Lark was in no hurry. At Oxford Street he took her arm in his and turned them west. The long street, lined with hundreds of shops of every sort, dipped and rose toward the distant corner where in centuries past the Tyburn gallows had stood.

She pulled back in his hold, offering him a questioning look. "I was thinking of Regent Street. Oxford Street…is…"

"Vulgar, gaudy, beneath your dignity?"

"There are pickpockets, aren't there?"

"Undoubtedly, but there are beadles to chase them away. You won't need your pistol."

She shot him a quick glare. "I know that."

"Trust me, for shopping pleasure, Oxford Street is what you want." He tugged her into motion again. "Regent Street jacks up its prices to convince buyers of the quality of its goods, and Bond Street pretends not to engage in trade at all, but merely to confer the mantle of fashion on the select few."

He waited. He'd got her thinking, revising her plan. He counted on Oxford Street itself to draw her with the sheer energy of so many Londoners in motion. In the jammed roadway, the rattle and rumble of individual sets of wheels merged into a single roar. On the pavement the bustling crowd streamed and eddied, snagged by shop windows full of goods.

Once again old memories stirred. Years before when Lark returned to London from Dav's country estate, Oxford Street, for all its bargains, had been above his touch. He and Rook had not been in the city a month before they'd sold the clothes Dav had given them to get their first room. Without those fine clothes, they had been out of place on Oxford Street, chased away, whenever they lingered, by shopkeepers' clerks and beadles. Lark shook off the memories. He was no longer that boy. One of the benefits of their charade was that

Lark could move freely among the most fastidious of shoppers even on Bond Street.

"First, slow down," he told Viv. "You want to notice details. You want to become part of the scene." Oxford Street was definitely a scene.

"Part of the scene? I'm an observer, a chronicler."

"You say you want women to move freely about London without being targets."

Viv nodded.

"So, they have to belong to the scene. They've got to be unhurried. It takes practice."

He slowed their pace to a stroll. Her skirts barely whispered. He liked having a hold of her arm. It made them a pair. They passed a window with a hundred pairs of shoes laid out like a splendid banquet, the merchant confident that the demand of London was great enough for even a shoe seller to make a fortune.

"You know," she said at a third window, "grazing cows in a field move faster than we're moving."

"Start noticing details."

"You think I'm not good at noticing details?"

He held his gloved hand in front of her eyes. "How many flower sellers are pushing their barrows our way?"

She was silent, her lips sealed in a tight line. He resisted the impulse to brush his thumb over those lips. This was her concentration mouth. He liked her mouth in all her moods. "Three," she said, a triumphant note in her voice. "There are two fellows with daffodils, and one with violets. And there's a man in an odd green suit with a cart full of tortoises lying on a bed of grass. Did I miss anything?"

He took his hand away. "Just a knife grinder."

She laughed and let him lead her onward. They swerved around a crowd pressed to the window of a silversmith's shop.

"Now you're ready for step two."

"And what is that?"

"You pick, at random, something you're likely to find in the scene to guide your steps."

"That sounds like an objective to me."

"Not at all."

"Enlighten me then."

"Pick a number, a low number."

"Three." No hesitation from his Viv.

"Now I'll pick a category of objects, say arched doorways, men in silk hats, or wild animals. After the third one, we take the next turn, whichever side of the street it's on."

"That's simply wandering."

He tilted his head her way, speaking confidentially. "It's letting the city take you to places you didn't know existed."

"If I pick wild animals," she said, challenging him as usual, "what happens to your game?"

He stopped, pulled her to the edge of the pavement, and pointed to the top of a building. A pair of beavers carved in stone faced the pointed center of the roof.

"No fair. You knew they were there."

"I've played the game before. See that lion up ahead, on his stout stone column. We'll turn there."

"Very well, for the sake of the game," she said.

At the lion, they turned into a narrow passage, and immediately left the crowd behind. On either side were neat dwellings, and at the end, a grand stone house with columns and pilasters surmounted by a tympanum where an ancient warrior in helmet and tunic grappled with a winged opponent.

In the little byway, Lark had no need to slow Viv. She was clearly charmed. They ambled to the end of the cul-de-sac to look up through bare branches at the imposing mansion.

She reached for her notebook. "Do you know anything about it? Who owns it? How old it is?"

"It's for sale," he said. "It's not too old, maybe fifty years. A man built it for his bride, and she left him for another man."

"You made that up."

"I didn't. The selling agent told me about it."

Her brow furrowed. "Do you talk to selling agents for the duke?"

He'd slipped, forgetting for a moment that Edward Larkin was a mere secretary to a rich man. "If he asks me. I do read the papers and get curious. Buildings have histories, you know. Are you ready to shop?"

She held his gaze, letting him know that she was weighing his words, noting the inconsistencies in that little self-revelation. Her keen attention was a heady mix of wanting her to truly see him, Lark, the man he was under the gentlemanly attire and fearing that she would. He kept his expression bland. At last, she spoke. "Let me make a few more notes."

He nodded, released from scrutiny. She wrote rapidly for a few minutes while he considered how to get her mind back on shopping. When she put away the little notebook, he offered his arm again.

"There are at least a dozen hosiers on the street, a straw bonnet maker, a corset and stay merchant, and one who sells brushes and combs. There's a shop for ladies' shoes and one for fancy French paper. What's your preference?"

"French paper," she said. "Have we stopped our wandering game?"

"Only while you purchase paper."

VIV PUT AWAY her notebook and accepted Mr. Larkin's arm. They retraced their steps to the stone lion on Oxford Street. Once again, he puzzled her. What he did for the duke changed with each of their conversations. For a rich man's secretary, he was knowing and haughty, and he probably rivaled his employer in finery. The little inconsistencies in his account of his employment reminded her of the earlier thought she'd had that he was perhaps an actor. But that couldn't be right either because he seemed almost to own the city.

At the corner, Oxford Street's incessant discordant rhythm recalled her to her task, which had nothing to do with the mysterious nature of her betrothed. Delivery van drivers urged their horses onward, angling this way and that, as they maneuvered past their fellows. The pavement pulsed with the staccato movement of passersby surging forward and stopping for shop windows. Oxford Street drew female shoppers with their billowing skirts taking up the walkway, but the atmosphere was far from that of Bath's genteel, ladylike Milsom Street where Viv had shopped with her aunt.

Mr. Larkin was right that Viv had been relying on what she already knew of shopping. She had not been open to discoveries. Her plan to find and name a few reputable merchants for the readers of their guide looked like folly in the face of the sheer number of shops.

And it struck her as odd that no one appeared actually to buy anything. "Why does no one enter the shops?"

"Ah," he said. "Looking is part of the game. Each shop preens a little, showing off its goods, asking you to linger and admire. It's supposed to be pleasurable."

"Pleasurable?"

They approached the corner of Holles Street. "How many shops did you wish to see?" he asked. "This is a nice stretch, a stationer, a tea dealer, and a chemist."

He steered her to the window of the tea dealer. Through the glass, orderly rows of black and green canisters each more than a foot high lined open mahogany shelves. There was an artistic flare to the contrast between the neat jars, with their vaguely foreign markings and hand-lettered labels, and a porcelain tea set in blue and white laid out on a white cloth-covered table as if ready for a lady to pour. The shop window told a little story of goods coming from the distant East to grace an English table.

Viv had not thought of shopping as pleasure before her time in Bath. In Weymouth, she or one of her sisters would be dispatched by their mother to procure a needed item, urged to hurry, and directed to one of the shabbier shops away from the Esplanade where merchants catered to fashionable visitors. She supposed that those experiences had defined her idea of shopping.

She turned to him. "How can anyone choose? Generally, I've not had much patience for shopping. One wants a thing…"

"Tooth powder, soap, shoes?"

"Exactly, and one does not need or want a hundred pairs of shoes to choose from."

He nodded gravely, but she detected a gleam in his eyes. "You want to enter a shop, look right, look left, make your purchase, and go. That's your method?"

"Don't mock. Someone needs to make sense of all this. A woman can't spend all day wandering as you put it. One simply wants merchandise of a decent quality at a price that's not too dear."

"No more wandering then." He turned from the window to look down the street. "What sort of shops do you want to see? And how many?"

Viv followed his gaze. On both sides of the wide thoroughfare, signs advertised goods of every sort. She could not possibly visit or catalogue all the shops she saw. The piece she had planned to write for the guide wouldn't work. A few shops would have to give her the flavor of Oxford Street. "I will concentrate on shops that cater to women."

"Milliners? Ladies' shoe sellers? Hosiery and glove merchants?"

This time Viv tugged him into motion, turning them east. "Yes. All those, and a few more, but the main aim of this outing is to find out where a woman can shop without interference."

"Without men annoying her, you mean."

"Yes! I'm sure you, as a gentleman, can walk the length of Oxford Street without some woman following you or pestering you to talk with her and treating you as if you..." She let the thought trail off. She wasn't going to explain it to him. She was too aware of his person. His mere presence stirred her in ways she did not wish to name.

"As if I what?"

"Knew things."

"Oh, *things*. As it happens, I do know *things*."

She risked a glance at him. He kept his gaze straight ahead. "Yes, but no one thinks the less of you for knowing them. No one imagines that you aren't a gentleman, or that your person is an item for sale."

"Are you proposing to walk the length of the street alone to discover whether some man thinks you know *things*?" He sounded as if he thought her mad.

"Not necessary." She pulled out her notebook again. "I just need to get a sense of the place to know what women shoppers will face. Give me the names of a few shops."

"Which way are you going?"

She pointed east.

"Try the Pantheon Bazaar, then."

She stopped. She had heard of the bazaar. Bazaars had become a sort of phenomenon in London, a place for merchants to sell their wares under one roof, while the organizer of the bazaar provided amenities like tea rooms and exhibits, dressing rooms and performances. The concept had its proponents and detractors. She would see for herself. "I will. Thank you."

He frowned. "If any man bothers you…"

"No matter. I'll handle it. Don't follow me." She set off. "Don't shoot anyone."

She sent him another swift glare over her shoulder. He stood with his hand pressed to his side.

"I'll give my ribs a rest," he said. "Meet me at the West End dining rooms in an hour, Viv, or I will come looking for you."

CHAPTER TEN

LARK WATCHED HER go with her chocolate silk bonnet and purposeful stride. When she reached the first crossing, it required a fair bit of resolution to turn the other way. He told himself that no real harm could come to her. There were men who might misread her singleness as vulnerability or an invitation, and he had seen a few pretenders to fashion who might approach her. But he hadn't spotted anyone on the game.

Oxford Street was familiar territory to him now. In the months since the fire, he had established himself as a regular in places like the West End Dining Room by the habit of stopping in for coffee and a roll and reading the papers. Still, he caught himself in front of a silk warehouse window, lost to his surroundings. His mind followed Viv. He pictured himself in the upper gallery of the Pantheon, looking out for her, watching to catch her reaction to the place.

He laughed at himself. He had tried to teach her something of his street-wise way of moving in London, but here he was, forgetting basic lessons in wariness that he'd learned as a boy under Dav. At least he was not fool enough to pull out his watch to check the time. The day was mild, and an hour was not so long.

He stuck to his promise. He strolled west, crossing and

turning east again only when he reached the end of Oxford Street. He was looking ahead down the walkway, hoping to spot her approaching him, when at Shepherd's Street, a body slammed against his, sending him reeling into the shadows of the byway, careening against a brick wall. His ribs screamed, and his hat went flying. He caught himself against the wall and turned to face his assailant.

From the middle of the lane, Rook glared at him, chest heaving, heavy fists balled at his sides. He was dressed as Lark had never seen him, in a brown wool sack coat and black tie, like a clerk in an office, his hair cut, his beard trimmed, and above all not reeking. In the shadows Rook looked almost respectable, as if he'd quit the game, but his angry bewildered face told another story. There was no one else about.

"What are ye playing at?" Rook demanded. "Ye think yer better'n me. Ye think ye can go places I can't."

Lark straightened. Any chance that his new appearance signaled a change in Rook crumbled like a snuffed candlewick. Sharp needles of pain pricked Lark's injured side. "I told you I don't do clicks. I'm about to go for coffee. Join me."

Rook shook his head. "I saw you with her, with the mark. Wot's yer new game?"

"No game," he said, and a preposterous idea popped into his head. *I am going to marry her.* It had to be wrong. The wall opposite was plastered with posters, advertising the great spectacles in London's theaters—*The Fall of Pompeii, Tom and Jerry, Madame Vestris' Tableaux Vivant.* The grandiose posters mocked the idea that his engagement was real. He was having a lark, like his name, playing at being betrothed.

Rook thrust his face forward. "Yer no gentleman. Ye don't belong here. This isn't our pitch." Rook shoved Lark against the wall. "I'm yer partner, not some bird ye just met."

Lark steadied himself. Under the anger, he heard the cry of betrayal. In the bewildered face, he saw hurt. "We can be partners again if you want. Let's go to Dav. He'll help us start a new enterprise."

Rook's lip curled. "Enterprise? Yer daft. We do prigs and clicks. We don't know 'ow to do naught else."

Lark didn't answer. He didn't say that he did know. He knew quite well how to invest small sums that paid off handsomely, and then larger sums, how to play a long game, how to keep money in the bank, instead of in a hole under the floorboards. Rook had never been interested in Lark's ideas about making money from money.

"Ye don't belong with 'er. Her kind is not our kind. Ye think she's better than Liza? Ye think there's something different under those fancy blue skirts of 'ers?"

Lark threw a punch, trained, accurate, measured. It connected with Rook's nose and snapped his head back. Rook's hand flew to his face. He stood stunned for a moment, his brow furrowed, his brain clearly slow to comprehend what Lark had done. With the back of his hand, Rook wiped the blood away.

"'Liza's better than you think she is," Lark told him.

The remark launched Rook at him. Lark countered the flurry of punches, random but heavy with anger, until one fist connected with the wound in his side. His consciousness dimmed, his knees gave, and he fell back against the bricks and caught himself.

Rook dropped his fists and stepped back. "Ye can't quit on me for some toffy-nosed skirt. I won't let you."

"Quit *with* me, if you want to be partners again." Lark knew as he said it that Rook would never take the offer. Rook had found his place in London. He was who he was. He did not search as Lark did for a lost self he was meant to be.

"I warn ye. Keep shut of 'er, or… or… I'll tell 'er who ye really are." Rook shook a fist and turned away.

The attack was over. Lark leaned back against the wall, his ribs rising and falling like bellows pumping air, his side throbbing with each gusty breath. He reached for his handkerchief and ran it over his face. The linen caught a small bit of blood from the inside of his lip. He pushed himself from the wall. A rush of energy flooded him, but he knew it would pass. He brushed himself off and straightened his tie. His hat lay on the stones a few feet away.

He took the necessary steps, one at a time, and then laughed at himself. He could not bend down for the hat. He put his hand against the bricks and bent his knees until he could just reach the hat. He dusted it off, straightened, and set it back on his head. He stepped back into Oxford Street, a few doors from the dining room. He did not see Rook, but he wanted to make sure that Rook did not find Viv. Rook was not likely to hurt her, but he would make good on his threat to expose Lark.

At the Pantheon, the porter let him in without a second look. He passed from the entrance porch through the vestibule with its sculpture display, and up a flight of steps, through the galleries to the upper story. The wound in his side objected to the stairs, but he gritted his teeth and kept going until he could look down on the crowded main floor below.

A throng of ladies and gentlemen moved through aisles created by the island-like counters with their array of goods. Gentlemen's black hats and ladies' fashionable balloon-like sleeves made a shifting pattern below, like a dance. Relief rose up in him when he spotted Viv's plain dark bonnet. She moved from millinery to lace to gloves, and he realized she was being followed, not by Rook, but by a twig of a man in a pair of lavender gloves. From his gallery vantage point, Lark could not tell whether Viv noticed the fellow at all. At a fourth counter, she at last made a purchase.

Unexpectedly, she looked up. He was not quick enough. She spotted him.

VIV MARCHED UP the steps to the Pantheon's upper gallery, fueled by a spurt of hot anger. She had been thinking how helpful he'd been and how grateful she was that he'd led her to Oxford Street. Now that he had broken his promise not to follow her, her distrust of him returned.

He stood, one hand on the rail, looking the picture of gentlemanly ease, nothing exaggerated in his dress, unlike the excess in many of the men around her in the bazaar. As she drew near, she realized that his easy elegance was an illusion. His face had a drawn look, and something was wrong with his mouth. She suspected that he needed to hold onto the rail. "We were to meet at the West End rooms."

"We can go together," he said. "You must want to put some thoughts in your notebook."

"You promised not to follow me."

"I spotted a fellow in lavender gloves dogging your steps…"

"Oh him. I saw him. A pickpocket, do you think?" She kept her tone light, but she wondered whether his wound was bothering him. There was a stiffness to his posture as if he had made some fragile truce with pain.

"Not in lavender gloves." He laughed, and winced. "Did he attempt to speak with you?"

"No. I thought he was someone's footman. He had that look of waiting for direction."

"It's a poor footman who neglects his own mistress to follow a stranger. Shall we go?"

"Something's happened to you." With one gloved finger she touched the corner of his mouth. She drew her finger back. There was a tiny dot of blood on the tip.

He gave her a tight smile. "I met a fellow who didn't like my hat. He knocked it off me. I had to set him straight."

"In Oxford Street? Didn't you say that that sort of thing didn't happen here?"

"It was unexpected," he said.

She tried to read his expression and knew that he was concealing whatever had really happened. "He hit you."

"But he lacked science." He straightened away from the rail, but it looked to Viv as if the move cost him some effort.

"Science?" She didn't know the term.

"Skill, training."

"And you are a judge of that sort of thing?" She moved to his side to take his arm.

"As it happens, it is one of the things the duke insisted we learn."

Viv thought *we* was an interesting word, but she did not press him. "So, all in a day's work for a duke's secretary, a bit of leisure and some violent amusement?"

"What are you thinking?" he asked.

"I'm just trying to understand who you are."

"You know who I am. I'm your betrothed, and your partner in these London expeditions."

"Perhaps," she said. "I do thank you for directing me to Oxford Street. I have lots to write about what I saw today. But first, if you can manage, I think we'd better get you sitting down."

"If you insist. I'm curious. What did you buy?"

"Ribbons for my sisters. To trim their hats, a bargain."

AFTER THE DECORATIVE exuberance of the Pantheon Bazaar, Viv found the West End coffee room sober. A clock hung on one wall and hat rail ran around the room above the dark wooden partitions of the booths. The scents of coffee, warm bread, and faint tobacco mingled. Most of the guests were single gentlemen immersed in their newspapers. But at one of the tables in the center of the room, a lady and her daughter, who looked to be the age of Viv's youngest sisters, the twins, Eliza and Anne, held a quiet conversation with the child's elderly nurse. Viv wanted to applaud the lady's serene assurance. From somewhere in the back of the premises came the clatter of pots and murmurings of the staff. A prompt waitress smiled at Mr. Larkin in a familiar way and showed them to a booth. He hung his hat on the rail, and Viv removed her bonnet, cape, and gloves. She pulled out her notebook and pencil. "I should make my notes," she explained.

He took up the *Morning Chronicle*. "You write. I'll read."

She wrote rapidly, trying to capture her impressions. The street was changing; shopping itself was changing. A shift was happening, so that the merely practical business of finding necessities was giving way to a form of seduction. Goods were displayed in playful abundance. In the bazaar, women with their wide skirts moved between the counters like ships navigating narrow straits, stacks of little luxuries making irresistible siren calls as they passed.

Viv considered what she should say to readers. Whatever the rules of female movement on the street, the shops were meant to give women pleasure and stir their senses. In the Pantheon a counter girl urged Viv to see the ladies dressing room area. Few public places considered a woman's need for a few minutes to put herself to rights after shopping. The story she wanted to tell was the story of the smart female shopper, who could steer her way through such enticements without getting caught staring, or dreaming of things beyond the capacity of her purse, and who was not so lost that she failed to attend to the perils of unwanted male attention.

Viv had encountered the sort of man to avoid. He had fallen into step with her, observed that she was alone, and insinuated that her singleness meant she was inviting male company. She wished for an umbrella with which to whack him. He looked something like a jacket-wearing turnip. She leveled a critical look at his striped trousers and embroidered green waistcoat, and suggested that he find a new tailor. He abandoned all semblance of gentlemanly behavior and called her a bad name. Now she needed a name for him. Perhaps, *Wickersham*.

She put down her pen and shook her writing hand. Mr. Larkin lowered his newspaper and watched her. She reached for her coffee, and found it cold. She had plainly lost track of time, but he hadn't interrupted. "How long have you been waiting for me to stop?"

He signaled their waitress to bring a fresh cup. "I had my newspaper to occupy me."

The waitress replaced Viv's old coffee with a quickness and eagerness to please that brought to mind an unwelcome memory of Viv's stepfather. Captain Pennington never lingered over his coffee and paper without demanding a dozen little attentions from her mother and sisters. They were always on the jump to bring him another slice of toast, more jam, his pipe, and a penknife he used to work at his fingernails. Then, after all their efforts, he would shove back his chair, scraping the floorboards, and announce that he was going out for coffee.

She took up the fresh cup of coffee and glanced at Mr. Larkin over the rim. He had none of her stepfather's restless impatience, and he was good at not drawing attention to himself.

"What?" he asked.

She put down her coffee. "Your lip is swelling, I think."

A fleeting expression crossed his face that she could not read. She expected him to touch the lip, but he didn't. He was keeping whatever had really happened to himself.

She took another sip of coffee. She had called him *Winkworth* in the little sketch she'd written of their meeting, but the name didn't suit him. With most of the people she put in her stories, she seized upon some element of the person's looks or dress that lent itself to caricature, a prominent feature, an outlandish bit of clothing, a mannerism or affectation. Her pretend fiancé was assured and self-contained. She hadn't found any obvious vanity in him except perhaps in his claim to know London particularly well. And that might be the result of his history, but when she thought about his story it all seemed too convenient, too like a fairy tale—the absent family, the undemanding job, the implausible past in which he'd been orphaned and then educated and provided for by a duke.

She turned her notebook around and slid it across the table. He'd had a chance to study her without her notice. She wanted a similar chance. "Will you give it a glance?"

His dark brows went up. He pushed his coffee away and drew the little notebook closer. "You're sure?"

She nodded. "Did I get it right, do you think?"

"You want my opinion?"

"You'll give it whether I want it or not." That drew a smile.

He turned the pages, his eyes lowered to her notebook. Over the rim of her coffee cup, she studied him. He moved about London with extraordinary freedom. He had changed her way of going about her researches. She had set out to find the stories that each street had to tell, but he made her realize that she was writing from an observer's perspective and not as one who was part of the scene itself. That seemed to be his particular quality. He was part of London, at ease there. He was a people watcher like her. He had spotted the man in lavender gloves, but while she had seen the gloves as a mere affectation, he had understood that a pickpocket would not call attention to his hands with purple gloves.

It was fanciful to think, but she wondered at the sequence of events that led to their odd partnership. She fully believed there to be elements of design in the marvelous workings of the universe, but she did not imagine that the grand scheme of things had been arranged to give her the chance to write her stories with a promise of publication. Every step of the way from her aunt Louisa's invitation to accompany her to Bath and to meeting Lady Melforth in the Pump Room to the Strydes' insistence on Lady Melforth's hiring a companion for her stay in London was a forward momentum in Viv's life utterly unlike her Weymouth days. Meeting Mr. Larkin in Babylon Street seemed no more remarkable than the rest of the story. It had all worked to Viv's advantage. Now she wondered what steps had led him to that meeting and what he was getting out of their bargain.

He looked up at last, his hand resting on the notebook. "You don't think female shoppers wish to be seduced?"

"I don't. No one wants to be…worked upon, to be buying who knows what because of the setting or the sheer abundance of goods. One wants to be in charge, making one's decisions based on one's actual needs and one's purse."

He straightened a little and pressed his free hand to his wounded side.

"Did your assailant hit you in the ribs?" she asked.

"We were talking about seduction," he said.

"We are talking about shopping, sensible shopping, about knowing one's needs and one's means and making purchases accordingly."

"You've never been seduced in Weymouth?"

"In Weymouth?"

"When the sky is blue and white clouds drift by and the sun sparkles on the sea and warms your face and the air is fresh? Can you tell me that on such a day, you've never closed up your book, put away your pen, and walked nowhere, anywhere, just to be part of the day?"

"Of course, I love—" She stopped and looked conscious of falling into his trap.

He stood and extended a hand to help her up. "Then you've been seduced," he said.

"And you," she said, "have reopened that wound."

CHAPTER ELEVEN

WHEN THEY REACHED the house, Viv tugged him gently toward the basement entry, where in the below-stairs world of Lady Melforth's servants, they could find a private place. She had noticed the hitch in his stride. He had a way of pretending he felt no hurt, but she suspected that he was covering up whatever injury his attacker had given him.

"You have to let me look at the wound to make sure this mystery attacker of yours did no serious damage." She gathered her skirts to take the stairs.

"It can wait for my...valet's attention." He halted at the top of the stairs.

"Your valet? The man who can't endure the sight of blood?"

"You don't fear the growing impropriety of our...pretense?"

She let go of her skirts. "What impropriety? You and I are wholly indifferent to one another. Surely, I can endure another sight of those stitches. I promise to be gentle. I've been tending Lady Melforth's foot for weeks."

"A lady's foot and a gentleman's"—he winced—"ribs are...different."

"So, you *have* taken a blow to the ribs! I can see it in

your walk."

"A random hit. I'll live."

"Maybe I need reassurance." She put a hand to his back and gave him a little push. It was the sort of encouragement she might give to one of her sisters, but Mr. Larkin had a lean, hard solidity to him. Just a brief touch, just her palm flattened against the hollow of his back, sent a wave of warmth through her. She dropped her hand and gave it a little shake.

"Feeling guilty over shooting me, Viv?" He watched her over his shoulder with knowing eyes.

She looked away. "Not at all," she lied. "Why are you permitted to call me *Viv* while I am calling you 'Mr. Larkin'? Aren't you a Ned or an Ed or a Teddy?"

"Teddy?" He laughed, but she caught him wincing. "None of those."

"What then? Surely your friends don't address you formally."

He turned, made a little bow, and with a sweeping arm gesture, invited her to pass before him down the stairs. She searched his face, but he didn't meet her gaze, his profile aloof, as it had been on the day they met. Her betrothed was not a man who readily gave up the details of his life. She held her breath. A footman in pale blue livery passed on the flagstones trying to control a bounding mastiff headed for the square. The usual clatter of carriages filled the air.

She passed him and headed down the stairs. From behind and above her she heard him speak.

"Lark," he said. "My friends call me Lark."

VIV STRODE DOWN the hall past the kitchen and larder and butler's pantry to a room beyond the servants' stairs. She opened the door to the shadowy darkness of the stillroom, and pulled two lamps from a shelf, setting them on the long deal table in the center of the room. "Wait here," she said. "I must find some water and plasters. Can you light the lamps?" She didn't look at him. "I'll be a few minutes."

"I can manage," he said. She detected some amusement in his voice.

She climbed the servants' stairs with quick steps. She was not fleeing. She was taking a moment to figure out how his name had so charged the atmosphere between them. She was used to giving names to the people she encountered on her walks. Once she named someone, that person became a character in the grand story of London that she and Lady Melforth were telling in their guide. Now, *Lark* had reversed the process. He was supposed to be *Winkworth*, the helpful gentleman she'd met on Babylon Street, but he had insisted on stepping out of the streets and into her life. By giving her his name, he had become someone else, someone who could know her back.

She gathered plasters from the medicine cabinet in Lady Melforth's dressing room and darted back to the servants' stairs and down to the kitchen for a basin of fresh water. She had so often collected the same items for dressing Lady Melforth's injured foot that the servants took no notice of her.

In the stillroom, he had removed his coat. He stood in

the lamplight, long and lean and unmoving, the white of his linen aglow, the champagne silk of his waistcoat a paler sheen. She set down her basin and turned to him. He was easily a head taller than she, neatly solid, his shoulders broad. Her person was separated from his by layers of silk and twill and buckram, by yards of fabric that ballooned around her, and yet those things were no barrier to the heady influence of his presence.

She wondered at it. It was commonplace to think that women were susceptible to handsome men, as if all handsome men possessed in equal measure some fatal charm. But the term was so general and so vague as to be nearly meaningless. The term was abstract. It did not explain the effect of a certain timbre in the voice or a particular laugh or the way a man's eyes lighted when a woman came into view.

At first glance looking at him, all she saw was the perfect gentleman, not like the men of Oxford Street, straining after fashion with their Cossack trousers and lavender gloves. Then she saw in the blue of his eyes a dancing bit of defiance, and in the ever-so-slight wayward curve of his nose a sign that it had once been broken, and in his fine-cut mouth, unexpected sensuality.

"You don't have to do this." He released the buttons on his waistcoat, little silk-covered buttons, each no bigger than a pearl, that his long fingers pried free with unhurried motions.

At that slow undoing, her pulse raced, and her stomach did a strange somersault. He was so calm. He must feel nothing, while Viv imagined a tension between them. She should be used to tending to him by now. "Sorry, here I am woolgathering. Can you show me the wound?"

He pulled the shirt free of his trousers, gathering the froth of linen in one hand and holding it up to reveal the plaster on his side. A single streak of red marred the crumpled linen.

She moved one of the lamps to illuminate his side more fully. The point was to see if his assailant had broken open the stitches. A livid red mark, the imprint of a fist, bloomed across the taut flesh where the plaster ended in a thin crust of dried blood.

She couldn't help a little cry.

"That bad, is it?" he asked.

"Forgive the editorial comment. You'll have quite a bruise, I think." She dipped a compress in the water and pressed it to the plaster. As she held the compress in place, the citrusy, woodsy scent of his soap took over her senses. All the other stillroom smells faded. She made herself call them to mind—comfrey, calendula, lavender, barley water, spirits. But it was no use. An odd state of frozen alertness possessed her.

A rivulet of water ran down to the waistband of his trousers. He shivered, and woke Viv from her trance. She lifted the compress, lay it aside, and peeled away the old plaster. He flinched with the first tug, and then stilled again.

"It is not as bad as I feared," she said, striving for a matter-of-fact tone. "The sutures are tight. The skin around them is puckered but not inflamed. Your ribs are very colorful, a mass of purplish brown, but there's only a trickle of blood where the fellow must have hit you. Why was he so angry with you?"

She reached for a towel to dry the area, glad for all the times she had tended Lady Melforth's injury.

"My attacker had a thick accent, and I didn't catch all that he said. I think he was insulted to be ignored."

She looked up at his averted profile. It was a neat explanation, but she knew him well enough now to recognize one of his evasions. It was a reminder to be on her guard. They were pretending to be engaged. They would soon go their separate ways. Whatever odd effect he had on her senses would pass. She applied the new plaster and wrapped a length of gauze around him. "There, done," she said.

"Where do you go tomorrow?" he asked.

She averted her gaze and tried to close her ears to the sound of cloth rustling as he restored his garments to order. "Oh," she said. "I'm not doing a walk tomorrow, just taking care of business."

"Business?"

"A visit to our publisher with some new pages. Then, of course, I really must work on my notes from today."

She looked up and found him regarding her steadily as he rebuttoned his waistcoat. She lifted her chin to meet that gaze. "Surely the duke has something for you to do?"

CHAPTER TWELVE

Lark found the offices of Dodsley & Sons at Number 86 the Strand between a chemist's shop with a striped awning, and a milliners with lacy confections in the window. Narrow, bright green glazing framed the panes of four tall windows through which Lark could see tables stacked with books, shelves crammed with more books, and standing behind a long counter, a young man in a maroon-and-gold plaid coat with a bold black velvet collar. Across the street he found a place to wait for Viv. Clouds streamed in overhead from the west, and it seemed the long dry spell was about to break.

Viv was easy enough to spot in her familiar chocolate bonnet and short, dove-colored cape above blue silk skirts.

At Dodsley's she stopped and peered through the windows, and turned away. She stood for a moment, clasping the bundle of pages to her chest and looking at the traffic. Then she squared her shoulders, drew in a breath, and turned to the door.

When she still hesitated to enter, Lark crossed the street. "Do you need me to go before and slay a dragon?"

She turned to glare at him, rising instantly to the bait. "You. How did you find Dodsley's? And, no, I do not need you to slay anyone."

He could not repress a grin.

"Yesterday you were the one under attack," she reminded him.

"I survived."

"Hardly a cause for self-congratulation," she observed. "I can't have you meeting Dodsley. We are trying not to have our arrangement exposed."

"It hasn't been," he said.

"Do not underestimate Lady Melforth because she didn't see through our...fraud at tea."

The word *fraud* sobered him. "I think you underestimate her."

"Me? Underestimate her? Never. She may look frail, but she is formidable. You'll see how we are treated by the publisher."

"You mean the one whose door you hesitate to approach?"

She shot him a sharp glance. "I may be a few minutes. I need to tell Dodsley what we want with these new pages."

"But his son, is it, is at the counter?"

"I can handle this. There's a coffeehouse not far from here. I can meet you there."

He opened the door for her. "Don't shoot anyone."

"You won't leave it, will you?" she said and swept past him. He was learning to judge her mood by the swish of her skirts. Sometimes they rustled gently, faintly stirred by calm and steady movement. Other times, they made an agitated sound like dry leaves in a gust of wind. Today a wind was blowing. He thought her fierceness better than her meekness the night of the tea. He hadn't quite figured out her relationship with Lady Melforth. On the one hand, Viv seemed to revere the viscountess, and Lark could see the advantages of Viv's position, but Lark thought the overbearing woman not simply cross, as a person might be with an injury, but jealous.

Viv strode to the counter and slapped the bundle of pages in front of the young man behind it. Lark pitied the poor fellow. Even unarmed, Viv was out to get her way about something. A white-haired gentleman in black appeared from the back of the premises, speaking to Viv and plainly, inviting her into an inner room.

Lark turned his attention to the crowded Strand. Since Viv shot him, he had avoided his old haunts by daylight. Rook's assault added another reason for caution, and he stepped back into the recess created by Dodsley's front door.

A steady stream of open-topped, horse-drawn omnibuses, packed with passengers, headed for Charing Cross. On the pavements, working men in butcher's aprons or rough fellows with sacks on their shoulders, mingled with gentlemen in top hats. Every man seemed intent on his own business. Dozens of signs proclaimed establishments doing business in an array of goods. Lark looked east toward the Temple Bar marking the entrance to Fleet Street, keeping an eye out for Rook, who could move unnoticed in such a crowd.

The thought of Rook on his own remained troubling. Their partnership had worked when they were boys because Lark had always been there to give Rook time to disappear after a pinch. The night of the fire had ended that. Lark had joined the men manning the pumps; Rook had picked pockets.

Rook refused to accept Lark's withdrawal from the partnership, and Lark's efforts to persuade Rook to leave the game had led to Rook's snatching Viv's purse and Viv shooting Lark. The encounter off Oxford Street proved that Rook was growing bolder, more reckless. Rook, acting on his own, could easily be taken up and hauled off to gaol.

As he had the thought, Rook came through the Temple Bar carrying a grease-marked paper parcel, almost certainly fish from his favorite shop. In an instant, Lark lost sight of him in the shifting crowd. Lark pulled his hat lower on his brow and concentrated on picking out Rook's wool cap bobbing in the sea of hats coming his way.

He was trying to gauge how far Rook had come toward him when Viv erupted from the shop in a violent swirl of silk. She brushed past him and charged off toward Charing Cross. Lark sprinted in pursuit. "What happened? What's made you so angry?"

"Dodsley wants to change our title."

"And?"

"He wants to call the book *Rambles with a Lady in London* or *Vignettes of London by a Lady*."

"You object to the term *lady*?" Lark needed to figure out the source of her anger.

"I object to trivializing our work, making it out to be mere amusement." She stepped off the pavement to pass a man carrying a sack, and Lark grabbed her elbow, pulling her back to safety as a dray rumbled toward her.

"What is the title you want?"

"*A City of Their Own, A Women's Guide to London.*"

"Ah."

"That's it? That's all you can say? *Ah*."

"Hasn't Dodsley published all Lady Melforth's books? He must have some understanding of how to sell them."

She stopped, and the stream of pedestrians parted, flowing around them. She fixed Lark with a glare. "That's what *he* said. He told me to look at his best sellers—*A Spinster's Tour in Genoa, Sketches of London Life, Notes of a Lady Traveler.*"

"So how did you leave it?" Lark turned her toward Charing Cross. Rook was somewhere close, and it wouldn't do to meet him in Viv's company. Lark doubted that Viv would recognize Rook, but Rook certainly knew her.

Viv started walking again with brisk, angry strides. "I couldn't make Dodsley understand what we are trying to do, how our book is a call to action, how we are encouraging women to make the city their own."

Lark suspected that Dodsley understood all too well and had no intention of promoting the free movement of women in London. "Does the title matter so much?"

"It does," she snapped.

"But, isn't the book going to call women to action whatever the title is?"

"What do you mean?" She stopped and turned to him.

For a brief moment he forgot what he meant to say under the influence of those lively brown eyes. Then it came back to him. "Some things you don't control, right? Dodsley decides the paper and binding and cover and print, right? He arranges for the book to reach booksellers, right?"

She let out a gusty sigh. "I don't like it."

He laughed. She wouldn't. "You control the writing, the words on the page."

She began to walk again at a quick impatient pace. Something else about the encounter was bothering her. Lark waited. The first drops of rain, cold and heavy, hit the cobbles and released their stony scent.

"Dodsley told me that he wanted to save me from the ill effects of any ignorant blunders I might make, being new to the publishing trade. He said the title didn't matter because Lady Melforth's *name* would sell books."

Viv charged on, oblivious to the increasing rain. People scurried for the edges of the pavement under awnings and overhangs. Lark wasn't sure she understood what Dodsley had revealed about her one-sided partnership with Lady Melforth. "What did you say to that?" he asked.

"I said he must deal with me. I must protect her, you know. She's always been so active, so intrepid, and now because she's confined to her couch, people want to take advantage."

Lark doubted that anyone took advantage of Lady Melforth, but Viv's admiration for her ladyship seemed to blind her to the woman's self-absorption.

She gave Lark a rueful glance. "At least I didn't shoot him."

"Then I'd say you won."

"I don't feel as if I've won."

They'd come to Charing Cross. The rain came down cold and thick, and Lark hailed a hackney cab. "Come on. I know a place that will cheer you up."

"Where?"

"Marie-Louise Christophe's house."

"Who?"

A cab pulled round to them, and Lark helped Viv scramble in. He swept his gaze over the area, but umbrellas had sprouted everywhere above the heads of the crowd, and there was no sign of Rook. He gave the driver the address and climbed in beside Viv. "The queen of Haiti, Marie Christophe. She lives abroad now, but she lived in London for a time, and there's a woman who remembers her every day."

"How do you know all this?" she asked as the cab jolted into motion.

"Stick with me. I know a great deal about London."

THE CAB STOPPED in a neighborhood a little south of Regent's Park near the entrance that led to the Zoological Gardens, and Mr. Larkin pointed to a square house with no pretensions to architectural grandeur. It stood on the corner of a modest street with a ground floor of white-painted stone, a shiny black door, and three upper stories of ordinary red brick. In front, a single plane tree shook its leafless branches in the April rain. All that distinguished the house from its neighbors was a bundle of dripping purple blooms hanging from the iron railing in front.

Viv turned to him. "This is it?"

"Wait," he said.

Viv kept watch through the slanting lines of rain. Then the woman appeared, tall and purposeful in her stride, wearing a day dress of printed lilac foulard and a fitted jacket of a deep aubergine shade. A straw bonnet tied with a chocolate ribbon framed her ebony face. She managed a black umbrella and a basket over her arm with a spray of fresh white blossoms. She stopped at the iron railing and reached to remove the wilted flowers.

Viv glanced at Mr. Larkin. "She came in the rain."

"She comes every day."

"Have you spoken with her? Do you know her reasons?"

"She honors her queen."

The woman held the new spray of flowers against the railing, deftly tying a bow to keep them in place. Then she stepped back and bowed her head in an attitude of prayer, speaking, though Viv could not hear the words.

"I didn't know Haiti had a queen. It was a French island, was it not, with enslaved people?"

"It was. The people freed themselves. They tried having a king and queen, but chose to be a republic."

"You have spoken with her. Will she speak with me?" Viv's mind ranged over all the women she'd been writing about, women, who, with their lives, had marked the landscape of London, but they were dead. To write about this bold living woman who moved freely about, to make her part of the story would change everything.

"She may not speak back," he warned.

"She spoke to you." Viv scrambled out of the cab. The rain was heavy, and she had no umbrella, but she dashed across the street and approached so that she might be seen and not startle the woman.

"I beg your pardon, ma'am, may I ask why you leave flowers here?"

The woman turned a proud eye to Viv and gave her a thorough scrutiny. Viv knew that look. It was the sort of gaze Lady Melforth gave to encroaching admirers. "Do I know you?"

Viv steadied herself, all her story-hunting instincts alert. Rain dripped from her bonnet. A cold drop ran down her neck. "My name is Vivian Bradish, ma'am. I write about London."

"I don't know you." The woman turned away toward the park.

"Wait," Viv cried. She hurried to catch up with the woman's long, elegant stride. "I don't mean to offend. You knew the queen, Marie Christophe?"

The woman glanced sharply at Viv. "What is it you want from me?"

"You must have cared about her."

"And what is that to you, Miss…"

"Bradish, ma'am, but it doesn't matter who I am. I write about the women of London, their stories."

"Women's stories?" The woman stopped, and her gaze turned amused. "If you want stories, stories I have."

"May I hear yours and hers, Marie Christophe's, if you know it?"

"And what will you do with our stories, Miss Bradish?"

"Tell them to other women."

The woman nodded. "And how will you do that?"

"In a book I am writing with Lady Melforth, the Traveling Viscountess."

"A viscountess?" The woman's brows lifted. "Are you sure your viscountess wants a story from the likes of me?"

Viv smelled of wet wool. The cold drops collecting on the back of her neck made her shiver. Later she would figure out how to persuade Lady Melforth to include the woman's story. "I think she must. Please, will you tell me your name?"

"My dear young woman, you are soaked to the skin. If you truly care to talk, come another day when the weather is not so...English. Good day."

"But I don't know how to find you."

"Your friend knows me."

Viv turned, and there was Mr. Larkin. He had removed his coat. He wrapped it around her as the rain molded his clothes to his body. "Let's get you home and dry," he said.

LADY MELFORTH'S DOOR opened, and Jenny dashed out under a serviceable black umbrella. "The Strydes are 'ere, miss," she warned. "Best to go in through the kitchen."

Viv whirled and led Lark around the iron railing down to the basement entrance. She hurried them into the long, dim hall with its half a dozen doors on either side, on past the narrow servants' stairs and into the herb-scented stillroom lit by its one high window. "They mustn't see you. Wait here."

Lark surveyed the dangerous little room. It smelled harmless enough like lavender and plants he couldn't name. Jars lined the open shelves, and bunches of dried herbs hung against the walls. But since yesterday, the room had figured in his imagination as a place of intimacy. He removed his hat and gloves, and set them on the plain deal table in the center of the room.

"I must get upstairs to Lady Melforth." Viv tugged at her bonnet ribbons, pulling them into an unyielding knot.

"You won't be able to help her in those clothes." He stepped forward and took the ribbons from her cold, stiff hands. "Let me."

She lifted her face. In her eyes, the excitement of their afternoon's discovery was gone, distress in its place. One damp curl stuck to the side of her flushed cheek. "It's only that they weary her so."

He teased the tiny loop of knotted ribbon with his fingers, but it wouldn't give. "Hold still and lift your chin. I'm going to use my teeth."

Her eyes flashed awareness, but she gave a nod and did as he asked. He leaned in, taking hold of the end of the ribbons, momentarily dizzied by the warm scent of her. She went perfectly still unlike her usual self. He took the loop between his teeth and tugged until the knot yielded. He pulled away, and finished untying the ribbon, lifting the wet bonnet from her head.

"Thank you." She studied him, unmoving.

"Don't mention it." He waited for her to come back to herself. Then, because he could not help himself, he thumbed the stuck curl back from her cheek.

His touch set her in motion again. She stepped back with a little shiver and removed her cape and gloves. "Wait here," she said. "I will bring…towels." She tossed her cape onto the table and spun away.

As her light footsteps faded on the stairs, a cold drop trickled down under his collar. He removed his jacket and waistcoat, stripped off his ruined tie, and hung them over an empty drying rack in a corner of the fragrant room. His lawn shirt stuck to him. He pulled it away from his body and gritted his teeth against a sudden chill. His false betrothal to Vivian Bradish was hard on his wardrobe.

His clothes and hers were soaked and dripping because she had seen something admirable in Lark's Haitian neighbor. Viv's single-minded determination to pursue the woman's story had meant she laughed at such slight inconveniences as rain. They had walked blocks in the downpour before finding a second hackney.

He circled the little room to warm himself. She had accused him of being an actor, and in truth, he needed to remember that he was playing the part of a lover. He'd almost lost his head for a moment, tempted to disappear into the role of Edward Larkin, as if Lark had never existed. She hadn't said his name once today, and he thought the omission deliberate.

After all, the ruse worked because Edward Larkin wasn't so different from Lark. Both knew London. Both had a head for figures and investments, and both had money in Hammersley's Bank. The time he'd spent in coffeehouses overhearing men boast of their shrewd dealings, and the hours he'd poured over the bankruptcy notices in the papers, observing their patterns, had prepared him for this imposture. He could go on pretending to be the gentleman of independent means that Viv Bradish thought him to be. No one in London would miss that other man, Lark. He could forget his search for Lark's past and add whatever he liked to Edward Larkin's history.

It was true that Rook wanted to pull Lark back into their

old life, but even Rook's attachment to their partnership would fade in time. The duke was a different problem. There was a good chance that Lark's masquerade would require contact with the duke at some point. He would devise a plan for meeting the duke later.

Lark shivered, his skin pebbled with the cold, a good antidote for folly. He came to a halt under the small window with its square of pale light. An unwelcome memory returned of the day he learned that Boy, their leader, was Kit Jones, a man with a family.

It had been a snowy day, Boy had led their gang of waifs across London to Bread Street, following a coach in which a woman lay captive and drugged. Ruffians carried her into the deserted public house at the foot of the street. For hours the boys played a desperate game in the deserted street, trying to wake the captive woman, feeling an unseen menace that hung over the scene. When she woke, they gave her an iron rod, with which to break out of her prison at Boy's signal. When the moment came, a man named Xander Jones appeared, and Boy directed him to the woman while Lark led their gang to the rooftop opposite. Then from the top of the street broke a flood of beer from a brewery's sabotaged tanks, and thousands of gallons of black, foaming brew roared down upon them.

From the roof opposite the pub, Lark and the others held their breath until the man named Xander and the woman emerged from an upper story window to clamber onto an adjacent roof. That had been the beginning of the end of their gang. Boy was not one of them after all. He had a family, a family that wanted to reclaim him from the streets.

And his was no commonplace family, for his father had been Lord Daventry, and he became not Boy or Kit, but Dav, a duke's grandson. No such transformation had waited for the rest of them.

Beyond the stillroom door, Lady Melforth's people came and went, busy with their household tasks. More than ten years had passed since Lark and Rook had walked away from Daventry Hall. Kit was no longer a lost boy like them. He was the Duke of Wenlocke. And Lark was still an outsider in the duke's world.

Viv returned with a lamp and a pair of towels draped over her arm. She set the lamp on the table and handed him a towel. He applied it to his head and stopped, finding her watching him. She still wore the damp gown.

"You'll catch your death," she said.

"No more than you. I thought you went to change."

"Jenny's bringing me a gown. Give me your shirt. Jenny will dry it for you."

He undid his cuffs and collar and pulled the damp linen over his head. A quick intake of breath from Viv made him pause. When he emerged from the shirt, she stood with her back to him. He lay the shirt on the table, picked up the towel, and slung it around his neck. The ends hung down over his chest.

"How is your wound?" she asked. "You removed the wrapping I put on."

He glanced at the plaster. It was wet and curling up at the edges. Even he knew it needed to be removed. He took hold of one ragged end and pulled. The wet bandage came away easily. He turned toward the lamp and glanced down at the wound, now a thin red line like a tightly closed pair of lips with the black silk threads crossing it at neat intervals, like careful tally marks. The doctor had done his work well. Only the faint yellows and purples of his bruises surrounded the area. Viv's mark on him was fading. Nothing much to hold Viv to him now, but he wasn't ready to let her go.

"It's red and swollen and there's something oozing from it." He spoke to her back.

She spun toward him, her eyes big with alarm, and stopped when she saw his side. "You wretch. Infection is not a thing to jest about."

He caught her hand and pressed it to the wound. Her fingers were cold as ice, the ring he'd given her loose on her finger, but he held her hand there, knowing with absolute clarity, that whatever happened if he were exposed and the masquerade ended without his kissing her, he was going to feel cheated.

"I'm going to kiss you," he said.

CHAPTER THIRTEEN

THE WORD *KISS* changed the atmosphere. Viv knew the effect of naming a thing, of giving words to the unspoken. Time slowed. Her soaked skirts hung so heavy that she could not summon the will to move. The dim little room smelled of lavender and wet wool. The lamp glow gave a golden edge to Mr. Larkin's shoulders. The ends of the towel hung down to his waist, leaving open to her gaze a curved plane of muscle divided by a shadowy cleft to the band of his trousers.

Viv had attended London's great exhibitions, had seen famous artists' representations of male flesh in paint and marble. She should not be affected by a mere man, but a hidden warmth ran through her under the cool surface of her skin. A bell rang in the hall summoning one of the servants. Upstairs, poor Lady Melforth must be enduring a barrage of censure from the Strydes, most of it directed at Viv for being absent.

She found her voice. "I shot you."

"I lived."

"I ruined your clothes. Twice."

"I do like a good waistcoat, but I can get another."

"You aren't thinking rationally. You can't behave like a footman stealing a kiss from the parlor maid."

"I can't think at all, with the lures you've thrown out to me."

"Lures! Of all the conceit!"

"The soggy bonnet, the drooping curls, the icy fingers, this private place. How is a man to resist?" There was laughter in his eyes but something else as well that made her pulse quicken.

"Be sensible. I led you here only to avoid the Strydes."

"Convenient those Strydes. I must thank them for driving you to such lengths."

"You know they would condemn me for…for being here with you. If a woman loses her respectability, she's not welcome anywhere."

"We're betrothed."

"But our betrothal is a…a ruse."

He pressed her hand more firmly against his side, his fingers warm over hers, his skin cool under her palm. "Your ring is no ruse. My scar is no ruse."

"I'm not good at kissing." His gaze narrowed to her mouth, and she moistened her lips. She'd made a mistake saying the word.

"You're bound to improve with effort." He tugged both her hands now, pulling her close, tangling her heavy skirts with his legs. "Tell me about that other time."

She choked back a laugh. "Oh you. I'll have you know I've been thoroughly kissed. In Bath in a moonlit garden with music drifting out from a ballroom."

"Did the man who kissed you believe your wits would dissolve under the influence of moonlight and roses?" he asked.

"Well, he might have," she admitted. "He believed I was an heiress."

"Did you disabuse him of that notion?"

"At once. The kissing was disagreeable, you see. There was something, I don't know, *practiced* about his…his lovemaking. Does that make sense?"

He nodded. "All the more reason to kiss me, to find out if kissing can be less…disagreeable."

"Without the moonlight and roses?" She searched his gaze.

"I'm not offering moonlight and roses."

At his voice, low and roughened, something uncurled in her belly. A spool of moments unraveled in her head back to the time in the hackney when she'd first pressed a handkerchief to his bleeding side. She had been so occupied with exploring London, making her notes, intent on her guide for women. Now she understood that his presence had altered the places they went. He had understood from the first her unwillingness to be satisfied with writing accounts of the great squares and eminent buildings, and her need to find the living stories hidden in London's multitude of lanes and dwellings.

She tried one last appeal to reason. "Jenny will return any minute now."

"We'll hear her on the stairs." He lifted her hand above her head, turning her in a dizzying whirl, like dancing, so that she faced the open door.

Viv held her breath. He'd changed his mind. He didn't mean to kiss her after all. She had only to step away from him, but he filled her senses, his solid warmth at her back, the low rasp of his voice, the scent of soap and rain on his skin. His hands tightened on her waist. He leaned in. His breath disturbed a curl behind her ear. Then his lips touched the side of her neck, a brief pressure that sent a violent shiver through her. *Lark.*

Hurrying footsteps sounded on the stairs. He stepped back, and Viv stood there, unmoving, her nerves registering his absence and a thousand tiny kiss shocks.

Jenny appeared, a plain blue kerseymere gown over her arm, a startled look on her face.

"I'll wait in the kitchen for my shirt to dry." He stepped around Viv and strolled down the hall, the towel over his shoulders, his shirt in his hand.

Jenny glanced from him to Viv. "Miss? Are you quite well?"

Viv came back to herself. "Help me, Jenny. I've got to get upstairs to Lady Melforth."

VIV ENTERED THE upstairs drawing room, her damp petticoat hem clinging to her ankles. Mr. Stryde filled a chair at Lady Melforth's right elbow, while Mrs. Stryde perched, her neck stretched high, on the ottoman beside Lady Melforth's injured left foot. Between them, they trapped her in her nest of pillows. In her ladyship's concealed hand and listless posture, Viv read the signs of an overlong visit. A cup of Doctor Newberry's soothing headache draught stood untouched on the tray of remedies by her ladyship's side.

Viv tugged the bell pull and moved to help her employer.

"Dear ma'am, how uncomfortable you look."

"Of course, she's uncomfortable," snapped Mrs. Stryde. "You abandoned her yet again. I wonder, Miss Bradish, that you dare call yourself a lady's companion at all."

Viv caught a mute appeal in her employer's gaze and refrained from rising to Mrs. Stryde's provocation.

"Thank you, Eustacia," Lady Melforth said. "It's been good of you and Arthur to keep me company, but Miss Bradish is here now."

"She may be here now, Aurora, but where has she been? Really, we cannot leave you to her care without some assurance that she is prepared to do the work she was engaged to do."

Viv ignored Mrs. Stryde, concentrating a tight smile on Mr. Stryde. "If you will move your chair a little, sir, I can help her ladyship to be more comfortable."

He looked surprised, but complied, and Viv leaned over her employer to help her to an upright position among the pillows. "You've not taken any of Dr. Newberry's draught, ma'am. Let me send Jenny for a fresh cup, and we'll have you feeling more the thing."

"Thank you, Viv. How was Dodsley?"

"He made only one difficulty today."

Lady Melforth laughed, her warm, throaty laugh turning to a dry cough. "You set him straight, I hope."

Viv nodded and cleared away the untouched cup.

"One difficulty?" asked Mrs. Stryde. "Yet you've been gone for hours, Miss Bradish, neglecting your duty, and I dare say, risking your reputation with no maid to attend you."

The justice of the accusation stung a little. In Viv's absence Lady Melforth had been plagued by her cousins, and the neglect was not in meeting Dodsley, but in the visit to Marie Christophe's house and that fleeting moment in the stillroom. Her thoughts had been centered on Lark. She resolved to banish him from her mind.

Jenny appeared, a little breathless from the stairs, and Viv handed her the old medicine, asking her to bring a new cup.

"The elderberry, miss?"

"Yes, thank you, Jenny."

"Should I bring more tea for the visitors?" Jenny whispered.

"Absolutely not," said Viv.

Jenny bobbed a curtsy and hurried off.

Viv turned back to Lady Melforth and her visitors, and pulled a chair up on the far side of the ottoman. "When I must do an errand for her ladyship," she explained. "I rely on Jenny. She's familiar with Dr. Newberry's instructions and very reliable."

Mrs. Stryde twisted round to frown at Viv. The stiff little curls at her cheeks didn't move. "Yes, but, a young woman, venturing unattended into those regions of London wholly devoted to commerce, is so indelicate as to no longer be considered a lady."

"In general, perhaps, ma'am, but a writer may always meet with her publisher quite respectably wherever his offices may be. Our most renowned lady writers have done so."

"Such boldness may be acceptable for writers of renown, but your name has not appeared in print. And respectable women cannot be too careful with publishers. Some, you know, produce the most scurrilous rubbish under the guise of informing the public of the very vices they promote." She turned to her husband. "Arthur, what say you?"

"Yes, my dear." He turned to Lady Melforth. "The Society has recently discovered a publisher on Babylon Street, whose premises are to be"—he gave a polite cough behind his hand—"investigated by the police."

"Investigated?" Viv asked. "You mean, invaded."

"Quite justly," said Mrs. Stryde. "The police know very well what this fellow is up to. The Society recently collected samples of the vile material he prints."

It occurred to Viv that the Society was quite keen to collect its samples. "Will the Society send members to Babylon Street to aid the police? Will you go, Mr. Stryde?"

Mr. Stryde swelled a bit in his chair. The drooping whiskers at the side of his face gave him the look of a startled fox. "It is our aim to offer the magistrates every assistance in the discharge of their duty."

"Mrs. Stryde, do you not fear that your husband may be tainted by a foray into such a neighborhood?" Viv asked.

"My husband is a gentleman, Miss Bradish, and a staunch member of the Anti-Vice Society. He can hardly be tainted by doing his duty."

"And you, will you do your duty as well? With no fear of being tainted?"

"In doing her duty a woman is always respectable."

"I'm glad to hear you say so. Exactly what I thought this morning when I called on Mr. Dodsley."

A warning look from Lady Melforth made Viv drop her

gaze demurely, the perfect lady's companion. It would not do for Mrs. Stryde to understand Viv's meaning too clearly.

"Really," said Mrs. Stryde. "We did not come to discuss the Society's work, but to consider what's to be done about your betrothal, Miss Bradish. We've not seen an announcement in the papers."

"Naturally, we are waiting to tell our own people first." Viv kept her voice mild.

"I thought Mr. Larkin said his was an old London family."

"Alas, his only family is an aunt in Somerton." As she said it, Viv realized Lark had no one but himself to vouch for his respectability.

"Has he told his employer of his betrothal?"

"That, of course, will be between them."

"Well, he can hardly have done so if the papers are to be believed, for they report that the Duke and Duchess of Wenlocke have gone into the country for the coming fortnight."

Viv felt Mrs. Stryde's usual effect on her temper. The Stryde's had made it their business to check up on her, and she was at a disadvantage because her betrothed had not informed her of his true situation. The *holiday* Lark had spoken of was not due to the duke's generosity after all, but to his absence. No wonder Lark could freely wander about London with her, and how odd of him not to tell her.

"You understand our concern must be for Aurora. No doubt you will resign your situation when you are married, for you can hardly be of any use then as a companion."

Jenny returned with a fresh cup of tincture of elderberry,

which Viv placed on Lady Melforth's table. Her ladyship managed a few sips before the cup wobbled in her hand, and she put it aside. Viv spoke at once. "Dear Mr. and Mrs. Stryde, thank you for keeping Lady Melforth company, but now we must let her rest."

Mrs. Stryde looked as if she might object, but glanced at Lady Melforth and rose. "Come along, Arthur," she said. "Don't worry, Aurora, we will never abandon you."

Viv saw them into the hall. As soon as the drawing room door closed, Mrs. Stryde turned on her. "Miss Bradish, we have been sadly mistaken in your character. I can only suppose it is your irregular upbringing that disposes you to be so careless of your good name."

"If Lady Melforth is satisfied with my upbringing that is all that matters."

"Aurora is too feeble to take you to task, but I assure you I am not."

"Please do not trouble yourself." Viv drew herself up to her full height. "Your husband, as Lady Melforth's cousin, has, perhaps, a right to speak directly to her, but for a person of so slight a connection as yours to her ladyship there is nothing to do. Good day to you both."

Mrs. Stryde opened and closed her mouth. The little curls at the side of her face shook. Her husband mumbled something and took his wife's arm. Viv clung to the banister at the top of the stairs, listening to their talk as they descended, letting her temper cool. She did not underestimate Mrs. Stryde. The woman wanted Viv gone. Viv's only satisfaction was the hope that their Babylon Street adventure might open their eyes to the true nature of London.

When at last she heard Haxton shut the front door, she returned to the drawing room. Lady Melforth's eyes were closed, but opened as Viv approached.

"They really are insufferable."

Viv sank down on the ottoman. "*She* certainly is. She's determined to spread misery wherever she goes. I am heartily sorry I took so long this morning."

Lady Melforth smiled. "You don't secretly admire her? I'm sure she quite rules Arthur."

Viv grinned. "Adding domestic tyranny to her other offenses does not raise her in my estimation."

"Ah, well, thank you for seeing them off."

"I will not abandon you again."

"Yes, but I still need you to deal with Dodsley. What was the problem today?"

"Dodsley wants to change our title, and we had a go-round about it. A note from you will help, I think." Viv explained Dodsley's alternative titles, pleased to see Lady Melforth taking more of the doctor's draught and even smiling a little.

"And after Dodsley's?" Lady Melforth peered at Viv over the brim of her cup. "You could not have been at his office all morning. You've changed your gown."

Viv plucked at her skirts. Under them, the damp petticoat stuck to her knees. "I confess, I took a quick look at a possible entry for our guide, and got a soaking."

"Oh, where is this?"

"It's a house on Weymouth Street, quite unremarkable from the outside, but it was once the residence of Marie Christophe, the former queen of Haiti."

"And that's what kept you?"

Viv hesitated. Now was the moment to confess that she'd met Lark and that it was he, who had led her to Marie Christophe's house. The outing was harmless after all, completely respectable, with everything public and permitted to a betrothed couple, until the scene in the stillroom.

She leaned forward, clasping her hands together. "There's a woman who comes to the house every day to leave a bouquet of flowers. I'd like to question her about her story and the queen's. It's a rare opportunity for us to present a pair of living women to our readers, models of female independence."

Lady Melforth shook her head. "I don't think so, Viv. I think it's time to finish the book."

"Finish? Without the full number of entries we planned?" Viv tried to contain her shock. Lady Melforth appeared tired, all her zeal for the book gone.

"How many do we have?"

"Eleven."

"And you have your notes from the other day, do you not?"

Viv nodded. She had only herself to blame for her ladyship's loss of interest in their book. While Viv had lingered in Lark's company, the Strydes had wearied and discouraged her ladyship. Worse still, Viv reproached herself, she had let herself be seduced, not in the vulgar sense of popular melodrama, but in her mind. In Lark's presence, she had not spared a thought for Lady Melforth, for the person on whom she depended, the person who had been generous and supportive, and who had made Viv a writer.

She offered her employer a bright smile. "I do have my notes. Twelve entries might work very well, an even dozen. Shall I put together what we have this week for you to look at?"

"Yes, that will do nicely. I think we could be wise to finish in the next fortnight."

CHAPTER FOURTEEN

Lark stood at the window of his small parlor. Rain descended on London in drifting gray veils, a rattling sort of rain that shook the windows and ran noisily in the gutters.

A true gentleman, when he woke at noon, would sit by his fire and let his servants bring him coffee and the morning papers. Wretches that picked pockets or cleaned street crossings or begged for a living would huddle in their hidey holes on such a day and wait for the sun to shine. Lark remembered that, remembered that in the old days Dav knew places to wait out a storm where the eaves of one roof overhung another, or where to find a bit of canvas to make a shelter of a corner where a pair of rooftops joined each other. And Dav knew how to wait.

Lark's rooms were perfectly comfortable. He should resign himself to a day without Viv. It was the smart thing to do, to keep up the pretense that he had an employer and work. She already suspected him of some deception about his connection to the duke.

The problem was that he wanted to kiss her again, to kiss her more thoroughly, and now he knew the thing could be done. The little room in the basement of Lady Melforth's house was a temptation, but there were other places they could go. He could write his own guidebook, a gentleman's guide to kissing girls in London.

He didn't want the false engagement to end. He sensed the ending was near, but he wanted to stay in the moment, in the world apart from his old life. Since he'd met her, he'd been drifting like a passenger in one of Green's balloons. For eight shillings a man could ascend with Green from Vauxhall into the ether, suspended in a basket beneath a great red-and-white striped silk balloon. For Lark the price of a ride was the wound in his side. For a fortnight he had been untethered from his ordinary life. To see London through Viv's curious eyes, to show her the things he'd discovered, was to see it as he'd not seen it before. He didn't want the ride to end. But it must, and his aim must be to end it gently, not in a wreck. He should put his mind to that, how to land the balloon and walk away whole. Not how to kiss her again.

It was unthinkable that their false engagement could become real, that he could step so far into the role he'd created as Edward Larkin that he could marry Viv. The thought of it was crazy, even scary. A real engagement meant he would have to tell her the truth about who he was.

He wasn't ready. The stumbling block was his parentage. He wanted to believe his mother had been a gentlewoman and that she had not abandoned him, but he had no proof, only elusive memories of her gentleness, of the ring on her finger, and of falling asleep in a warm, well-appointed carriage somewhere in London. And there was Rook, a real tangible obstacle to any claim of Lark's to being a gentleman.

He had thought that wandering with Viv he might come

across the place he'd been searching for. Instead, he'd abandoned his search for the spot. In the months since the fire, he had searched dozens of streets, but he had yet to take his search as far as the great West End parks and beyond.

Today would be a good day to return to the search. Riding with Viv in Lady Melforth's carriage, being in the house on Henrietta Street had sharpened his memories. He believed his mother had left him in a carriage to enter a building, not a private house, but an edifice that dominated a square. If he could find the place where that parting had taken place, he could unravel the mystery of his birth.

He would call to see that Viv had come to no harm from the Strydes' visit. He wouldn't try to see her. He didn't know how she felt about that kiss. She had participated in a surprised sort of way, but he knew her. She had now had hours to think about it, to feel awkward or uneasy in his presence.

ON THE MORNING of a third day of rain, Lady Melforth crumpled to the floor in her bedroom. Viv was at her desk working on the guide when Sarah, her ladyship's maid called for help. Her ladyship revived almost at once and insisted that she had taken no harm, that it was only her pesky foot giving way underneath her, but she allowed them to help her back to bed, and Viv sent for Dr. Newberry.

The doctor spent nearly an hour with his patient before joining Viv in the upstairs drawing room. He looked grave as he entered, but his expression brightened when he saw Viv at the tea table with a teapot and plate of biscuits.

"Thank you for coming like this," she said. "How is she?"

The doctor took a seat and accepted a cup of tea from Viv. "Rebellious, I'd say. She's planning a dinner party."

"A dinner party?" Viv had forgotten, but apparently Lady Melforth had not.

"To celebrate your betrothal and the completion of your guide."

"Oh dear, is she up to it?" Viv made some rapid calculations. She would have to reach Lark. She would have to see him again. She had been trying so hard to put him out of mind. To forget the kiss. To invent the speech she meant to give to end their false betrothal.

"I don't think anyone can stop her, but I do think a day in bed won't hurt her."

Viv dragged her runaway thoughts back to Lady Melforth's situation. "Is it usual for a broken bone to take so long to heal? The lack of progress seems to lower her spirits. She no longer writes, you know."

"She doesn't?" The doctor put down his cup and took up a biscuit, turning it round in his fingers as if deciding whether to take a bite. "When did she stop?"

"Not long after we came to London. I can consult my notes, but I took over her correspondence in February. Is it significant?" she asked. Newberry looked grave and he wasn't meeting Viv's gaze.

"I'm sorry to hear it. It gives us a measure of her spirits. I hadn't realized she was feeling quite so low."

"You always cheer her. I think she puts on an act for

you."

He took a bite of the biscuit. "Does she?"

"I must ask about visitors. May she have them?"

He gave her a quick sharp glance, amusement glinting in his eyes. And it occurred to her that though he could be called handsome, her pulse never quickened in his presence. "You don't want a dinner party? Or you want an excuse to turn away the Strydes."

"Am I so obvious?"

"Perfectly, but you need not worry. The Strydes may not call for some time."

"Why? What's happened? What do you know?"

He grinned at her. "You haven't heard? Mr. Stryde was taken up in a police raid of a shop on Babylon Street."

"What? Oh my! I knew they were planning something of the kind. They told Lady Melforth that it was their duty to assist the police. Mr. Stryde claimed that his evidence alerted the authorities to the publisher."

Newberry offered her a grin. "He may have been over-zealous in collecting it. He stuffed his pockets with a very different sort of guide from the one you and her ladyship are writing. I believe it's called *The Swell's Night Guide to London's Bowers of Venus*. Illustrated, one shilling. The police thought he was a regular customer and another witness claimed to have seen him in the shop before."

"How embarrassing for him." Viv could picture him sputtering and protesting his innocence. She wanted to tell Lark. It was almost a habit now, the desire to tell him things. She carefully placed her teacup on the table, afraid that if she met Dr. Newberry's gaze, he would see where her thoughts had strayed.

"It gets worse," he said. "Mrs. Stryde was with him."

Viv could not help looking up at that.

"She whacked a constable over the head with her umbrella and was taken up, too."

It was too much. For a minute, they just laughed until he rose to take his leave.

"There's a letter in the *Chronicle*, describing their mistreatment at the hands of the authorities and expressing the Society's outrage that their members in the pursuit of duty should be so mistreated."

"Oh dear, the Strydes will be furious with me."

"With you?"

"I encouraged them to do the raid."

"Ah," he said. "Well, best to deny them Lady Melforth's company for a few days if they do call. And watch out for them, Viv. They would see you sacked."

"I know."

With a quick bow he was gone, back to his busy rounds.

HOURS AFTER DR. Newberry's visit, Viv returned to her desk. Outside the rain had subsided to a drizzle. Lady Melforth was sleeping peacefully while Viv was anything but at peace. The dinner party was going forward. Without consulting Viv, Lady Melforth had drawn up a small guest list including Viv's aunt Louisa and her uncle Sir Oswald, the inevitable Strydes, and ambitiously the Duke and Duchess of Wenlocke. While Viv had been working to complete their guide, Lady Melforth had turned to Haxton and her maid Sarah to send invitations for the following Wednesday. Viv was to turn the final draft over to Dodsley, and they were to celebrate.

She needed to consult Lark. It was the prudent thing to do. She had no idea whether in his vague position with the duke, Lark would see the invitation. Surely, if they worked together, the duke would speak of it. But if, as the Strydes reported, the duke was not in London, how would the invitation reach Lark? She had discouraged his visits to Henrietta Street with a note delivered to him by Haxton, when Lark had stopped by the day after their kiss. As far as Viv knew, he had not called again, and she still didn't know where he lived. If he did not know what they faced, how could they carry on their charade in company with the Strydes? If they were exposed, she did not know what would happen to her part in the book. She really had to find him.

He must have a bachelor set of rooms somewhere, not in the most exclusive sort of place like the Albany, but somewhere not far from Henrietta Street. She realized he was always on foot. To her knowledge he didn't keep a horse or a carriage or a groom. He had never offered to take her up in even a hired carriage. He didn't pretend to great wealth though he looked as fine as any other gentleman of taste, finer than many. His mode of dress had alerted her to the excesses of others.

The kiss remained a problem. His name remained a problem. Those things had troubled her even as she bent her mind to working on the guide. He had changed her approach to writing. With him she discovered more on each of her walks. She wrote with him in mind as well as those female readers who were to be inspired by their book, those readers who were to be shown how not to be cowed by London, by its history and grandeur, its rowdy, boisterous streets, its fondness for male privilege. She had discovered living women who acted in the assumption that men might be superior in their circumstances but not in their character.

She looked at the pages piled up on her desk. Each walk was numbered, and each had its own set of notes plus any questions she still had about the route and the places to see along the way. She wanted to go back over those early entries with what she had learned since meeting Lark. She had worked their river adventure into the walk from Green Park to Westminster Abbey. And she thought perhaps there was a walk into which she could fit the Haitian woman leaving flowers for her queen. She went back to her notes on the walk from Regent's Park to Marylebone.

Her notes were thin. The rain, Lark's kiss, and the visit from the Strydes had driven the woman's image from Viv's mind. She needed more details. She needed a real story to tell before she could put the absent queen's former house on the route. A point in her notes abruptly struck her. The woman had known Lark, and of course, Viv remembered, he was used to seeing the woman leave her floral tribute. She closed the little notebook. If she found the woman again, she could get her story, and she could ask about Lark. It was possible that he lived in the neighborhood of the Haitian queen's house.

Outside her window, shafts of sunlight were breaking through the clouds. Rain drops sparkled on everything. Viv stuffed her notebook and pencil into her favorite bag.

CHAPTER FIFTEEN

As the sky began to clear, Viv hooked her umbrella over her arm. Puddles glinted everywhere in shafts of sunlight, reflecting back the fleeing clouds. The breeze tossed bare tree limbs and scattered bright drops. Viv made three circuits of the neighborhood, noting possible bachelor's quarters, before the tall woman with the flowers appeared.

This time she carried yellow flowers, and wore a green gown. Like Viv, she had an umbrella over her arm, but also a sturdy traveler's case. Viv waited for the woman to put down her burdens and replace the spray of flowers on the railing. When the new flowers were in place, and the woman had said her prayer, Viv approached.

"You again. I suppose you want that story now. Miss Bradish, is it?" With smiling eyes in her heart-shaped face the woman bent to retrieve her bag and umbrella.

"I do, ma'am. If I may have it."

"Your friend, Mr. Larkin, tells me I may trust you."

Viv kept her smile in place. There was the proof, if she needed it, that Lark lived in the neighborhood. "He's a good neighbor then?"

"He is." The woman's eyebrows went up. She pointed. "He's just there with the bachelors."

Viv made a mental note of the number.

"Walk with me, Miss Bradish. And I'll tell you my story."

"May I know your name?"

"I was born Adele St. Clair in Cap Francois, like the queen." It was a simple beginning, but at once Viv had a thousand questions.

"Did you know her in Haiti?"

"No. I came to London as a girl before Marie Christophe became queen. My father sent me when I was twelve because there was great violence against our people then, and everyone said the land was a powder keg." Adele had a faraway look in her eyes.

Viv fell into step beside the older woman. "How did you come to know the queen in London?"

"My husband is a customs clerk. He heard of her arrival as I was beginning my business, and he encouraged me to seek her favor." Something in the memory made Adele smile.

"You smile, ma'am. Tell me more."

"I was not sure I should put myself forward, she, a queen, and I, a seamstress, but my husband said, 'Who else should sew for her but her own countrywoman?' And he had an idea of how I could win her favor."

They came to the park's York Gate and turned west along the road, passing a row of new terraced houses. Through the park's iron fence, the little lake sparkled and the trees made a lacy open canopy of branches about to blossom. Viv admired the storyteller's craft with which Adele had stopped the narrative short leaving her listener with an unanswered question.

Beyond the row of terraced houses was an island in the

road with shrubs around a bench. To Viv's surprise Adele produced a small rug from her bag to lay over the damp surface. "Sit, girl," she said.

When Viv complied and Adele joined her on the bench, she asked, "Are you particular about your coffee, Miss Bradish?"

Viv nodded, momentarily confused by the aside from the main story. "I prefer a cup prepared the Turkish way."

Adele nodded. "In Haiti, the coffee cherries are as red as your English holly berries, and the roasted beans, as black as my hands. You use a *pilon*, a large mortar to turn the roasted beans to powder." Adele made a gesture with her hands. "So, at my husband's suggestion, I brought the queen beans from home and a *pilon* and offered to sew for her and for her daughters, Améthyste and Athénais."

Viv could see the cleverness of the appeal to a shared experience, and the intimacy of such a connection. A woman's seamstress knew her tastes, her figure, her very attitude toward her appearance. Viv itched to pull out the notebook from her reticule, but there would be a time for that. First, she must simply listen.

"That's how we came to be friends. Over coffee. When I came to bring cloth or designs or to measure and fit, we always had our coffee and our talk. So much talk. I cannot begin to tell it all."

"Please, can you tell me about her? The queen?"

For a time, it seemed to Viv that Adele St. Clair was lost in memories, then she smiled again. "She was Marie-Louise, as she grew up in her father's hotel. Cap Francois was like another Paris then. She told me of all the people she met there as she came up. It was her father who first thought she would make a queen. In some ways her father was like mine, believing his daughter could learn anything, be anything. But they did not always see eye-to-eye. Especially about her husband who worked in the hotel's stables, until Marie taught him, and helped him buy his freedom and become a soldier."

Adele paused looking out over the park. "The great struggle with the French came and afterward with the factions. The queen lived underground for nearly three years with her children. Her time as queen was brief, but she had dignity and grace."

Viv did not know the story of the distant island and the struggles of its people. "And then?" she asked.

Adele sighed, but her voice took on a powerful quality. "Her husband died, and their home was to be destroyed. She saved his body from harm. Her sons were killed, and she fled with her daughters. All they had known was lost."

It sounded like the end of the story, but Viv knew there was more. "And so she came to London?"

Adele smiled again. "Yes. Marie has a saying. *Je renais de mes cendres.* I am reborn from my ashes. Like our country."

"But she did not stay. Why did she leave?"

"The London air. The soot and smoke made her daughter Améthyste very ill."

It was plain to Viv that Adele's visits were a tribute to a female friendship, like the one between Lady Melforth and Viv. From the corner of her eye, she saw a gentleman approaching with a rapid stride. He headed straight for them.

"Now, you know why I must come to her house. In Haiti we do not eat the food of forgetfulness. It helps me in London to remember the one who was good to me, who brought me many ladies as clients. Not all great ladies are as kind as she."

"And your business?"

"It thrives thanks to her."

The gentleman reached their bench and tipped his hat. He had a head of red curls, blue eyes in a freckled face, prominent ears, and a blade-sharp nose. "My love," he said, addressing Adele. "I see you've made an acquaintance."

"My husband, Bob Kirby, Miss Bradish."

Bob offered Viv a little bow while she tried to collect her thoughts, at the overthrow of her own expectations.

"Has my girl been telling you about her queen?" he asked with merry eyes.

Viv nodded.

Bob offered a hand to Adele, who rose gracefully. "But has she told you we disagree a good deal about queens?"

"No." Viv glanced at Adele to see how she was taking her husband's humor and caught the flash of her eyes.

"We do," said Bob. "She thinks a queen likely to bring stability to a nation, to reign a long time."

"You must admit, my dear husband." Adele took her husband's arm. "That you men change governments as often as you change your neckcloths."

Viv thanked Adele again and watched the husband-and-wife pair stroll away, their laughter blown back on the breeze in little bursts. When Viv had first seen Adele St. Clair, she had never imagined a Bob Kirby in her life, but Adele apparently felt no contradiction between her independence and her marriage. Her eyes lighted at her husband's appearance, though he was far from handsome, and the two of them played teasing verbal games that they had obviously played before. Adele took her husband's offered arm, and together they made a picture of marriage as Viv had not seen it. Adele's rug had left a dry patch on the bench, and Viv pulled out her notebook and began to write.

She was sure she could convince Lady Melforth that the story of the heroic Queen Marie Christophe, a story of courage and resolve, hidden in a quiet corner of London, belonged in their guide. They could include Marie's house in Walk Number Nine. But as Viv wrote of Adele St. Clair's queen and benefactor, it was Adele's story she found herself telling, the story of the protégé who had made her own way in the world. Adele was the model of the independent woman of London who deserved to be celebrated. Adele's story would inspire the readers of their guide. Viv filled three pages of the little notebook with details, before she stopped to read over her notes.

Her portrait of Adele St. Clair had been written not for the Lady Melforth or the women of London. It had been written for Lark. He had led her to Adele St. Clair. She would not have written the story of Adele's independence if she hadn't met Lark. She closed her notebook. Lark was not her writing partner. She could not add Adele's story to the guide without consulting Lady Melforth. Her partner was Lady Melforth. As Dodsley had said, Lady Melforth's name would sell their book, not Viv's.

She hugged the little notebook to her chest. She had become chilled sitting on the bench in the breeze. And she had yet to leave a message for Lark at what she believed to be his lodging. There would be a porter or a maid with whom she could leave her note. She scribbled a few lines on a page torn from her notebook, tucked away the notebook, and took up her umbrella.

When she turned to cross the road, she froze. Lark was standing on the opposite flag way, the wide busy thoroughfare between them. One of the great square omnibuses, a new invention from Paris, rumbled past. It must be the heavy vehicle that made the pavement under her feet tremble. Lark's appearance was merely convenient. That was all. Now she need not find his lodging. She could simply explain their dinner party dilemma.

He made his easy, unhurried way through the traffic. "What brings you here?" he asked.

"Adele St. Clair," she said.

"Ah. Did she tell you her story?"

"She's remarkable."

"More than her queen?"

She glanced at him, wondering at the ease with which he understood her. "To be sent to London alone by her family as a young girl and to keep her head, find her way, and make a successful business …"

"And a marriage," he said.

"That, too." Viv wasn't going to admit to him how struck she had been by the way Adele and Bob teased one another.

He offered his arm. She hesitated, then took it as they crossed the road. "Is something troubling you?" he asked.

"Did the duke mention an invitation to dinner at Lady Melforth's?"

"No." He didn't meet her gaze. "What dinner party?"

She made herself keep walking in spite of the evasion. It was a reminder that he was not perfectly open with her. "Lady Melforth has invited a few friends to celebrate the book's near release and our betrothal." She expected him to groan, but his thoughts seemed elsewhere.

They reached the high street and began to stroll south toward Mayfair before he spoke again. "A large or small party?"

"Small, but nevertheless, we must keep up our…pretense." What bothered her about the party was that it felt like an end rather than a celebration.

"Are you worried you might slip up?" he asked.

She stopped and turned on him. "Me? Why would I slip up?"

He was looking at her lips. She clamped her mouth shut.

"You might not know about the duke's once notorious mother or his famous brothers. Or what happened to him as a boy."

"What did happen to him as a boy? You never mentioned that before."

He shrugged. "Ancient history. Who is on the guest list?"

"Besides the duke and duchess? My aunt Louisa and my uncle Sir Oswald Atwood, the Strydes, and Dr. Newberry."

He whistled. "We will be in dangerous waters!"

"Especially with the Strydes. There's something I must tell you about them. They are quite likely furious with me." She knew he would appreciate the story.

"More than usual? Why?"

"They were arrested."

His brows went up. "Whatever for?"

"They went to Babylon Street."

"To have their pockets picked?"

"To aid the police in a raid on a publisher." Viv grinned at him. "Mr. Stryde had a guide to the *Bowers of Venus* in his pocket, and Mrs. Stryde whacked a constable with her umbrella to save her husband."

He gave a short, sharp bark of laughter, his eyes alight with unholy merriment. "And you have been enjoying the sweet satisfaction of their embarrassment. But now, you fear their revenge. Have they been released?"

"Yes, Dr. Newberry told me the Anti-Vice Society protects its own."

"Ah," he said, sobering at once.

"What's *ah* supposed to mean?"

"Newberry looks out for you, does he?"

"I suppose he does. Anyway, Newberry doesn't matter. What matters is that we need a plan for this dinner."

"You mean our *Waterloo* strategy. It's worked before."

Viv thought he was entirely too confident. She did not know how they might be exposed, she just felt the danger. She could imagine the conversation coming to a halt and all eyes turning on them, seeing through their pretense, Lady Melforth's trust in Viv drying up like puddles on the paving stones. "You like risk. You think we can just sprinkle *Waterloo* into the conversation like salt at every uncomfortable turn."

He straightened his tie and cleared his throat. "As easy as

a waterman navigating the Thames under the *Waterloo Bridge*."

"Not if Mrs. Stryde masses her forces against us."

"Like Napoleon's Imperial Guard at...*Waterloo*? She's doomed I'd say."

"And if my kind, but curious aunt Louisa simply wants to know how you changed my mind about marriage?"

"I'll say it was a near-run thing, but like Wellington at *Waterloo* I had reserve forces ready to throw at any stubborn, last-minute resistance you might throw at me."

"Where does all this *Waterloo* knowledge come from?"

"The United Service Museum, one shilling admittance, and a great model of the field and battle." He stopped and turned her toward him, tilting her face up, his gloved fingertips soft under her chin. He was inviting her to play a game with him, as he had from the first when he'd gone down on his knee before her in Lady Melforth's drawing room. It was a heady prospect. Together, they could defy those who would keep them down. If only she could read him as well as she thought he could read her.

"I know you're worried, but no one knows the true state of our feelings but us. Now, if someone wants to know how you feel about your fiancé's desire to kiss you again ..."

"I'll say, there are some things we will never know about...*Waterloo*."

CHAPTER SIXTEEN

Lady Melforth's dining room was brilliant with light, and overwarm from a blazing fire in the hearth. Lark couldn't say that the evening was already a disaster, but it was headed that way. The only thing he had not had to worry about was a meeting with the duke and duchess, who were away from London.

Candlelight from a dozen tall white tapers gleamed and sparkled on silver and porcelain. And pearls. Those pearls shook the certainty in which he had dressed for the evening, the certainty that as Viv Bradish's fiancé he had become a true gentleman. Tonight, she seemed impossibly distant from him, not the partner of the past fortnight. Listening to empty talk in the drawing room, the pearls had caught his eye, and the old professional habit of assessing weights and clasps had taken hold.

Lady Melforth's long triple strand hung nearly to her waist, its clasp concealed by a lace collar. Viv's aunt Lady Louisa wore a glittering pearl and diamond bib with a box clasp, and Mrs. Stryde's heavy double strand, weighted with a bloodred garnet cross, was tied with a matching velvet ribbon like the stripes in her gown. Viv's single pearl in a gold filigree setting hung on a delicate chain that closed with a toggle clasp, easy for a man to undo as he brushed his lady's hair aside.

Now Lady Melforth stood at the head of the table in an emerald gown with tall black plumes in her fiery hair. She waved away Dr. Newberry's assistance as her guests found their seats. Lark distrusted her ladyship's forced gaiety. For half an hour, she had stood in the midst of her guests, calling the evening a grand celebration. There had been champagne for all and a pointed salute to Viv, which, to Lark's ears, had sounded bitter and dismissive. "To Viv, who has taught me the value of having an assistant for the tedious aspects of the business so I could concentrate on the main work."

They were a small party, and the dining table further shrank the boundaries of the conversation. Lark was on one side between Lady Louisa and Mrs. Stryde, while Viv was opposite him between Mr. Stryde and her uncle Sir Oswald Atwood, Baronet. Newberry was at the foot of the table opposite Lady Melforth. Almost any topic could trip Viv and Lark up. Between them, mid-table under the chandelier, was a sort of silver tree, over a foot tall, its branches holding scallop-edged glass bowls filled with fragrant pink blooms. He tried not to regard the seating arrangement as a further sign of impending catastrophe. Begging Lady Louisa's pardon, he leaned to his left and mouthed their signal to Viv. *Waterloo.* She gave him a faint smile in return. He straightened and caught a hostile stare from Newberry.

At Lady Melforth's nod to Haxton, the servants sprang into quiet action, and over a vivid green pea soup, Lady Louisa turned to Lark. She was a tall woman in lavender silk and black lace with a long plain face, lively hazel eyes, and an amiable, no-nonsense manner. Her genuine interest in others seemed to Lark as much a danger as Mrs. Stryde's malice and Newberry's suspicion.

"Viv tells me that your only relation is an aunt in Somerton."

"Yes, ma'am. She's quite good to me, though I rarely see her."

"And, is it in Somerton that you made Wenlocke's acquaintance?"

"It's where I did my schooling, ma'am, with his help."

"Oh. Privately then." Lady Louisa looked across the table to Viv. "What did you tell me, Viv dear? The old duke or the current duke?"

Viv's voice came from behind the silver centerpiece. Lark could see the blue of her sleeves, but not her face. "Well, I suspect I've got my dukes mixed up, Aunt. It was after…Waterloo, so it must have been the…"

"The current duke, ma'am." Lark supplied the answer.

"After his return to his family then. You must be near in age, Mr. Larkin. And your friends call you *Lark*, do they? From childhood? It puts me in mind of something I wanted to ask you about the duke, but it's gone out of my head." She smiled at him and dipped her spoon in the soup.

"No doubt it will come back to you, ma'am," he said, keeping his expression blank.

For the rest of the soup and fish course, Lady Louisa talked with Lady Melforth about mutual friends, but when the bowls were removed, she turned to Lark again.

"I'm surprised that some enterprising playwright hasn't turned the duke's story into a drama. *The Lost Heir Restored* sounds rather suitable for the Adelphi Theatre. I don't suppose, Viv, that you want to try your hand at that sort of thing?"

"Not my style, Aunt."

"Are you thinking of another guide, then?" Lady Louisa smiled in Viv's direction, but Lady Melforth stiffened, wineglass in hand.

"Under Lady Melforth's tutelage, I may," Viv replied. "I've learned so much from her. I think you'll like the chapter on shopping, Aunt."

"Ah, you know me well, my dear."

Lady Melforth set aside her wine. "I'll see to it that you have a copy, Louisa, but it's far too soon to speak of another guide. Who knows what Viv will do when she and Mr. Larkin wed."

"I quite agree, Aurora," said Mrs. Stryde on Lark's right, "I fear that you've allowed Miss Bradish to expose herself to the worst sorts of persons in pursuit of her duties at no small risk to her writing ambitions."

"Whatever do you mean, Eustacia?" Lady Louisa asked, looking past Lark at Mrs. Stryde. "If our intrepid Viv has had adventures in the great city, I'm glad to hear it."

"I'm sorry to tell you, Lady Louisa, but Miss Bradish went the length of Oxford Street unaccompanied and had…encounters with men on the street."

"Viv," said her aunt laughing, "I hope you know how to wield an umbrella or a hatpin when gentlemen get out of line."

"It's no laughing matter, Lady Louisa," said Mrs. Stryde. "A woman who wishes to have public support for her writing, must safeguard her reputation. What lady can allow herself to be guided by an authoress with a reputation for vice?"

There was a most awkward silence. Lark had a clear recollection of the fellow with the lavender gloves following Viv in the Pantheon, and realized the man had likely been a tool of the Strydes. He waited for Lady Melforth to defend Viv, but the lady appeared absorbed in moving bits of a lobster cake about on her plate.

"I think I may vouch for Viv, ma'am," he said, ending the silence. "If she put herself in situations that ladies of London too often face, she did it to show how a sensible woman handles such nuisances."

"Bravo, Mr. Larkin." Lady Louisa gave him a warm smile.

"I beg you, Lady Louisa, not to be deceived." Mrs. Stryde clutched her red garnet cross. "It is not guidebooks, but the work of the Anti-Vice Society that preserves female safety and decency. It is the society that strives to make headway against the godlessness and decadence of this city."

"Godlessness and decadence," said Sir Oswald. "Is that what you call it? I suppose this Anti-Vice Society of yours goes after sport on Sunday and that sort of thing, and a man won't find a decent mill or a horse race anywhere."

Mr. Stryde cleared his throat. "Our main aim, Sir Oswald, is to stop licentious publications."

"You mean salty books?" asked Sir Oswald.

"Exactly. There are hundreds of them. We have recently shut down a Babylon Street publisher."

"The raid was a success then?" Viv asked.

"The police bungled it of course, but everything has been

put to rights." Mrs. Stryde glared at Viv.

"Do you think London is growing worse, then?" Lady Louisa asked.

It was an opening Mrs. Stryde could not resist. "You can hardly understand the depths of depravity in London until you see it for yourself. Filthy pollution circulating in the post, doxies boldly parading our streets, pickpockets on every bridge."

Sir Oswald turned to Dr. Newberry. "Won't it be boring for you, Doctor, if the Strydes succeed in purging London of its vices? What will happen to the doctoring business, if no one falls ill, or gets shot?"

"Oh, there's no danger yet that disease will go away, Sir Oswald. And we're not so dull as you imagine. I treated a gunshot wound in this very neighborhood, not a fortnight ago." The doctor stabbed a bit of venison pie with his fork.

"Really? Now that improves my opinion of London. Is there a story to tell?"

Newberry looked up from his plate, glanced at Lark and coolly shifted his gaze to Viv. For her the doctor would keep silent. "Another time, Sir Oswald, have you tried this pie?"

VIV HARDLY KNEW what she ate. Somehow, she had offended Lady Melforth. The effort to put on a gaiety she did not feel was wearing. She told herself she should be glad that a book, largely of her words, was nearly complete, and relieved that her counterfeit betrothal with its awkward intimacies was nearly at an end, but the evening felt dismal rather than celebratory. She hardly recognized Lady Melforth as the friend who had laughed at her stories and encouraged her efforts. Tonight, her ladyship had reduced Viv to the role of obscure assistant, rather than partner. It made no sense. Even with the new pieces Viv had written, she could not think how she had offended her benefactor.

The dinner passed through two courses in a blur of talk and the clinking of flatware. For a brief moment, while the footmen shifted the great silver epergne to remove the cloth and lay out the dessert, she exchanged a glance with Lark. He gave her a cheeky grin, as if he were enjoying their peril, but he was not the one who could lose his situation and all that he had worked for.

She pulled herself together. So far, she and Lark had avoided catastrophe. The worst moment had come with Sir Oswald's asking about the gunshot wound, but Dr. Newberry, whatever his suspicions, had not given them away. Abruptly, Newberry pushed back his chair, his eyes fixed on the head of the table. Viv followed his gaze.

Lady Melforth rose to signal the ladies to withdraw so that the gentlemen might linger over their claret or port. As she stood, the feathers in her headdress tilted over her left ear. Her mouth froze in a downward turn. Then her ladyship's eyes closed. She went limp and sat down hard. Viv was on her feet at once. "Haxton, her ladyship."

The butler lunged forward with undignified haste to catch his mistress and stop her sliding from the chair. Viv knelt at her side and took her hand, giving it a squeeze. "Ma'am, can you hear me?"

Her ladyship's eyelids fluttered. Newberry appeared next

to Viv and took her ladyship's other wrist, feeling the pulse. "We must get her upstairs," he said.

"What's happening?" cried Mrs. Stryde. "Arthur, see to your cousin."

Mr. Stryde, who sat mopping his brow, struggled awkwardly to push his chair back from the table. Lady Louisa stepped up to Viv, holding out a glass of wine. "Won't it be easier if Aurora revives a bit first?"

Viv gave her ladyship's hand another gentle squeeze. "Ma'am, do you wish to say good night to your guests?"

Lady Melforth's eyelids fluttered again, and she stirred, clutching the arm of her chair. Her eyes opened fully and her gaze took in the three people hovering over her. "Oh dear," she said, "I'm afraid my leg gave out on me. Too much standing before dinner."

Newberry took the glass from Lady Louisa and offered it to Lady Melforth. "A quick swallow will do you some good, ma'am. Then we'll get you upstairs to rest that leg."

A look between doctor and patient told Viv the collapse had been expected. Lady Melforth drank some wine, but her grip went slack, and the doctor caught the glass. He spoke to Haxton, who summoned two footmen to lift her ladyship's chair back from the table.

She waved to her guests. They were all on their feet now except the Strydes. "Carry on, dear friends. Don't let my pesky foot keep you from Mrs. Brandle's sponge cake."

Between the doctor and Haxton, Lady Melforth regained her feet. The two men assisted her out of the room, Doctor Newberry speaking quietly in her ear and keeping a steady hand under her arm.

Viv cast Lark one quick imploring look before she and Lady Louisa followed the doctor.

LARK UNDERSTOOD THAT look. Viv wanted the Strydes gone. Easier said than done. Rank dictated that Sir Oswald take charge. Lark waited for the older man to break the silence. Sir Oswald stared regretfully at the sponge cake on its glass stand. The remaining footman stood stiffly by the door. Mr. Stryde still mopped his brow.

"Arthur, don't just sit there, do something," cried Mrs. Stryde.

Her husband levered himself out of his chair. "My dear, I hardly ..."

With a sigh Sir Oswald glanced up from the cake and came round the end of the table. He took hold of Mrs. Stryde's chair to assist her. "It seems our dinner party is at an end, ma'am." He turned to Stryde. "Perhaps, Stryde, you'd best take your wife home to wait for news of how the patient does."

"Oh no," said Mrs. Stryde, twisting in the chair to confront Sir Oswald. "I refuse to let you send Arthur away."

"My dear," her husband protested.

"Be quiet, Arthur," she snapped.

"No need to trouble your husband, ma'am," said Sir Oswald. "Dr. Newberry knows his business."

"Does he? Why does Aurora's foot not heal?" Mrs. Stryde turned her glare on Lark. "This collapse is Miss Bradish's fault. She's been gadding about London in a most improper way, neglecting our dear cousin's health until it's come to this. Arthur is Aurora's cousin. He is family. He should be at her side, not that shameless girl."

She started to rise from her chair, but her skirts apparently held her back. She reached out a hand for balance and Lark caught it. "Steady, ma'am," he said.

She shook off his hold, but her pinned skirts held her in place.

Sir Oswald rolled his eyes. Lark gritted his teeth. From the first time he overheard the Strydes speaking to each other in the entry hall, he knew they wanted Viv sacked. Now, Mrs. Stryde seemed to have found a way to do it, to blame Viv for Lady Melforth's collapse. Mrs. Stryde bent over to free her skirts, tugging violently. The burgundy velvet bow around her neck grew taut with her efforts. In a flash Lark saw a way to divert her attack on Viv. The act was done in an instant.

"Ma'am," he said, kneeling beside her chair. "It may be that the chair is holding your skirts down. If you will allow Sir Oswald to tip it back, I will free your hem."

"Young man," cried Mr. Stryde. "That would be most improper."

"Don't be absurd, Stryde," said Sir Oswald. "Do you want your wife stuck in this seat forever?"

Mrs. Stryde straightened and nodded. "Oh, very well," she said.

Sir Oswald gripped the frame of the chair, and tipped. Lark dropped to one knee, pulled the yards of silk forward, and finished the job he'd started. "You can let her down now, Sir Oswald," he said.

Sir Oswald let the chair down, and offered a hand to Mrs. Stryde. She took it briefly, rose, and strode toward her husband in an angry swish of skirts. "Come Arthur, we must go to your cousin."

Her husband simply stared at her, pointing at her chest. "My dear, what's become of your cross?"

Mrs. Stryde looked down, pressing a hand to her bosom. "My pearls," she cried. "I've been robbed."

"Have some sense, woman," snapped Sir Oswald. "You've not been robbed in Lady Melforth's dining room."

"Where are my pearls then?"

"Ma'am," said Lark. "Shall we have the footman look under the table? It's likely that your necklace came loose as you tried to free your skirts."

Mrs. Stryde turned slowly, her hand still pressed to her unadorned bosom, and stared at Lark. He knew that baffled look, when, in spite of plain fact, a mark could not understand how her possession had simply vanished.

Lark met her gaze with an innocent one of his own that said he wanted only to help.

"Good thought, lad." Sir Oswald clapped Lark on the shoulder and summoned the footman to their side of the table. "Let's shift these chairs, Mr. Larkin, and let the fellow look."

As the footman went down on all fours to peer under the table, the door opened and Newberry entered, escorting Viv and Lady Louisa. Newberry leaned close to whisper something in Viv's ear and gave her shoulder a squeeze. She smiled, and he slipped out of the room. At the familiarity of the exchange, Lark, who had seen Viv enter rooms many times in their brief betrothal, caught his breath. Only now did he see her clearly in her proper setting among the people to whom she belonged.

An accident of time and place had connected Viv and Lark on Babylon Street. The small, round ball with which she had wounded him had set them on a path neither intended. Now they must return to their separate spheres. The idea that he could propose to her a second time in all sincerity died. He was a man who, to protect her, used the first means that came to mind, a click, a pinch. He was not, and he never would be, a gentleman.

"Oswald, dear," said Lady Louisa, "what's going on?"

"Nothing really. Mrs. Stryde's got herself in a state over a missing necklace. How's the patient?" asked Sir Oswald.

"She's much restored," said Viv, her gaze meeting Lark's. "Dr. Newberry has elevated the foot, and she's resting comfortably. She begs your forgiveness for her indisposition and hopes you'll call on her in a few days."

"Good, good," said Sir Oswald.

"Found it, sir," came a muffled voice from under the table. The footman backed out from under the table and stood, holding the double string of pearls, the red velvet ties dangling from his gloved hand. Viv's puzzled glance rested briefly on those velvet strings.

"Take it to Mrs. Stryde, boy," said Sir Oswald. "You see, ma'am, nothing to get worked up about."

Mrs. Stryde snatched eagerly at the necklace. "Come, Arthur. We're leaving, but we know our duty to Aurora, and we will return." She swept her husband through the dining room door.

"Damned difficult female that," said Sir Oswald. "Did our best to get her out the door, and then such a fuss when she couldn't manage her skirts and lost her necklace."

"Ready to go home, my love?" asked Lady Louisa, holding out her hand to her husband.

"Yes!" said Sir Oswald. He turned to Lark. "May we drop you somewhere, Mr. Larkin?"

"Thank you, no. I'll walk."

AS LARK LEFT the house, he met Lady Louisa coming back for something she'd forgotten. He joined Sir Oswald on the pavement to wait for her return.

"Are you sure we can't take you up, lad?" Sir Oswald asked.

"Thank you, no. A walk will clear my head."

"Right you are, boy. After that woman made such a fuss, a man's head needs clearing."

The door behind them opened, and Sir Oswald turned to his wife. "Never even had my cake. You don't suppose, Louisa, that they'd send a bit of cake round to us, do you?"

"My dear," she held up a small basket. "The heroes of the hour deserve some reward."

"That we do, eh lad?" As Sir Oswald took the basket, a substantial black town coach came to a stop at the curb. A servant leapt down to open the door, and Sir Oswald extended a hand to his wife. "In you go, my dear."

Lady Louisa took her husband's hand and offered Lark a parting smile. "We are glad Viv found you, young man. We thought she'd never think of marriage." She shook her head. "Fond as I am of Aurora, her illness makes quite a tyrant of her."

Lady Louisa and Sir Oswald climbed into their coach, and when it vanished round a corner into the London night, Lark's old memories stirred to life. Somewhere in the great city was the spot where he had been a sleepy passenger in another coach as it rumbled away from the building that had swallowed up his mother. In the months since the fire, he had been certain that he would know the place when he found it, and that finding it would change him, give him knowledge of his true self. Lately, he had imagined that other self, the person Edward Larkin was meant to be, proposing to Vivian Bradish a second time with no pretense. Now he knew he would not, could not. A thief could not propose to a lady.

But he could not stop thinking of her. He tried. He stood, firmly rooted to the pavement in front of her door. He counted the windows of neighboring houses, bright rectangles of yellow light. He counted the gas lamps, ranged at intervals down the street, each a smaller glowing globe. He tried to name a familiar tune that came from an upper room across the way, where someone played the pianoforte with heavy, determined fingering. He worked to put words to the posh accents that came and went in snatches of indistinct conversation. He counted the bells that tolled the quarter hour not quite in unison, marking another bit of time that could not be got back again.

A long-forgotten conversation returned to him, an exchange he'd had with the duchess, when she was merely the grinder that Dav had hired to teach their boy gang. Robin, the youngest of them, had found a toad in the hall that spring day and claimed it was a baby dragon. She wanted to preserve the boy's illusion, his *delight*, she'd called it, in the squat little creature. Lark had known then that illusions were dangerous and that the world held no lasting delight for boys like them. The argument came back to haunt him now, and he clenched his fists against a rising sense of loss.

Behind him, inside the house, Viv would not think of Lark. Her thoughts would be of Lady Melforth. The woman was clearly more ill than she was willing to admit, and it would be Newberry at Viv's side with the right to calm her fears.

The door behind him opened again, and he glanced over his shoulder. "You."

Viv came down the two steps toward him. He turned and took her hands in his. He knew why he'd lingered on her doorstep, and he tried to crush an absurd hope that she felt the same. "What is it?"

"Thank you."

Her gratitude was not what he wanted. "For what?"

"My aunt told me how you and my uncle kept the Strydes at bay. They make things so much worse for her ladyship."

"She's quite ill, isn't she?" He could see the worry in her eyes.

"She's not herself. One minute she blames Newberry for not curing her foot, and the next she insists that we finish the book tonight. But I fear..." Viv drew in a long, slow breath and squared her shoulders. "Newberry will consult another physician tomorrow. He thinks she has developed a palsy."

Lark gave her hands a squeeze. The demands on her would be greater now. A woman as proud and independent as her ladyship would not be easy to care for. He knew there was another fear. "You worry that the writing will come to an end."

"I do," she admitted. "For her, as much as for me. She's always been a writer. I've just begun. But you give me courage."

"Courage?" He wanted to laugh. He doubted that the woman who shot him needed courage. His wound was nearly healed. He no longer wore the plaster, and soon the spent ball and the slight scar on his side would be the only reminders of their brief betrothal. He wanted more to remember, much more. He released her hands and slid his palms up her arms. Her eyes widened, and she shivered under his touch. He watched her mouth, knowing from the way she drew in her lower lip that she was concentrating, trying to hold onto some idea. He took hold of her shoulders, making his own intentions plain.

"Wait," she said. "Let me finish what I meant to say. The courage I get from you is the courage to keep writing, and to write what I truly see."

It was sweetly sincere, but it was far from what he hoped for. "Finished?"

She nodded.

"Good." He kissed her, and his senses narrowed to her. He lost himself in illusion. It didn't matter that he was a thief and she, a lady. For the moment she was his Viv, not soft and yielding like some imagined lover, but fiercely alive and meeting him kiss for kiss. She clutched his coat, bunching the wool over his ribs in little pulses of movement that echoed the pounding of his own pulse. He moved to cup her face and slide his fingers into her hair and hold her where he could taste the sweetness and boldness of her spirit.

For the moment there was only Viv, and he could believe she knew him, the man under the layers of disguise. Her kiss lifted him up. The old London, which had rated him as nothing without knowing him, faded away, its stones dissolving under his feet. He inhabited a new London, in which he was no longer a pickpocket, only the man who loved Viv Bradish.

The tune from across the way ceased, and an unseen audience clapped mightily. The spell broke.

Viv slipped from his grasp. She lowered her head. "I must go in. I'll leave word with Haxton when we can meet again. To...to finish things."

He nodded, unable to speak.

ALMOST AS SOON as he began to walk, Lark knew he was being followed. His pursuer hung back when traffic was light and moved closer as Lark approached Cavendish Square. Lark passed his usual turning, and headed away from his lodging. As the view opened up across the square, Lark slowed his pace, listening for the man's footfall. There was no mistaking Rook's heavy tread. Rook had been waiting in the shadows, watching.

Lark headed down Regent Street toward Piccadilly. In

his evening finery, he could stroll unremarked. He would put people and carriages between himself and his pursuer. He would lead Rook into the very heart of temptation among London's jewel-studded West End pleasure-seekers with their diamond stickpins and fat gold watches. Once Rook was distracted, Lark would give him the slip.

Eluding Rook took the length of Regent Street and a good bit of Piccadilly, but at last Lark stood in the darkness of the park, free for the moment, but knowing Rook would return to the house where Viv lived. The Rook who had assaulted him and followed him was not the friend and partner of the old days. Lark did not think Rook would do Viv harm, but he could not be sure what this new Rook's intentions were.

There were servants to prevent him from entering the house either through the front door or through the basement, and Haxton would not hesitate to summon the constables if needed. But Viv, who had no idea of Rook's existence, could leave the house alone, and be followed and accosted. In her own neighborhood, consumed with worry about Lady Melforth, Viv would not think to carry her pistol.

Lark should warn her, but he could think of no word of warning that would not reveal the truth about their first meeting. That was the rub. *I know you think I'm the kind gentleman who came to your aid when another man pinched your purse, but I was that man's accomplice for years.* If they had to part, if their sham betrothal had to end, he wanted her to go on thinking of him as Edward Larkin, a gentleman. He would have to be sharp and alert to prevent Rook from getting to her.

CHAPTER SEVENTEEN

TWO DAYS PASSED without a visit from Newberry's fellow physician. Neville Pridmore reportedly had royal as well as noble patients and a full schedule. Viv spent the time at her desk or at Lady Melforth's side. Although Lady Melforth kept to her room, she read over pages of their draft and kept Viv busy making small changes and sending them off to Dodsley. Newberry came twice a day to urge his patient to rest rather than write. He said nothing to Lady Melforth of his suspicion that she was subject to a particular palsy, but with Viv, he shook his head and looked grim. The Strydes called often and were turned away on Newberry's orders, and once Viv heard Mrs. Stryde's angry voice, warning Haxton that he would be gone as soon as the house was hers.

The night before the consulting physician's visit, Lady Melforth could not sleep. She insisted that she alone would meet him. She asked Viv to retrace the steps of their walk through the Green Park. Walk Number Six was meant to refresh a woman's senses and encourage her to enjoy the freedom of a country ramble in the city. Now Lady Melforth worried that the walk was too taxing for a lady, and wanted Viv to walk the route again. Viv knew she was being got out of the way, so that her mentor could face the new doctor alone, but she agreed to go, so that her ladyship could at last sleep.

Viv sat beside the great canopied bed and turned to the other matter on her mind, ending her betrothal. She would ask Lark to accompany her to the park. There, away from others, she would find a way to end their betrothal with dignity and gratitude. She had thought of little else in the few minutes that were hers while attending Lady Melforth and working on the book.

Briefly their engagement had seemed real. His feelings seemed to have changed from the moment when he'd challenged her to accept the ruse. He had said no moonlight and roses, and had kissed her on the pavement in front of the house with someone playing badly in the background and the odors of horses and trash bins in the air.

She had kissed him back and clung to him in that moment. Without meaning to, she had come to regard them as being in league together, taking on the great city and making it theirs. But days of tending to Lady Melforth and holding the book's pages in her lap had brought Viv to her senses. She had come to London to become a writer. She owed everything she had learned to Lady Melforth. Tomorrow or the next day, she would take the last bits of the book and all the notes and revisions to Dodsley. In days, the proofs would be in her hands.

She knew there were girls who dreamed of seeing their names in the marriage register of some grand church next to a mister or an esquire or even a lord. Not Viv. She had dreamed of opening the cover of a book and finding her name in print. She knew just how their London guide would look now that Dodsley had accepted their title.

A LADY'S GUIDE TO LONDON IN TWELVE SELF-GUIDED WALKS

A FAITHFUL DESCRIPTION OF ROUTES AND PLACES

TO ASSIST WOMEN IN KNOWLEDGE OF THE METROPOLIS

WRITTEN BY LADY AURORA MELFORTH, THE TRAVELING VISCOUNTESS,

AND MISS VIVIAN BRADISH

LONDON: PUBLISHED BY DODSLEY & SONS, 86 THE STRAND

AVAILABLE AT BOOKSELLERS IN ENGLAND, WALES, IRELAND, AND SCOTLAND

It was an old dream, now close to coming true. And Lady Melforth needed her. Viv had no business turning away from her when the caring had become more difficult.

THE MORNING OF the doctor's expected visit, Lady Melforth woke early, insisting that she must be up and dressed hours before he was scheduled to arrive. Sarah, her maid, sent for Viv at once. Together they helped her ladyship to her dressing table, where Sarah had placed her ladyship's cup of morning chocolate. Sarah offered further help, but was sent to bring her ladyship's clothes from her dressing room. Viv was ordered to gather the latest pages from her ladyship's bedside.

Her ladyship stared at the mirror, apparently lost in thought. She lifted her hand and rested it on the edge of the dressing table, then with a sudden jerk of the hand, swept the cup of chocolate from the table. She gave an anguished cry and shouted for Sarah. With her shaking hand, she clutched her dripping skirts, scattering drops of chocolate.

Viv's heart lurched. All of Newberry's hints that her ladyship might be seriously ill came to mind. She dropped to her knees at her ladyship's side and put a steadying hand on her trembling arm. Once the tremor subsided, Viv retrieved the cup from the carpet. Sarah came running. "Sarah, please bring some towels and send for Jenny."

Viv applied a napkin to the worst of the dark spill on her ladyship's dressing gown. "Don't worry, ma'am. Jenny will take care of the spill. Let's move you to the bench and get you out of this wet gown."

Lady Melforth released her hold of the gown, and allowed Viv to help her to her feet. Together they managed the few steps to the bench at the foot of her ladyship's grand canopied bed. Viv helped her ladyship to put a hand to the scrolled arm of the bench and stiffly lower herself down. She looked up at Viv with anxious eyes.

"How silly of me to be nervous about this fellow Pridmore's visit. He's just another sawbones, no matter how puffed up he is by having exalted patients."

"Exactly," Viv agreed. "You know Newberry only wants to be sure that he has not overlooked anything that may be done for you."

Jenny arrived, and whatever she thought of the dark brown stains on the ivory skirts of the dressing table or the puddle of chocolate on the pale blue carpet, she went to work at once with soap and cold water to remove evidence of the spill. While Sarah and Viv helped her ladyship to dress, Jenny turned the skirts on the dressing table to move the stain to the back. Together Jenny and Viv moved the table a few inches forward to conceal the drying spot on the rug.

When all was in order, Viv and Sarah helped her ladyship back to her dressing table, and Sarah began gently to brush her ladyship's fiery hair into some sort of order.

"Now, Viv," said her ladyship, her gaze once again clear, meeting Viv's in the glass, "you'd best get going if we're to have those last revisions to Dodsley by the end of day today."

"Of course, ma'am." Viv gathered up the pages, gave a mock salute, and turned to go. Outside the bedroom, she leaned against the door, and made a brief, silent prayer for strength for her ladyship.

WHEN VIV DESCENDED, she found Lark waiting in the hall. It was plain that he and Haxton were now on good terms. Even the least of her acquaintances would feel something when the pretend betrothal ended, perhaps nothing very great, a bit of confusion, a passing sympathy for Viv, but something.

Lark's questioning gaze met hers at once, and he moved toward her at the bottom of the stairs. "Something's happened, hasn't it? Is she worse? You don't have to tell me, but I am at your service today."

"Are you? Again? When I meet your duke, I will be sure

to tell him that he is a most lax employer." She accepted her cloak and bonnet from Haxton.

"That he is! Where are we off to today? Your publisher?"

She settled the bonnet in place, noting the familiar evasion at the mention of his work. She took a minute to hide a slight disappointment as she donned her gloves. She had no business feeling disappointed that he hid something of himself from her almost effortlessly. Her plan was to end their pretense of a betrothal. "Lady Melforth wants me to check the time and distance on one of our early walks through the Green Park."

"Your carriage awaits," he said.

At that, she did look up. She hadn't ordered it. "Do we need a carriage? It's a perfect spring day."

"Which, we'll enjoy in the park. You'll have a more accurate account of how fatiguing the walk is if you haven't walked a mile or more first."

"Miss." Haxton opened the door, and they passed through into the bright cool day.

Taking the carriage made perfect sense, but again Viv sensed that his preference for taking the carriage concealed something. She cast a quick glance around her as she climbed into the coach. Henrietta Street looked ordinary. Nothing in the air, the sunshine, or the sky suggested cause for alarm. It was a rare spring day.

When they sat facing each other and he signaled the coachman to go, she noted a passing expression of satisfaction in his eyes. "What are you not telling me?" she asked.

"Nothing," he said. "You want to return to Lady Melforth in good time, don't you?"

"I do," she agreed, still trying to name the thing that bothered her and wanting to protest that she could easily walk three miles or four in London and hardly needed to be carried to her destination. But the protest never made it to her lips. With the motion of the carriage, she yawned, prodigiously, helplessly, a long shaky exhalation. She clapped her gloved hands over her gaping mouth.

Across from her, he grinned. "Her ladyship running you ragged?"

"It's not as bad as that."

"I can see that you are worried about her," he said, sobering at once.

"She's restless at night, so I read to her, her own books mainly. That's what's so heartbreaking. I think she fears that she'll never write again. And..."

"And..." he said gently.

"And that would be like losing her voice, losing who she is." Viv straightened on the velvet seat. "That's why it's important that we get our book finished. More than any doctor or medicine, having the proof copy in her hands is bound to do Lady Melforth a world of good."

"Well, then. Let's get to it."

The carriage let them down in Piccadilly near the entrance to the park. Viv and Lady Melforth had chosen the smaller park as a walking destination without the bridle paths and carriage ways of the larger, more popular Hyde Park. The route they'd planned was about a mile along the Queen's Walk, past great houses like Spencer House, and humble lanes like the old passage for milkmaids to the milk stalls in St. James's Park, down to Buckingham House, and on down Constitution Hill to the tip of the park across from the Duke of Wellington's Apsley House. The whole leisurely excursion was meant to take an hour, allowing time to admire the different prospects, and offering women the freedom of a stroll in the country in the heart of the city. Queen Caroline, George II's wife, had envisioned just such outings when she'd designed it.

The carriage rolled away, and they entered the park. A clump of Narcissus nodded their white heads at them. There would be no other flowers in the park itself, just a rolling expanse of green with the tracery of faintly green-tipped branches overhead. Viv reached for her notebook and pencil.

"I'll watch the time if you like," he offered.

"Thank you." She set off briskly, and almost at once, moderated her pace because he was with her, his presence a reminder to allow for observation and for enjoying the freshness of the air and greenness of landscape and the freedom of easy motion. It was a scene into which Lark fit perfectly, every inch the gentleman.

At each stop, Lark gave her the time to jot in her notebook. And she considered their surroundings. No spot seemed quite right for announcing the end of their engagement. There were too many people about. The sun was too bright, or the shade too deep. He was being too helpful. She wanted to keep to their schedule. By the time they reached the little shrub-surrounded lake below the front of Buckingham House, she had resolved that the best place to end their betrothal was in Lady Melforth's green drawing room where it had begun. In a few days, Viv would have a handsome copy of the book to give him and could inscribe a brief message expressing her gratitude for the ways he had helped in making it. That would be a perfectly fitting way to end things between them.

Swans glided on the lake and ladies in white gowns echoed their movements on the surrounding path. Children and small dogs ran this way and that, chasing sticks and balls. Looking toward Buckingham House itself one saw columns upon columns and a view obstructed by the great marble arch in the forecourt. The arch had been built to memorialize England's great victory over Napoleon. Viv consulted her notebook. One couldn't exactly commend the house as an inspiration to women.

"Are you wondering what to say about it?" Lark asked.

She nodded, turning to look toward the east. "The arch is too near the house, and obstructs the view. Of course, the king doesn't live there, so I suppose it's no inconvenience to him. At least the arch is not blocking traffic."

"The king probably doesn't want to live with a monumental arch to another man's achievement on his doorstep."

She frowned. "You think the king is offended by the monument?"

"He tried to give the house away to Parliament," he said. "But the members apparently refused to take it over as a meeting place. You could simply omit it from your guide."

"But how could a monument to a national achievement offend the king? He's the head of the nation, isn't he?"

Lark was silent for a moment, the teasing look gone from his eyes. "What if," he said at last, "the king doesn't feel that he was truly a part of the great effort of beating Napoleon. What if the monument makes him feel like a mere onlooker, an idler, as if he doesn't quite belong among the happy throngs of Englishmen glorying in their splendid victory. A man has to take part in order to belong."

"Oh dear, I can't omit it. It's there, isn't it? It makes a fine backdrop for Londoners out on a stroll, something for a painter to capture." She caught his glance, now laughing again, and realized he'd meant to provoke her defense of the place. He was dangerous in the way he had of anticipating her thoughts.

They turned and made their way down the final stretch of the proposed walk toward the western tip of the park where three great thoroughfares came together, and that other, vaster park began. Viv slowed her steps, reluctant to come face-to-face with Apsley House. Carriages and horsemen passed in all directions and a shifting crowd gathered to admire the Duke of Wellington's famous abode at Number 1, London.

Apsley House stood at the end of a row of grand houses on the north side of Piccadilly. A little island of green with a few trees on it lay between them and the house. People paused before the house, pointing to its features and paying their tribute of awe to the duke and to the men who'd fought with him at Waterloo. Viv could see without feeling the swelling pride and unity of the crowd in the near environs of the great man who had led England to glory on that day. Lark's words about belonging or not belonging were fresh in her mind. She could not share the thrill or celebrate with others, not because she had not been at the great battle, but because for her June eighteenth was no victory. It was both her birthday, and the day her father died, the day her mother's widowhood had begun.

It confirmed what she and Lady Melforth had been striving for in their guide. The grand monuments and sights of London might have different meanings for each traveler.

As she stared at Apsley House, she realized that she'd lost Lark somewhere in the crowd. She turned to look for him and found a rough-looking man with a dark brown beard, bear-like in his size and ferocious appearance, his huge fists clenched, his menacing gaze fixed on someone beyond her. She followed the hostile gaze and found Lark looking away from Apsley House, unaware of the man. Lark stood transfixed, the only word for it, staring at a plain building of yellow stone and red brick on the opposite side of Grosvenor Place.

She moved closer to him and put a hand on his sleeve. "Lark, what is it?" she asked. "Do you know that building?"

He didn't answer. Viv glanced at the building that had captured his attention. Two signs across the upper stories proclaimed in bold lettering: PENITENT WOMEN'S HOSPITAL and VOLUNTARY ADMITTANCE.

Viv turned and found the bearded man still glaring at Lark. She tried to catch the man's eye and warn him off, but he turned his back to her. That broad back in a plain brown sackcloth coat reminded her of the fleeing pickpocket of the day she met Lark. But they were laughably far from Babylon Street, surrounded by fashionable Londoners. People strolled past, unhurried, unalarmed. The bearded man moved on as if he meant to enter the park. Viv slipped her arm through Lark's and gave a gentle pull.

He seemed to feel her presence then, but turned a blank

face to her, his mind clearly on some inner vision. She tugged his arm again. "Let's return to Piccadilly," she said. On Piccadilly, there were always crowds, and perhaps there would be a constable, someone to turn to if the bearded man approached again. Lark fell into step next to her, but said nothing, withdrawn into himself. She thought walking must help, must bring him back to himself and to her. She could not imagine why the building had overset him.

They had gone a very few steps when a harsh voice reached them.

"I'm warning ye. Ye'd better do a click. Ye and yer fine friends can't dodge me furever!"

Viv couldn't be sure she heard right. She looked over her shoulder as Lark pulled her along. The bearded man stood alone in the middle of the walkway, rigid with fury, people swerving around him as they passed by. "Does that man know you?"

"I doubt it. Come along, Viv. It's time you met the duke."

WHATEVER THE WOMEN'S Penitent Hospital meant to Lark, seeing the building had changed him. His face was grim, and there was a reckless gleam in his eyes. He was no longer the easy gentleman out for a stroll in the park that he had been. Instead, he kept them moving at a brisk pace up Piccadilly and into Mayfair, winding through its streets, a man with a purpose and direction.

Several streets and turnings later, he stopped at an imposing stone house, five bays wide, and taller and more austere in its lines than its neighbors. The individual who opened the door came as a surprise to Viv. He wore a grin as if he'd been enjoying a good joke.

"Miss Bradish is here to see the duke," said Lark.

The man did not go all stiff and haughty on them. Rather, some quick assessment went on behind the professional glance of friendly curiosity, and they were let into a warm and comfortable entry hall and cordially asked to wait a minute. From somewhere above them came squeals of youthful laughter.

Then they were led to the back of the house and admitted to a sunny, book-lined study in which, in the middle of a fine Turkish carpet, stood a castle constructed of books and children's blocks surrounded by tiny figures of mounted knights arrayed for battle.

Viv's gaze shifted at once to the man standing behind the castle. He was tall and fair with piercing blue eyes, broad shoulders, and a lean torso encased in a waistcoat of figured blue silk. The cuffs of his white lawn shirt had been rolled up, presumably as he did some work at the large desk to one side of the room. Viv saw the ink stain on his middle finger, the telltale sign of a writer at work. His alert gaze was all for Lark, and some unspoken communication passed between them.

"Your grace," said Lark. "May I present my fiancée, Miss Vivian Bradish." He turned to her. "Miss Bradish, His Grace, the Duke of Wenlocke."

Viv dropped into the expected curtsy. He was something, this living duke, not quite what the word *duke* might conjure in the public imagination, far too young, too fit, too vigorous, almost like a pugilist in his figure, but undeniably powerful with an easy authority of manner. There was no evident surprise in the duke's expression at Lark's announcement, but Viv guessed that the man had taken some cue from Lark. She could hardly decide which of the two of them behaved with greater composure.

"Pleased to make your acquaintance, Miss Bradish." The voice was deep and sure. "Forgive me if we had an appointment, it must have slipped my mind. What brings you to Wenlocke House today?"

"Miss Bradish has something she wishes to say to you," Lark prompted.

Viv reddened, remembering her threat of the morning. "I, too, am pleased, your grace. What Lark, that is, Mr. Larkin, is wishing me say, may sound presumptuous." She paused, but met the duke's gaze squarely. "You, sir, are a most lax employer if my fiancé is to be believed."

A corner of the duke's mouth twitched ever so slightly, and he glanced at Lark. "You doubt him, then, but if Mr. …um…Larkin has neglected his work of late, surely I may blame that on you."

A light knock sounded on the door, which opened behind them without ceremony. A woman entered, who could only be described as a fairy princess, petite and golden-haired, shimmering in a pale rose-colored silk gown, a small beribboned pin on one shoulder. She stopped when she saw them. "Oh, I came to return this." She held up another of the knight figures. "I didn't realize you—"

She broke off, catching sight of Lark. Her eyes lit up.

"Lark!" The word came out on a gust of a sigh. She moved toward him with her hands extended.

"Your grace." He bowed his head and allowed her to take his hands. "I have been remiss," he said. "I came to introduce my betrothed."

The duchess sent a questioning glance to her husband and caught some message from him as Viv tried to make sense of what she was seeing and hearing. Her mysterious betrothed was well known to both the duke and the duchess, but he was no mere secretary handling matters of book collecting. Indeed, the books in the study appeared to be arranged to suit small castle-builders rather than a collector of rare volumes.

The duchess turned to Viv. Again, Lark made the introduction, and Viv curtsied to the lovely duchess, who seemed to recover from her surprise.

"I believe," she said, "that we should have met sooner. Lady Melforth's invitation did not reach us, as we were in the country for the birthday of our middle daughter. A new pony was involved."

An awkward moment followed. Viv was sure the duke and duchess were waiting for some clue from Lark, but he had withdrawn into himself with the look of troubled distraction his face had worn since he'd seen the Penitent Women's Hospital. At last, he spoke.

"Thank you for seeing us, sir, ma'am. I apologize if our visit has inconvenienced you. Miss Bradish has had her doubts about my connection with you since we met, and as we were walking nearby, I thought to stop and put her mind at ease at last."

"Do not trouble yourselves. You see how informal we are here." The duke accepted the small figure from his wife and stooped to place it in front of the castle.

"Shall I send for some refreshment?" asked the duchess.

"Thank you, no," said Viv. "I must return to Lady Melforth directly."

"Ah, well," said the duke, coming forward, and offering an arm to both ladies. "Let us send you home in proper style, Miss Bradish. Lark can see to having a carriage brought round."

Viv murmured her thanks, and they made their way back to the entry hall. Her brain buzzed with questions about her betrothed. It was plain that the duke and duchess had closed ranks to offer him some sort of protection. From what she could not imagine.

For a few minutes they stood in the entry, the duchess asking questions about the guide Viv and Lady Melforth were writing, just the sort of easy questions to keep Viv's mind occupied and not wandering to the much larger questions the day had raised.

"We must invite you to dinner here," the duchess was saying when Lark returned. They made their farewells, and Lark led Viv to an elegant open carriage standing at the door with a liveried driver on the box. Viv thanked the duke and duchess, and Lark helped her into the carriage.

"You're not coming?" she asked.

"I'm afraid you reminded my employer how very undemanding he's been, and now he has things for me to do. Go. Lady Melforth needs you. You have a book to finish."

She nodded. She had only a brief glimpse of his troubled

face as he turned away.

He was right, but behind him the duke's door stood open, a door to all that was mysterious about her betrothed, all that he had concealed. It made no sense that he had been so very modest about his connection with the duke and duchess. His ties to them appeared quite deep. But then there was the bearded man in the park who seemed to know him. And the puzzle of the change in him wrought by the sight of that hospital. Her pretend fiancé was a dizzying set of contradictions.

Viv leaned back against the cushions. She should be thinking of Lady Melforth. Her duty was to her ladyship. The new doctor must have made his visit by now and perhaps offered her ladyship a course of action or medication to deal with her troublesome symptoms. He might even have given her ailment a name.

VIV'S CARRIAGE PASSED from sight with no sign of Rook, and Lark returned to Wenlocke's house. He must think of Dav as Wenlocke now, though he imagined that his old companion found it distasteful to go by the title of his vengeful grandfather.

The pleasant butler readmitted Lark to the lofty entry hall where the duke and duchess waited. Without hesitation the duchess came forward and enfolded him in a warm embrace. He steeled himself to bear it. He could not turn her away.

The hug was quick and light, like a passing cloud of

goodness and sweetness. He knew the duchess had had her share of sorrows. She still wore the small pin and faded ribbons on her shoulder that Lark and Rook had once lifted from her pocket in the schoolroom at Daventry Hall where she'd taught them reading and maths.

"I will leave you two gentlemen to understand one another." She gave her husband's hand a squeeze and ascended the stairs.

"Come," said Wenlocke. "We'll have beer and sandwiches and you can tell me what really brought you here today." He nodded to the butler and turned back toward his study.

Lark followed. He had expected exposure not kindness. Kindness from those he had once wronged would be his undoing. He knew how to mimic kindness, how to offer it to strangers, and how people, all sorts of people, even the most unlikely, drank kindness in as if they were parched for it. He hadn't thought he was someone who needed or deserved kindness.

And now he'd come face-to-face with shocking evidence of his true identity. His fragmentary memories of beringed fingers and upholstered carriages had deceived him. The hospital revealed his mother's shame. She had been a drab, one of those women shuffling along London's lowest streets, concealing poxy faces behind leaden paint and reddened lips, until they could no longer dupe potential clients.

In his study, Wenlocke gestured to an armchair. Lark waited for the duke to be seated. Wenlocke laughed, and pointed to the child's castle in the middle of the room. "You see that we live quite informally here. And you must know that you are welcome."

Lark remained standing. "After twelve years? You must think me daft to come here. I...I...would not have except that..." He could not say what he'd discovered about his mother. "I thought you'd likely expose me."

One of Wenlocke's fair brows quirked upward. "You thought I might begin by asking Miss Bradish why she has pledged her troth to a pickpocket, though an uncommon one, and one who's not done a click in some time."

Lark could not hide his surprise. "How did you know?"

"Sit down, would you."

Lark complied. He could not help it. The energy that had propelled him away from the hospital, away from Rook's anger, suddenly left him.

"I've been following your...career. Robin, you remember him, has joined Peel's new detective force. He keeps me informed. If you were ever taken up, I would want to act."

"You would do that? Even after the way we left?" In addition to his other sins, Lark could add thinking ill of Wenlocke.

For a moment Wenlocke studied his hands, saying nothing. "I know what you did that day, the day of the match. The duchess told me. When you called out my opponent as a cheat with weighted hands, you saved my life, and because, mine, hers. We always hoped you would come back."

While Lark sat stunned by what he was learning about his old companion, a footman knocked and entered with a tray of beer and sandwiches. When these were set down and the fellow had left, they were free to resume their conversation, but Lark could not begin again. His life had never unfolded in a smooth progression. It was no broad straight avenue, but a maze of narrow winding ways, sudden turns, and blind alleys. He had thought himself prepared for life's blows, but the sight of that hospital had shaken him. He had come to Wenlocke to end the farce of his betrothal.

"So tell me." Wenlocke took up a cup of beer. "What's happened? What brings you back to us? Your engagement?"

Lark regarded the tray of refreshments, but they seemed quite beyond his reach. "I discovered the truth of who my mother was."

Wenlocke lowered the ale cup in his hand to the table, his expression sobering at once. "And what is that truth?"

"She was admitted to the lock hospital on Grosvenor Place. That night was the last time I saw her." Saying the words hurt. In ancient times a lock hospital had been for lepers. Now such a place was for women who had the pox. The hospital had overturned all his fantasies of the fine coach and his mother's beringed fingers turning the pages of a storybook.

Wenlocke didn't speak. Instead, he rose and moved restlessly around the room, stopping at the mantel to shift a ceramic duck nearer its mate and at the desk to straighten a pile of papers. At last, he turned and faced Lark.

"Are you sure? Tell me everything you remember about that night. It was night?" He took his seat again.

"It was night. We came in a closed carriage. Posh, I think. At least with soft cushions. Father, Mother, and I. It was late, and I must have dozed in the carriage. I think my mother fell asleep as well."

"Go on."

"When the carriage stopped, another man opened the

door, not a servant, at least not in livery. Together, my father and the other man helped my mother from the carriage. I saw the building through the open door." That much had come to him almost at the first glimpse of the hospital before Viv tugged his arm and Rook shouted. The images rearranging themselves in his head had fled in the face of the insistent present.

"Can you remember any talk? Anything that was said? Did your mother speak?"

"There were only men's voices. I must have tried to follow, but my father told me not to move."

Wenlocke appeared to consider Lark's account, leaning forward in his chair, his brow furrowed, his powerful shoulders hunched, his hands steepled together. "I can guess what you're thinking. You imagine that your mother was a mere doxie and that when illness rendered her unable to ply her trade any longer, she had no recourse but to abandon you, perhaps in the vain hope of saving you both."

Lark nodded dumbly.

"I doubt it. Think, man. From what you've told me so far, it's unlikely that your mother entered that hospital voluntarily. The nighttime admittance. The carriage. Your father's presence and some sort of accomplice. Your mother's sleepy condition. Your own abandonment. All those details suggest a different story."

"You think my father was a villain?"

"We can't rule it out. We can return tonight if you like, and recreate the circumstances exactly. You may remember more." Wenlocke paused. "I think you should attempt it. Are you willing?"

Lark sat stunned. It was a risk. All the time he had pretended to be Edward Larkin, he had expected that the truth, when he found it, would confirm that he was a gentleman, one worthy of Viv Bradish. He had imagined, walking in that park, that he could simply step into the identity he had invented for himself. He could shed the years as a pickpocket because he had been born a gentleman. The hospital undid that history. Now, again, with Wenlocke's offer, the path of discovery took an unexpected turn toward a dangerous hope. He could not see whether it would end in his elevation to respectability or cost him a true betrothal to Viv.

He looked up and met Wenlocke's gaze. "I'll do it."

CHAPTER EIGHTEEN

WHEN THE CARRIAGE drew to a stop, Viv turned her mind from the troubling questions about Lark's history and connections. Haxton admitted her to the house and confirmed that Neville Pridmore had come and gone. Her ladyship was resting. Haxton's sober countenance gave Viv little hope that the doctor's visit had produced good news. She went directly to Lady Melforth's bedroom.

Her ladyship sat propped up against her pillows with a stack of papers in her lap. Sarah occupied Viv's usual chair beside her ladyship's bed, and oddly, she, too, had papers in her lap.

"Now, Sarah—" Lady Melforth broke off. "Ah, Viv, what did you discover? Does the Green Park chapter need any changes?"

"Perhaps a word or two about Buckingham House, but that's all."

"Excellent. If you will add those details and give your pages to Sarah, we'll send everything to Dodsley this afternoon." Lady Melforth sank deeper against the pillows and waved a hand in Sarah's direction. "Go, Sarah, you know what to do."

Sarah rose and collected the papers from her ladyship's lap and passed Viv with a low murmur but without a glance.

Sarah's manner, furtive and almost ashamed, puzzled Viv. For months they had worked together keeping her ladyship's spirits up. Sarah's realm had been Lady Melforth's clothes and hair, and Viv's had been her writing and correspondence. Sarah had never looked at the book as far as Viv knew.

Viv remained where she stood. "Ma'am, may I ask how Dr. Pridmore's visit went? Did he have anything to prescribe for your comfort?"

Lady Melforth turned her head fitfully against the pillows. "The man was quite useless. And conceited. He made me play silly finger games. I had to make my fingers look like his, hardly scientific."

It didn't sound scientific, but Viv wondered what Newberry would have to say about the doctor's approach. "So, the doctor had nothing to recommend?"

"Carriage rides. As if shaking my bones would steady my nerves. I told him a donkey cart might give me a good shaking, if that's what I need."

"Did Dr. Newberry say anything?"

"He left me to my fate. Watched that fellow as if the man were a genius."

"Oh dear." Viv's shoulders sagged. She had hoped the new doctor would suggest a way forward. She had no doubt that Lady Melforth's complaints were in proportion to her dashed hopes at the doctor's unhelpfulness. "How disappointing!" Viv moved a few steps closer to the bed.

"How useless!"

"But you were able to work after he left?" Viv tried to suggest a ray of hope.

"With Sarah's help. Now, Viv, you be sure to get your

Green Park pages to Sarah today. She has all my instructions for Dodsley."

"Should I not go?" Viv worked to keep the surprise out of her voice. It made no sense to send Sarah to Dodsley. In the last couple of days her ladyship and Viv had worked together steadily to put the finishing touches on the manuscript. Viv had read key passages aloud and detected no dissatisfaction with her share of the work.

"No." Her ladyship's voice was sharp. "It's all settled. Just do those pages."

"Of course. Is there anything I may bring you?"

"Nothing. I'm going to rest now." Lady Melforth closed her eyes.

Viv shut the door as softly as she could. Her throat ached with a sudden sorrow. Somehow, she had lost her best friend. She found Jenny waiting for her in the hall. "Dr. Newberry is in the downstairs drawing room, miss."

"Oh Jenny, thank you. Could you send tea?"

Jenny nodded, and Viv's spirits lifted. She trusted Newberry to give her a better picture of the situation and some idea of how to help her ladyship.

In the green drawing room, Newberry stood by the mantel. He turned to her at once.

"Where were you this morning? We could have used your help."

Viv halted, taken aback by his brusque manner. "She sent me off on an errand. She did not want me present for her meeting with your colleague."

"Hmmph," he said, his expression still cold.

She sat, expecting him to do the same, but he remained

standing by the mantel.

Jenny appeared with a tea tray and set it on a low table in front of Viv. When Jenny left, Viv nerved herself to ask about the meeting with the specialist. "The meeting did not go well, I take it."

"She refuses to accept that anything is wrong other than her foot."

"But your colleague believes otherwise?"

"She didn't tell you? Pridmore told her she was seriously ill." Newberry came away from the mantel and sat opposite her. She hoped it was a sign that he was letting go of his anger. "He suspects, as I do, that she has the shaking palsy. A fellow named Parkinson identified it in a paper about twenty years ago. There is a better understanding of the disease now, of course, but no cure."

Viv's spirits sank under the dreadful news. For the Traveling Viscountess to be confined, to be unable to move freely in the world was a terrible fate. "Is there nothing that can be done for her?"

"The French have developed ways of relieving some of the symptoms."

"Like carriage rides?" Viv poured a cup of tea and offered it to him.

He took the tea. "Did she give you her opinion of that idea?"

Viv nodded. "What is the thought behind the rides?"

"Apparently, vibrations can calm the tremors, even for several days. But the disease is progressive and ugly. Over time it takes away the voluntary control of muscles. There's much more to be studied, including the effects on the brain."

Viv took up the teapot, seeing in her mind the spilled chocolate on her ladyship's dressing gown. "What does she need?"

He put down his cup and answered, his gaze cold and hard. "She needs a great deal of care and compassion and a companion who is present, not gadding about London with her betrothed, if indeed he is your betrothed."

Viv put down the teapot. "You doubt him?"

"The only E. Larkin I can find in London is an Edmund not an Edward and he's a married greengrocer in Islington. So, I doubt that your Mr. Larkin is the Duke of Wenlocke's secretary or book dealer or whatever he claims to be. Whoever he is, what matters is that you've had entirely too much freedom to run about with him. I never thought I would side with the Strydes, but since that man arrived, you've neglected your duties shamefully. Perhaps you only took employment to find yourself a husband."

Viv's anger rose in response to his, but she did not attempt a defense to which he would not listen. He did not understand the writing fellowship that she and Lady Melforth had shared. He did not understand how they had laughed together and how telling stories and finding the right words had been a shared venture. He did not understand how finishing the book was a way of supporting Lady Melforth.

He rose again and returned to the mantel, leaning an elbow on it, staring down at her. In his angry countenance, she hardly recognized the ally she had relied on for months. "I've read the introduction to your so-called guide for ladies," he said. "Apparently, you have no idea of the behavior proper to a lady or of the sphere in which a lady belongs."

Viv wondered if he understood that he was condemning Lady Melforth as much as he was condemning Viv. It was time to end the conversation. She rose. "The manuscript of the book, written under her ladyship's direction and with her full approval, goes to the publisher this afternoon. I am now free to attend fully to her ladyship's other needs. If you have anything to add to her regimen for her comfort, it will be done."

She turned and moved to the door, looking back only to say, "You're wrong, you know. Whatever you have come to believe about me, I have met Mr. Larkin's duke, and there is no doubt that they are bound together by the closest ties."

By the time she reached her room, Viv shook with suppressed anger. Her world had gone mad. No one was who she thought they were. She had apparently mistaken everyone's character, even Newberry's. The doctor was not the friend she had assumed him to be. Lady Melforth was changing before Viv's eyes perhaps because of her illness. Even Sarah had altered. And Lark remained the biggest mystery of all. She had defended him against Newberry's attack, but she did not understand how both the rough, bearded man from the darker regions of London, and the lofty Duke of Wenlocke could claim a hold on him. One minute Lark was her easy gentleman companion, the next he was lost in contemplation of the Penitent Woman's Hospital, which held some meaning for him.

She needed to settle her mind, and finish the last bit of work on the book. She had promised Lady Melforth not an hour earlier that she would get it done today. Now it seemed even more vital that their guide be published. She crossed the room to her desk, and stopped dead.

Her desk had been cleared. The manuscript, which Viv had arranged in neat piles, one for each chapter, and a pile each for the front and back matter of the book, was gone. Not even the chapter on the Green Park, to which she meant to add her notes, remained. There was a scrap of paper with a note in Sarah's hand. DON'T WORRY. I'VE TAKEN IT ALL TO DODSLEY AS LADY MELFORTH WANTED.

WENLOCKE GAVE SOME last order to his coachman and climbed into the carriage beside his wife. Whatever their plans for the evening had been, and Lark had not thought to ask, the duke and duchess had entered fully into the scheme of recreating Lark's experience of losing his mother. Across the coach from Lark, the duchess made a shadowy female figure. For the memory experiment, she had subdued her radiant beauty, dressing somberly in an old gray gown, blue wool traveling cape, and a black bonnet that obscured her golden hair and pale face. She wore a pair of rings on her right hand.

"Ready?" Wenlocke asked, taking his seat beside his wife, and glancing at Lark.

Lark nodded, a mad hope surging in him that the memories would come at last. He would either go to Viv a gentleman or part from her a thief.

Wenlocke knocked on the roof to signal the coachman, and the carriage rolled into motion. The duchess lay her head against the duke's shoulder in feigned sleep.

Lark, too, closed his eyes and leaned back against the squabs, letting conscious thought go. Against his closed lids, light flickered from gas lamps. His body rocked with the steady motion of the coach. Street sounds faded in and out of notice. His mind played with snatches of conversation from the long afternoon of talk about their early days together.

Lark had sold his shoes and coat and acquired a rusty knife before he met the gang of boys led by Wenlocke, who was then simply *Boy*, Robin's name for him. In those first weeks in the streets, Lark had learned to say little to avoid being marked as soft, as prey, and above all to avoid being collared by bigger, rougher men. He had moved west through the city, seeking familiar streets, away from the docks where he had wakened alone. Wenlocke told him that on the first day he had noted both the quality of Lark's remaining garment, a pair of wool trousers, and the smell of the docks that lingered in his hair and clothes. The gang had offered him food and showed him how they moved unnoticed on the rooftops of the rookery they called home. Lark had slept warm that night for the first time in weeks. He soon abandoned his search for his past life.

Now memories of those days swirled in Lark's mind as the coach rolled on. Streets and turnings became indistinct, the well-mapped London of his waking searches became shifting shadows, shafts of light, and spells of darkness. He let his hands fall slack against his thighs, let his head sway to the motion of the coach, emptying his mind, becoming again a drowsy child safe in the company of his parents.

The journey lasted minutes or hours before the coach made a wide turn and slowed to a stop, the horses blowing slightly, harness jingling, leather creaking. Lark opened his eyes to dark figures in motion, low male voices, and the woman being half-lifted from the coach, her body listless. One of her boots caught against the doorframe. She made an incoherent murmur, and the men carrying her lifted her slightly to pass through the door. For an instant the figures blocked the open carriage door, plunging the interior in darkness. When they moved, light broke through, and Lark saw the hospital behind its iron railing.

Somewhere deep in his head a man's voice spoke. *"Don't drop her, for God's sake, Sneath."* Another voice replied. *"Not this cargo, eh Cap'n. Worth 'er weight in gold she is."*

The words cleared the fog in Lark's mind. Understanding snapped into place. His mother had been a victim. His father, a captain, had paid a man named Sneath to assist him in locking her up. Lark was in motion before the next thought formed. *She could be there yet.*

He hurled himself from the coach past the duke and duchess, intent on reaching the hospital entrance and pounding the door down. As he reached the steps, Wenlocke snagged his arm in an iron grip, hauled him back, and pinned him against a stone pillar marking the opening in the railing. Lark tried to shake him off, but could not break Wenlocke's hold.

"I take it," said Wenlocke, "that you remembered something."

Lark's chest heaved, a muscle throbbed in his jaw. His breath came and went in gusts. He worked to free the words in his head. "You were right. My mother did not go voluntarily."

"Good man." Wenlocke did not release him at once.

"What if she is in there?" Lark asked, the words a hoarse whisper from his constricted throat.

"We will get her out."

For a moment Lark simply stared blindly, as if bricks and stone could be peeled back to reveal his mother. Then his gaze returned to Wenlocke, a man who knew what it was to be a captive. Wenlocke had said *we* as if they were again rooftop companions.

"Pardon me." Lark shuddered. "I thought I was prepared for…anything."

Wenlocke released his hold and stepped back.

They returned to the coach, but Wenlocke gave no signal to drive on. Both he and the duchess regarded Lark somberly. "Can you tell us what you remembered?"

Lark repeated the words that had echoed in his head. Wenlocke congratulated him again.

"We will begin tomorrow. If there are any patients who have remained in care since you were abandoned, we will find them. If your mother is not among them, we will check the hospital's admittance records for the year you came to us."

"I don't know her name," Lark said.

"You know that your father was a captain. You know he had help from a man named Sneath. We will question any staff from that time who remain. Someone may remember the unusual circumstances of your mother's admission. I expect that when she recovered her senses, she protested her confinement." He paused. "If she left the hospital, there will be a record of her leaving."

"And the authorities will just open their doors and their books to our scrutiny and allow the hospital staff to be questioned?" Lark asked. He still liked the idea of pounding down the door.

The duchess gave him a gentle smile and tucked her hand through her husband's arm. "He is a duke, you know, and dukes are quite looked up to by heads of institutions that depend on charity. Never underestimate the power of a duke with funds to bestow."

"If we have no luck tomorrow with our first inquiries," said Wenlocke, "we'll find fellows to do more record checking, parish registers, Navy and Army rolls. Do you remember Finch? He's a clerk in a law office now and knows other clerks who are always hungry for a bit of extra work. And—" His wife checked the rush of her husband's thoughts by kissing his cheek. "That is," he finished, "if you want to continue the quest to find your mother and find your people."

The search for her, for them, had consumed Lark since the great fire. Now he saw that his search had been a selfish one. His only thought had been to prove himself a gentleman. He had never imagined that his mother's suffering had led to his abandonment.

Wenlocke signaled his driver, and the coach began to move. By the time the coach reached his lodging, Lark knew only that he had to make sure that his mother, if alive, was not confined to that hospital or another. Then, it would be time to decide whether he wanted the whole truth about his past. Before Viv Bradish, he would not have hesitated. Before Viv Bradish, he had wanted the truth to raise him up. Now he needed the truth for his mother's sake whatever the cost.

Wenlocke stretched a hand across the coach, and Lark took it. "You're back, man. We're glad."

The duchess added her smile. "You are not a lost boy anymore," she said. "You're one of the duke's men, always welcome in our house."

Lark climbed out of the coach into the night. The coach rumbled off, a brief disturbance in the quiet street. Astonishment kept him standing on the flagstones. Wenlocke's powerful grandfather had tried repeatedly to deny his grandson's legitimacy, to erase his very existence, but Wenlocke had refused to be erased. In time, the truth had come to light. Now Wenlocke offered the same chance to Lark, the chance to find out who he truly was. And with that knowledge he would go to Viv.

CHAPTER NINETEEN

THREE DAYS AFTER meeting the duke, Viv sat at her desk at dawn, a letter from her aunt Louisa before her. Putting aside the letter and pulling her wrapper close against the morning chill, she watched pink wisps of cloud flee to the east across a pale golden sky.

Aunt Louisa had warm praise for Mr. Larkin and strongly advised Viv to move forward with her plans for marriage, pointing out that Lady Melforth would soon be in need of a professional nurse rather than a companion, and that Viv would need an establishment of her own if she did not wish to abandon her dreams and return to her mother's crowded household. The advice made perfect sense, and if Viv were truly betrothed to Mr. Edward Larkin, the support of her kind and resourceful aunt would be invaluable. As the matter stood, Viv's stomach knotted at the thought of seeing Aunt Louisa later in the morning when they were to take Lady Melforth for the doctor's recommended ride in Aunt Louisa's landau.

The falseness of Viv's position now struck her as an evil. She had passed from one small deception to an ever-growing string of them. What began with putting pebbles in her purse to deceive a potential pickpocket had led to firing a pistol at Mr. Larkin and becoming betrothed to him. In the beginning the pretense had been necessary to preserve her position as a companion and a writing partner for Lady Melforth. Now the book was finished and at the publisher, and with her palsy, Lady Melforth needed Viv more than ever, yet each day Viv piled lie upon lie, alienating Newberry, and involving her aunt and uncle in her deception. It was time to tell everyone that her betrothal was at an end, but she hadn't ended it. She had planned to end it, but when the opportunity arose, she had not acted. She didn't understand herself. *Did she love him?* Surely, she could not love a man she did not truly know. But it was impossible to deny her part in the kiss in the street. In the heat of that moment, she had known herself, unafraid and seeking, curious and alive, and she had wanted to go on kissing him, hungry for more, until the jarring piano note had brought her back to herself. Now he had simply vanished. *Vanished* was perhaps too strong a word, but he had stopped calling and sent no messages. She should count herself lucky.

She looked at the ring on her finger. She had grown used to the feel of it, as she had grown used to a certain energy she had in Lark's presence, an eagerness to show him that women could handle whatever London threw at them. But she had got things wrong. He was not the man she thought he was. She did not know the real Edward Larkin or Lark. That man, whoever he truly was, had abandoned their betrothal as if he had tired of a game, and returned to his other life, the one he'd had before they met, a life that included the Duke and Duchess of Wenlocke.

When she looked back on their ruse, she saw how very careful he had been in presenting himself. He never claimed to be a man of rank or fortune. Rather, he allowed her to think that his circumstances were similar to hers. He let her believe he was a gentleman on the edge of fashionable society, perhaps a younger son, obliged to take a paid position, constrained to marry advantageously. The story he told of his dead parents and his maiden aunt was so conveniently vague that she could not place him in any rank of society.

Then their visit to the duke had unsettled what little she thought she knew. When she examined, moment by moment and point by point, the exchange between the duke and Lark, she could only conclude that in the duke's study as in Lady Melforth's drawing room on that first day, her pretend fiancé had slipped into a role.

He let the duke know what role he played by his careful announcement to the duke's butler, by the way he introduced Viv, and then by the way he set her up to tell the duke that she regarded him as a lax employer. If she knew anything true about her betrothed, it was that he was good at pretending. That first day when he'd made his sham proposal, she had thought him an actor. Now she considered the possibility again.

At that point, her tumultuous thoughts took another turn when she considered the duchess, who greeted Lark with genuine delight and relief, as if she had been waiting for him to return from a great journey. Her warm welcome did not fit what Viv knew about the condescension with which exalted persons like dukes treated ordinary people in their employ. Rather, it seemed to Viv as if her grace's taking Lark's hands in hers had broken some resistance in him. He and the duke stood measuring each other, two strong men, slightly at odds, squaring off, neither willing to yield. By welcoming Lark, the duchess had changed the mood, made them both bend a little.

Viv shivered in the thin wrapper. Her ruminations on the mystery of her betrothed always led so far before her thoughts ran into a wall of unknowns like the angry bear of a man in the park, the effect on her betrothed of the Penitent Women's Hospital, and the puzzle of what he wanted from the duke.

Outside her window, the clouds were breaking up. She folded her aunt's letter and tucked it away. She was foolish beyond permission to moon over a man she meant to break off with, and she needed to find a way to tell her aunt the truth.

AT THE UNFASHIONABLE hour of eleven, Lady Louisa's well-sprung landau, pulled by a pair of magnificent black horses, wound through Hyde Park. To see the two old friends side by side on the seat of the landau made Viv realize how frail Lady Melforth had become. She was far from the commanding figure Viv had met in Bath the previous September. Under the influence of a mild April sun, a light breeze, and cheerful conversation, Lady Melforth unbent so much as to smile from time to time. Her smile had changed from a broad, confident parting of the lips and turning up of the corners, to something more like a bared-teeth grimace. Only a softening of her eyes made the expression recognizable as a smile. At least the trembling hand relaxed as the ride progressed.

If Lady Louisa noted the shocking change in her friend, she gave no sign of it, but kept the conversation to happier times. "Aurora was always our leader," Lady Louisa confided to Viv. "We thought her quite daring. One night, she led us out of a very dull ball, where gentlemen were scarce, through a garden and a mews to the site of a famous elopement, the very window from which the heiress, Miss Tudbury, descended to run off with her dashing lieutenant of the Guards."

"What became of you all? Did you resolve to elope? Did you return quietly to the ball?" Viv asked, doing her part to keep the conversation light.

Lady Louisa smiled. "I'm sure I had Miss Tudbury in mind when I told my papa, your grandfather, Viv, that I would marry my Oswald, a mere baronet! By the time my brother Richard married your mother, Papa was quite used to his children going their own way in matters of love."

"You would find me a sad case, now," said Lady Melforth, "if I tried to lead you anywhere."

"Not at all," said Lady Louisa staunchly. "You may be at a low ebb momentarily, Aurora, but I know your spirit. You will rally. You must make use of my landau as often as you like when Oswald and I return to Atwood."

"Are you leaving London, Aunt?" Viv asked. So far there had been no opportunity for a private moment to confess the truth.

"Tomorrow. But we will return to celebrate when your book comes out."

Lady Melforth, who seemed not to hear them, looked down, plucking at her gown, and made no answer. Viv's spirits sank, but she reminded herself that the actual proofs must cheer her ladyship. Viv was counting on it.

Lady Louisa turned to Viv with a determined look. "And, now dear girl, you must tell me your wedding plans. Oswald and I quite liked your Mr. Larkin."

Viv offered her aunt a faint smile. Lady Melforth was perhaps not fully attending, but Viv did not want the truth of her deception to add to her ladyship's distress. They had reached the park's southern gate and turned toward Mayfair, and Viv thought of a perfect way to shift the conversation, the Women's Penitent Hospital.

"Ma'am," she said to Lady Melforth. "Can you endure a few more minutes of shaking?"

"If you really think it does some good."

"That's the spirit, Aurora," said Lady Louisa.

Viv turned to her aunt. "Aunt, may we take a turn along Grosvenor Place? I want to ask you both, from your knowledge of London about an institution there that I came upon in our Green Park walk."

"You've made me curious, dear girl," said Lady Louisa. She spoke with her coachman, who turned the horses at the appropriate corner.

"Here," cried Viv, as they came upon the Women's Penitent Hospital. "Do you know anything of this place?"

The coachman stopped the carriage. Viv's companions stared first at the hospital and then at her. Except for the large signs proclaiming the nature of the building, it might have passed for a block of apartments or a tradesman's warehouse. A pair of stone obelisks marked an opening in the iron railing separating the building from passersby. Viv was not entirely ignorant on purpose of such a place, but she could see nothing in its plain brick and stone exterior to overset her pretend fiancé.

After a shocked silence, Lady Louisa spoke. "I have to say I know more of its charitable supporters than of its inmates. What do you say, Aurora? Aren't the Duke of York and the Marquis of Hertford benefactors?"

"What is your interest in this place, Viv?" Lady Melforth demanded. "I thought you meant to show us a museum or an exhibition hall. You didn't mention the Penitent Hospital in the book, I hope."

Viv had a fleeting thought that her ladyship must know that Viv had not written about the hospital, but then she remembered that Sarah had taken the draft to Dodsley before Viv could revise that section.

"Of course, not, but our sixth walk ends just across the way, and when I looked about, I could not miss those signs. I suppose it made me curious about the hidden lives of other women." There seemed to Viv a great gulf between the three ladies in silk in the open landau and the world behind the hospital door. Those other women were perhaps a subject for another book about London. For a moment, Viv only half heard the conversation around her.

"I suspect that many a young woman who has been debauched and abandoned may have recourse to such a place," said Lady Louisa.

"Is that how they come to be here?" asked Viv, returning her attention to her companions. "Is it a program, as the sign proclaims, of voluntary admission?"

"Really, Viv," said Lady Melforth. "What an odd topic to take up! I am tired now. I want to go home."

Before Viv could answer, the ladies' attention turned to the opening of the hospital door. Three men emerged, the tallest of them, Viv saw at once, was the Duke of Wenlocke with his unmistakable wheaten hair. A somber man in a clerical black coat bowed to the duke and withdrew. Then duke turned and strode toward them, speaking to a thin man trying to match the duke's rapid stride.

Viv wanted to sink. It made no sense that the duke should be there, that he and she should be drawn to the same place, but instantly the thought occurred that he must have come on some business connected with Lark. She didn't care to be caught gawking at the place. She bowed her head, hoping the brim of her bonnet would conceal her face until the men passed by.

"Viv." Her aunt tapped her wrist gently. Viv looked up, blushing, to find the duke standing at the side of the landau, regarding her with frank curiosity.

"Miss Bradish, ladies, taking the air?" His piercing blue gaze seemed to read Viv's mind, and her cheeks burned.

She barely remembered the civility that was required. "Your grace, may I present my aunt Lady Louisa Atwood, and my friend Lady Melforth."

They exchanged bows, and the duke introduced his companion, Mr. Finch, a wispy, thin sort of young man, perfectly the gentleman in appearance, but perfectly dutiful. Everything about Mr. Finch proclaimed him to be a sort of secretary. She was mulling over how unlike Mr. Finch and

Mr. Larkin were when the duke began speaking to her companions. "A pleasure to meet you, Lady Louisa, and you Lady Melforth. Your fame as the Traveling Viscountess precedes you."

Lady Melforth offered the duke one of her diminished smiles.

"My wife regrets that we missed your dinner party, Lady Melforth. She would be happy to see you after so many years. May she call on you?"

Again, Lady Melforth smiled, and Viv could not help sending the duke a grateful look.

Lady Louisa said, "Your grace, I understand that your book collection played a part in Miss Bradish's betrothal to Mr. Larkin."

At Mr. Larkin's name, meek Mr. Finch started and cast a quick curious glance at Viv.

Wenlocke caught Viv's eye with a kind of warning, and she steadied herself. "A modest part, but one I am glad we could play. If you will forgive me, ladies, I must bid you good day, my business is pressing. I hope my wife may call, Lady Melforth."

Lady Melforth nodded, and with a brief bow, the duke and his companion turned away.

"Extraordinary meeting him here. I suppose he must be a benefactor," said Lady Louisa.

"I didn't think you had met him, Viv," said Lady Melforth.

"Just briefly in passing the other day," Viv admitted. Her aunt Louisa's glance said she was not fooled for a minute.

"We must get you home, Aurora." Lady Louisa signaled

to her coachman, and the carriage began to move.

As Lady Melforth sagged back in her seat, there was no more talk until they reached Henrietta Street. There, in passing from the carriage into the house and attending Lady Melforth up to her room, the opportunity for Viv to confess the truth passed.

ONCE LADY MELFORTH was comfortably settled for a nap, Viv went to her room. She would write to her aunt without delay and put the letter in the afternoon post. At least, then, one person would be undeceived.

The empty desk momentarily dismayed her. For weeks the sheets of paper she had folded into little booklets of twelve leaves had held her stories about their walks. Most pages had been marked with her pencil notes where changes needed to be made. She reminded herself that when the proofs came, she would have another chance to make corrections and perhaps to restore her friendship with Lady Melforth.

She opened the drawer and withdrew pen, ink, and paper. She didn't know quite what to say, but she trusted that the words would come.

Dear Aunt Louisa,

I write to thank you for your kindness to me. From the time you brought me to Bath and introduced me to Lady Melforth. I have had opportunities I little dreamed of in Weymouth. Today, I am especially grateful to you as the publisher's proofs of our London guide are expected this afternoon. It is not possible for me to exaggerate the benefits of Lady Melforth's guidance and generous support. As her companion, I have learned so much about the course I long to pursue as a writer, and remain eager to continue the work.

I am glad, too, that you could meet Mr. Larkin. In his own way, he has contributed to my writing. Nevertheless, Aunt, I must tell you that we have decided to end our betrothal....

Viv put down her pen. Some explanation was needed, one that would not lead to further inquiry or further deception. And yet Viv did not know what to say. The ruse was not entirely her secret, but Lark's, as well. She could hardly reveal that they had been complete strangers, and that she'd shot him as he tried to help her. Or that, in the event, she had felt a particular duty to bring him to a doctor, as her purse, for which he'd endured an injury to his clothes and his person, had been full of gravel.

She might write that she and Mr. Larkin had decided they did not suit. Her aunt would accept such an explanation, but not without feeling wounded that Viv was concealing something. Aunt Louisa and Uncle Oswald had seen how Lark routed the Strydes. And unfortunately, Aunt Louisa had now met the Duke of Wenlocke and heard him proclaim his gladness to be a part of the match.

That was another wrinkle in Viv's plan to undeceive her aunt. She twisted the ring on her finger. She had no idea what Lark had said about their engagement to—she still had to call the duke—his employer. The duke's appearance at the

Penitent Women's Hospital had deepened the mystery of Lark's connection to him. By stealing a glance at her, the duke's companion, Mr. Finch, seemed to confirm that he, too, knew of the betrothal. Viv could not believe that their meeting there had been a mere coincidence. From the building, Lark had gone directly to the duke in great distress of mind. Her instinct said that the duke was now helping her absent fiancé in some way.

A soft knock on her door interrupted her worried thoughts. She tucked her letter away, and went to the door. Jenny stood there, looking unsettled. "The Strydes are here, miss. No one could keep them out. They're waiting in the upstairs drawing room to take tea with Lady Melforth."

"Is her ladyship awake, Jenny? Does she know they're here?" Viv's letter would have to wait. She would simply send it in the morning directed to her aunt at Atwood in the country.

"Yes, miss." Jenny hesitated. "'er ladyship is that flustered, miss."

"I'll go to her directly, Jenny."

Jenny bobbed a curtsy and turned to go. Then stopped. "Oh, and, miss, there's a package for ye from the printer. Shall I bring it up?"

Viv nodded and gave her appearance a quick glance to make sure she was equal to the Strydes' scrutiny. She took a deep breath and stepped out into the hall.

NEITHER THE STRYDES' encounter with the London police

nor the seriousness of Lady Melforth's condition lessened their determination to secure their place as her near relations. For half an hour, Mrs. Stryde made insistent inquiries about the consulting doctor and the level of care her ladyship was receiving. Even in the face of such an onslaught, Lady Melforth's tremor was gone for the moment, and her eyes were bright. And Viv was glad of their earlier carriage ride.

"Eustacia, do stop," said Lady Melforth. "I am quite able to judge a physician's skill, and of course, I have Newberry, on whom I may rely without doubt."

"But, Aurora." Mrs. Stryde cleared her throat. "Don't you think, propriety calls for a skilled nurse, rather than a male doctor?"

"I have Sarah and…Viv."

"To be sure, but won't Miss Bradish be leaving you soon to marry?"

All eyes in the small party turned to Viv.

"We have set no date," she said.

"Your young man is still dillydallying, is he?" said Mrs. Stryde. "No announcement, no word to your parents? One wonders whether you mean to marry at all, Miss Bradish."

"I am simply glad to be of use to Lady Melforth while I can be."

"Yes, well, Aurora," said Mrs. Stryde turning, "we have done some looking and some careful screening of potential candidates, and we believe we've found the very nurse for you, a Mrs. Coates."

"Thank you, Eustacia. If I find myself looking about for a nurse, I will consider your candidate. For now, I shall go on as I have been doing. Viv, will you ring for Sarah? I should like to return to my room. Oh, and please see my cousins out."

Viv rose and crossed to ring the bell, with only a little pang at being left out of her ladyship's confidence once again. Her ladyship was and was not herself. She could be imperious and strong when facing the Strydes, but the former warmth of understanding and friendship between her and Viv had cooled.

In the hall as the Strydes prepared to leave, Mrs. Stryde turned to Viv. "Your days here are numbered, Miss Bradish. You had best make your conjugal arrangements while you can."

"Thank you, Mrs. Stryde. I will take your advice to heart."

When they were actually out the door, and in the carriage, and when it began to pull away, Viv breathed again. The Strydes were a very good reminder that if Viv did not wish to be ruined, she would be wise never to reveal the nature of the deception she and Mr. Larkin had practiced. She would tell her aunt that they had decided they did not suit.

She returned to her room to take up her letter and found the printer's package on her desk, wrapped in string and brown paper and addressed to her in a hand that was not Dodsley's, the printer's, she thought. For a moment she simply rested her hands on the package. She had imagined weeks earlier that she would open it with Lady Melforth and share some celebratory cake from Mrs. Brandle or perhaps even champagne. But now Viv merely wanted to see that the book existed, that unlike her betrothal and her tie to her ladyship, the work had not vanished.

She pulled the ends of the strings and unfolded the paper. The book had come from the printer with a dark-green cloth binding and a gold-edged square of paper with a sepia-toned print of a London street on the cover. She paused to admire the handsome binding, feeling the thrill that notes and jottings could be transformed into such an object. She opened to the title page, and sat down hard, her heart hammering, her breath sucked out of her. It had been changed.

> A Lady's Guide to London in Twelve Self-Guided Walks
>
> A Faithful Description of Routes and Places
>
> To Assist Women in Knowledge of the Metropolis
>
> Written by Lady Aurora Melforth, The Traveling Viscountess
>
> London: Published by Dodsley & Son, 86 Strand
>
> Available at Booksellers in England, Wales, Ireland, and Scotland

One had to look carefully. Title and type and layout all looked the same. Only a single line of the original seven was missing, the line with Viv's name. Where her name had been there was a space. The gap looked intentional as if meant to separate the title and the author's name from the lines about the publisher and the booksellers.

It could not be deliberate. It had to be a mistake. Dodsley had got it wrong, or thought Viv's name unnecessary when Lady Melforth's name alone was sufficient to sell books. Viv steadied herself. She must not jump to the conclusion that she had been deceived or used. She opened the book and paged through to the walk on Babylon Street. There were her words telling the story of having her purse with its false contents plucked from her arm. She had not been written out of the book. The title page must be in error.

Viv turned next to the preface and experienced a second, deeper shock. Lady Melforth wrote of being called upon by her public during an extended stay in London to give an account of traveling in the great metropolis. In response therefore, she had endeavored to describe from actual experience how a lady traveler whether native or foreign might safely navigate London's streets. A brief sentence thanked those in her household and on her staff for their support and assistance. Viv had seen a very different version of the preface before the dinner party.

She jumped up and began to pace. With astonishing rapidity, scenes from the previous weeks flashed in her mind. Lady Melforth insisting they finish the book, her coldness at the dinner party, Sarah's sitting at Lady Melforth's side with pages in her lap, Lady Melforth's sending Sarah, not Viv, to Dodsley with the final drafts, Newberry's telling Viv he had read the front matter of the book, and Viv's empty desk with Sarah's note on it. Viv stopped dead, facing the empty desk and a most unwelcome conclusion. At some point, Lady Melforth had decided to treat the work as if it had been hers alone, as if Viv had had no part in it. That couldn't be right, but what else could explain the changes? It was theft. Lady Melforth was willing to put her name to Viv's words.

The idea devastated her, that her friend, the woman who had encouraged her, the woman she'd laughed with, could serve her such a turn. Viv had urged Lady Melforth to keep writing even though her hand shook and she couldn't get around in the way she was used to travel. Together they had planned the walks. Lady Melforth had encouraged each of Viv's outings and together they had strategized on everything from which points of interest to include to the best words to describe a scene. In every case Lady Melforth had encouraged Viv. Those times had been full of laughter.

But the laughter had stopped. Viv could see that now. She had offended her ladyship or disappointed her. She recalled the dinner party and her aunt's cheerful assumption that Viv was very much a partner in the writing of the book, and Lady Melforth's cold response. Now Viv's cheeks stung with mortification. She had done something wrong. She had made her ladyship feel that Viv was using her, taking advantage of the Traveling Viscountess to gain a reputation of her own. She shuddered to think that she appeared to her ladyship like the clinging Strydes, that she had missed the hints to remain in her place.

She opened her desk drawer. There was the Toby pistol, her ladyship's gun, one she had used long ago in Italy against bandits. She had lent it freely to Viv that day, sending Viv out into London's streets to become an intrepid female traveler. And Viv had done it. She pushed the gun aside and reached for her pencils. She would not remain in her place, where she was invisible, where she had no prospects. She had come to London to escape her place, to learn, to establish herself as a writer, to win her independence. She could not go back to the house of her mother and stepfather.

There had to be a compromise. Without Lady Melforth there would be no publisher, no curious public, but without Viv there would be no words on the page, no stories of pickpockets or shopping or the river. Viv had contributed to their guide, and she would have recognition for her part in it.

She would correct the proofs and take them to Dodsley in the morning. She would sit at her desk and light her lamp and take up her pencil. She opened the book. At once she saw a new difficulty. Her drafts were gone, carried to Dodsley by Sarah. Viv had only her notebooks with jottings from each of the expeditions. She would begin with those, make as many changes as she remembered if she had to work all night.

CHAPTER TWENTY

As Lark approached Lady Melforth's door, a carriage pulled away from the curb. His gaze narrowed to Viv slumped on the front steps in the morning light, her head bowed, a brown paper package clutched to her chest, her blue skirts trailing against the stones. The first time he'd seen her he'd thought a piece of the sky had fallen to the ground. Now his heart lurched. She had fallen somehow. He hurried his steps.

The house looked as it always did with its neat stone exterior and iron railing, its windows glinting in the sun. He glanced at the door knocker, but no black cloth shrouded it to explain her dejected state. Her gloves, bonnet, and shawl proclaimed that she had been out on some errand or was about to begin one. He stopped, facing her. "Viv? Why are you sitting out here?"

She looked up, blinking against the light. He moved to shield her face from the glare and caught his breath at the expression of blank wretchedness in her eyes. "The Strydes are here. I saw them enter."

So, she *had* been out. He knew she avoided the Strydes when she could, but usually they brought out the fight in her. Their presence did not explain her downcast state. "May I?" he asked.

She seemed not to understand him. Carefully, he brushed her skirts aside and joined her, setting his hat on the stones. He wasn't sure she noticed that he sat beside her. "Can you tell me what's wrong besides the Strydes?"

Carriages and vans rattled by on Henrietta Street, casting moving shadows over them as they sat. A passing gentleman and the lady on his arm gave them a quick puzzled glance. Lark waited. The morning's brightness exposed an odd contrast between the shine of his boots and the bedraggled hem of her gown. At last, she spoke.

"Where have you been these past days?" She sounded mildly curious, as if his absence had been a matter of little importance.

"Did you think I'd forgotten you? The duke—"

She twisted, putting a gloved hand to his lips, shaking her head sadly. The brown package slid off her lap down her sprawling skirts. "Don't," she said. "The duke is not your employer, is he? And you do not manage his book collection, do you?"

He met her gaze as steadily as he could.

She took her hand away.

"I never lied about knowing him. He saw to my education."

She gave him a sad, searching look that made his heart shrink. He wanted to protest that it hadn't all been lies. His feelings had not been a lie. But as he tried to think of more truths he could tell her, his thoughts scattered. "I do not depend on him for...my...income. I bank with Hammersley's, as I told you." He tapped the package beside her with his forefinger. "Is this making you sad?"

She pushed the package off her skirts onto the stone step. "The proofs from Dodsley."

"You're disappointed." He knew he was stating the obvious, and the word was far too mild for whatever devastating blow had fallen. Something had knocked the bright spirits out of her. He stole a glance at the package of proofs. The explanation must lie in them. "Did Dodsley change the title, or worse?"

"It doesn't matter." She began to tug off her left glove. "It's good that you are here. We have come to the end of our arrangement, have we not?"

He watched her pull at the glove. It snagged a little on his garnet ring, but she tugged again to free her hand. He took her hand in his, hers, icy cold, the ring loose on her finger. She was going to end their betrothal, while he had come to ask her to continue a few more days, at least until he knew the whole truth. He already knew that his mother had not had the pox, nor had she lived by selling the use of her body.

He rubbed Viv's hand between his own warmer hands. If he could delay this talk of ending their betrothal, he could get to the bottom of what had happened to bring her so low. "Can you tell me what has caused your distress? Is there anything I can do? Shall we go to Dodsley?"

"I've just come from Dodsley. He isn't the problem." Her hand lay lifeless and cold in his. Her gaze was remote as if her thoughts were far away. Then she turned and looked at him with such piercing directness, his heart hurt. "I want no more deceptions," she said.

He swallowed. It was too soon to undeceive her. He

needed more time. Even a day or two could make all the difference. His mind raced through what he already knew, what he could possibly say. His mother had a history, though she did not yet have a name.

Wenlocke had been the key. With the duke's backing, the hospital had allowed Lark to question the oldest serving members of the staff. An ancient nurse remembered the night arrival of a woman so dosed with laudanum the doctor feared she might not revive. When prompted to explain a matching record that Finch found, the matron acknowledged that the woman must have been admitted mistakenly. The matron insisted that the hospital bore no blame because the woman had been troubled with delusions of a husband and a son though her record said otherwise. She had been sent to a private hospital in Surrey. Meanwhile, Robin had discovered that Sneath was well known to the authorities for various frauds. Fury and guilt plagued Lark with each discovery, and each maddening delay now that he was so close to finding the truth.

He roused himself from his thoughts. Viv was in distress. He must help her first. A large shadow fell on them both and didn't move. Lark looked up.

Rook stood on the flagstones in front of the house, his stance wide and challenging, his fists clenched, his bearded face screwed tight in anger.

"Tell 'er the truth. Tell 'er 'oo you are, or I will." His voice boomed out.

Viv's hand slipped from Lark's, and she turned a faltering gaze from him to Rook. "You followed us in the park that day."

"Tell 'er," Rook said, ignoring Viv, his stare fixed on Lark.

"She knows who I am," he said. Lark readied himself to push Rook back away from her.

"Hah! She thinks yer a toff that dresses swell and talks fine. Yer liars, the pair of you." Beside Lark, Viv shuddered.

Rook dipped a big hand into the pocket of his worn brown coat and pulled out a scrap of blue velvet, crushed and dirt-smudged. "See this!" He took a heavy step forward and dangled the little blue purse by its strings, thrusting it at Viv's face. "Yer nothin' but a cheat. Ye think yer that clever stuffing it with stones."

Lark sprang from the step and gave Rook a quick shove that rocked him back on his heels. Rook staggered, grabbing hold of the iron point of a railing to catch himself.

"Say what you came to say. Your quarrel is with me, not her." Lark positioned himself between Rook and Viv and glanced to see that she was unharmed. Her gaze was fixed on Rook with a look of dawning comprehension in her eyes. "You took my purse that day in Babylon Street."

Rook shook his head and offered her an evil grin. "We did." He let go of the railing and pointed to Lark. "We're partners. Rook and Lark."

Viv flinched as if he'd struck her, but that didn't stop Rook.

"Lark, 'e spots the marks. I do the clicks. Then Lark makes 'em forget they ever saw me."

Viv's gaze shifted back to Lark, alert now, accusing. She came slowly to her feet. "So that's how it's done. It's distraction, isn't it? That day you were distracting me, not helping me. You were protecting him, your partner, letting him get away. You let me think..."

Her eyes, those deep brown eyes of hers, were wells of pain. She said no deception. He offered none. "You wanted to meet a pickpocket. Now you have."

"You let me believe... Was it all lies then?" Her voice sank to a low whisper. Her face was drawn and colorless in the chocolate depths of her bonnet. She didn't wait for an answer. She tugged the ring from her finger and held it out to him.

Everything inside him protested, but he opened his hand and she dropped the ring into his palm. For an instant he simply looked at the red gleam of it in his hand. Then he closed his fist and dropped the ring in his pocket. They were back at the beginning. The mad spell of being Edward Larkin was at an end. His past had claimed him.

Rook clapped Lark on the back and slung an arm around his shoulder. "Yer free, man. Ye can come 'ome now. You and me. It'll be like it was."

He shook off Rook's hold. "No. I told you I wouldn't go back." Viv might not have him, but he had one more thing he could do for her, a thing only a thief could do. He bent down to sweep his hat up from the stones, turned, and strode off.

VIV STOOD STUNNED. The bearlike man shouted, "Laaaark!" His cry, like the wail of a wounded beast, was swallowed up in the noise of Henrietta Street, but it rang in Viv's ears, reverberating hollowly inside her.

His name was Rook, and they had been pickpockets together. Rook turned on her with his frown-creased brow and his face full of baffled pain.

"It's yer bleeding doing. Ye spoilt it all," he cried. He advanced toward her, but she lifted her chin and stood her ground. She didn't have her pistol, but in the house, they would hear him shouting. Any minute the door would open. He halted in front of her, an imperfect mirror in which to read the truth. She, too, loved Lark.

"'e was my partner. 'e was my friend." Rook pounded his chest with one beefy fist. "'e doesn't belong with the likes of ye."

"You are better off without him." She meant it.

"Ye twisted 'im. Ye made 'im think 'e was a toff. He was a thief like me."

She shook her head, denying it. He was a thief, but not like Rook, nothing like Rook. Lark had been Edward Larkin from the moment he spoke to her on Babylon Street. He had not belonged to her or to the wounded bear in front of her. The door opened behind her.

"Miss?" Haxton cried. He held a poker in one hand and shook it at Rook. "You," he shouted. "Be off now, or I'll have you taken up."

Rook shouted one last invective, threw the soiled velvet bag at Viv's feet, and ran.

Viv picked up her ruined bag, and turned to gather up the proofs. But the steps were empty. The proofs were gone.

CHAPTER TWENTY-ONE

VIV STORMED INTO the hall past an astonished Haxton still wielding the poker, and a trembling Jenny, wringing her hands.

"Miss!" cried Jenny. "Are you unharmed?"

Viv flung her gloves and the soiled velvet purse onto the demi-lune table, and tore off her bonnet, moving toward the stairs.

"Perfectly unharmed, Jenny, thank you. But oh he's a liar and a thief and I shall—" She railed at his perfidy. She did not know what dreadful fate could possibly satisfy her wrath. Really, the whole barbaric idea of four horses pulling his disemboweled body apart seemed reasonable at the moment except for the distress to the horses.

Behind her Haxton closed the door. "Shall we call for the constables to apprehend the ruffian, Miss Bradish?"

"Yes! He will have gone in the direction of Weymouth Street." A burly constable taking him up would be a good first step. A cell in some low, dank corner of Newgate would be a start. Leg irons would be a nice touch.

"Weymouth Street? Very good, miss."

Viv reached the foot of the stairs and turned back, her thoughts racing. "No. He'll go to Wenlocke." He would go to his grand friend the duke who would protect him from the law, and from Viv, too.

"The duke, miss, that ruffian?" Haxton plainly thought she had taken leave of her senses, and perhaps she had. Somewhere deep in her was a place where a monstrous hurt lay coiled and waiting, and if she stopped being angry even for an instant, it would spring and eat her alive.

"No. The ruffian is a man named Rook. He is Mr. Larkin's partner." Only he wasn't a *mister* Larkin. He had told her he was *Lark. My friends call me Lark.* He meant his pickpocket friends and his titled friends. It made no sense that he'd told her such an intimate thing. Her knees threatened to give. She grabbed the newel post and pulled herself together to speak plainly, to name the betrayal. "Mr. Larkin is the thief. First, he stole my purse. Now he's taken our book proofs."

Haxton and Jenny stared at her with complete incomprehension.

"Oh, truly, believe me, he is a thief, a common pickpocket. I can't explain right now."

A rustle of skirts on the landing above made Viv look up. There stood Mrs. Stryde, the little black curls on the side of her face as tight as ever, her lips compressed into a thin red downward bow.

"Who has taken the book proofs, Miss Bradish? They were your responsibility, were they not?"

"Good morning, Mrs. Stryde."

"You'd best come up, Miss Bradish. We've been waiting for you."

"Directly." She turned to Haxton and Jenny, still standing confused and distraught. "Thank you for coming to my aid. There's no need to send for a constable. Lady Melforth will decide how she wishes to deal with the thief."

Viv gathered her dignity, clutched her dirtied skirts in one hand, and began to climb. The corrected proofs had been her last tie to her ladyship. In the night at her desk, Viv had restored the copy as closely as she could to the original, the one that had emerged from their work together, from hours of exchanging ideas and playing with words and laughing. Viv had worn out her pencil making those changes. In the end it was as if she had recovered those lost good times. But Dodsley had refused to look at Viv's corrections. He had his orders, he said, direct from Lady Melforth. The Traveling Viscountess was the name that sold books, and he was going to publish the guide as she wrote it. Only she hadn't written it. That was the rub.

Viv had wandered for some time, hugging the corrected proofs to her chest, thinking about her mother's house, about the room she shared with her sisters, about the daily round of errands and chores that kept their meager household going, about scrimping and saving for paper and pencils, about her mother's weariness and her stepfather's demands. She did not want to go home, but she could see no way forward in London. She could take the guide to a rival publisher or to the law, but any claim she made of her role in the writing of it would expose Lady Melforth as a liar. Or, more likely, given her ladyship's established position, would land Viv herself in jail as a fraud.

The garnet ring on her finger had mocked her as she wandered. If Viv's betrothal had been a real one, if Lark had truly been open with her about his situation, if he had once said that he loved her... But those were not the facts. She hardly knew how she found her way back to the house.

The act of climbing the stairs steadied her. She had been in a fog, and now the fog had cleared. By the time she entered the upstairs drawing room her mind was made up. They were all there, the Strydes, Lady Melforth, and Dr. Newberry. Lady Melforth stretched out on her favorite couch supported by pillows. Her jutting nose gave a cold, unbending expression to the pale, sunken face. Plump, bewhiskered Mr. Stryde sat in a chair by her feet, while Mrs. Stryde in another of her endless striped gowns hovered over a tray of medicines on the side table. From the hearth Newberry shot Viv a scornful glance that took in her dragging skirts. She knew she would receive no support from him.

"You look a right mess, miss. Where have you been this morning?" Lady Melforth's frown deepened.

Viv waited. They all looked at her, expecting her to wilt or crumble under their censure, but she had nothing to lose. She met Lady Melforth's gaze. "I took the proofs that arrived yesterday back to Dodsley for correction. He, of course, refused to make any changes."

Lady Melforth's eyes flashed with a quick gleam of recognition and alarm. Her hand shook and she glanced aside. Her ladyship understood what it meant that Viv had read those proofs. "But Mrs. Stryde has just said they were stolen." Her voice quavered.

"From your very doorstep, by Mr. Larkin, working with a partner to create a diversion. It's a method pickpockets commonly use."

Mrs. Stryde gasped. Her glance flew to her husband. "I

told you my necklace was stolen."

Newberry shoved away from the mantel, moving to stand beside Mrs. Stryde. "You were sharper than the rest of us apparently, Eustacia. You recognized the man as a fraud from the beginning."

"Your necklace was not stolen, however. You still have it," said Viv, insisting on the truth. She would not have Lark condemned for something he didn't do.

"But my proofs are gone," said Lady Melforth, her brow furrowed in perplexity.

Viv lifted her chin and stared her ladyship down. "You may pursue the thief, of course, but I'm sure you can have no use for the corrected proofs he took. Dodsley should be able to supply you with another proof copy, a copy more to your liking."

"Insolent girl," hissed Mrs. Stryde. "How dare you speak to your employer in such a manner."

"I do dare. I resign my position. I thank you, Lady Melforth, for your many past kindnesses. I will stay only as long as it takes for you to engage someone to take over my duties."

A brief stricken look passed over Lady Melforth's face. It might have been a plea for understanding, and Viv waited for her to say that it was all a mistake, but her ladyship's hands closed on the silk coverlet over her legs, and she looked away.

Viv went cold. She understood the choice to lie in the moment when there seemed no other way, when everything, one's position and reputation, could be lost forever, but to enshrine the deception, to carry on deliberately in the lie, was something else. The woman she thought her dearest friend, now knowingly denied the work they'd done together. Her mind flashed to Lark. How odd that the pickpocket in such a desperate moment had simply admitted the truth and lost everything.

It was Mrs. Stryde who spoke next. "Foolish girl. Where will you go? Your thief of a fiancé can't help you."

"Where I go can be no concern of yours, Mrs. Stryde. I am not without resources." With a quick curtsy she turned and left.

WITHIN MINUTES OF leaving Henrietta Street, Lark altered his course twice. As long as he didn't stop, the loss of Viv would not catch up with him. Part of his mind went on working, guided by the instinct to avoid pursuit. She would quickly discover the theft of the proofs, and she would be furious. She would think that he and Rook had been in on it together, and Lark could not plead his case. He could not argue that he had ended his partnership with Rook months earlier. He could not change what he had done that first day, stepping into Viv's line of fire to save Rook. He owed Rook that. He would do it again. And he'd made sure that Viv would send the constables after him, not Rook. Angry and wounded, Rook would plunge ahead, do some reckless click, follow it up with an evening of drink, and stagger back to their old lair.

Viv would have Haxton summon a constable. She knew enough to find Adele St. Clair to ask where Lark lived. He could not go to his digs, nor could he go to Wenlocke, as Viv could as easily send constables to the duke's house. He did not want to embarrass Wenlocke. Maybe it had been folly to steal the proofs. Lark wouldn't know until he had a chance to look at them and discover why they pained Viv. As he moved, a plan formed. He knew a place where no one would think to look for him and where he could take all the time he needed to examine the proofs. He turned his steps toward Isaacson Brothers Fashion Emporium.

When he reached the East End square dominated by the Emporium, he could see that business was good. Old Mr. Isaacson and his brother had built a retail palace, with an elaborate portico at the entrance and floor-to-ceiling windows along the front that showed a crowded interior. Lark made his way around to the back alley where goods were delivered and asked the porter at the door for his friend Ezra, Isaacson's son.

Within minutes Ezra showed up, dressed for the shop floor in a fashionable gray coat, pin-dotted white cotton waistcoat, drab trousers, and a lavender floral tie that managed to merge the colors into a single scheme. Lark guessed that Isaacson's would sell dozens of those silk ties based on Ezra's appearance alone.

"You are unfair to your customers, Ezra," Lark told his friend.

Ezra let him in. "How so?"

"You make them think they will look as dashing as yourself."

Ezra grinned. "What brings you back to us? Twice in a fortnight! You've not been shot again?"

"Worse. I must avoid the constabulary for a few days. Can you put me up?"

"That bad, is it?" Ezra gave Lark's face a closer scrutiny. "You look done in, as if we ought to fit you up with black bands for your hat and sleeves."

"It's nothing. A minor wound." Lark did his best to hold Ezra's gaze.

"You know the room upstairs behind the cutting floor? Will that suit you?"

Lark nodded, and Ezra led the way up the back stairs they'd often used since they first met. That day they had been vying to buy the same coat from a slops seller in Monmouth Street. Lark actually wanted to wear the fine custom-made coat formerly belonging to a bankrupt tea dealer. Ezra wanted to take it apart to understand its construction. They'd compromised, and Lark had followed Ezra to the Fashion Emporium.

"Here we are." Ezra opened the door to a spacious plain room with a small window to the north, no carpet, no curtains. "What have you nicked this time?"

"A book." Lark noted a daybed covered in a red-and-blue Kilim rug, a plain deal table and chair under the window, and a tall blue-painted wardrobe. The place was ideal for his plan.

"Books aren't your usual style." One of Ezra's dark brows went up. Another of the reasons customers bought whatever Ezra chose to wear was that he was a handsome fellow with a head of dark curls and an easy, unaffected manner. "Is it a rare manuscript?"

"It's the key to a mystery. I need time to read it." Now

that Lark had stopped moving, the hollow in his chest had begun to ache.

"Oh, you'll have time. In case you've forgotten, we close for Shabbat in a couple of hours. The place will be a tomb until Saturday night."

"More like a grand mausoleum. I'll be ghost then."

Ezra sobered. "I can't keep you company. A good son has to be at his mother's table, but I'll leave you some food and beer."

"What about paper and pencils? And candles? And have you got a boy who can take a message for me?"

"Now you expect me to be a hotel. I'll send a boy to you. Stay out of sight. I don't want Father to think I'm breaking Shabbat for the likes of you."

"You do eat and light candles, don't you? No one will know I'm here."

"Fine. But don't leave until we talk. I want your opinion on some cloth Father bought to use for a new line of trousers."

"He's not going to make Cossack trousers, is he?"

Ezra shrugged. "Customers want them, but they offend my father's sense of what an English gentleman ought to wear."

"That's because they are a high crime against fashion."

Ezra laughed. "An abomination, Father calls them. I'll be back in a few minutes."

Lark set the paper package with Viv's manuscript on the table. There was enough light for him to begin, but he would wait until he had his supplies and sent his message. He looked about the room again. The plainness suited him.

From the window the view north across rooftops reminded him of London as he'd known it with Wenlocke and the others. He recognized St. Botolph's narrow cone of a steeple rising upward from the irregular pattern of slate and chimney pots stretching out to the horizon.

Ezra returned with a basket of food, three bottles of porter, and one of the firm's messenger boys. He also gave Lark a box of candles, paper, and pencils, taken from the designer's workshop. Lark wrote a note to Wenlocke, giving the boy strict instructions for its delivery and a coin. Then Ezra was off for his family's weekly observances.

LARK PUT ASIDE his gentlemanly trappings, his hat and gloves, his coat and tie, and settled himself at the table. He had dressed himself in the borrowed robes of a fiction for too long. It was time to face the truth. Edward Larkin did not exist. He, Lark, was a thief with a stolen treasure, a thief who could help the woman he loved. He unwrapped the package and found a dark-green cloth-bound book with a sepia drawing of a London street affixed to the cover. He opened the book to the title page and saw at once what had left Viv slumped and bereft on Lady Melforth's doorstep. Inserted into the blank space between the printed title and Lady Melforth's name was Viv's name in pencil. The contrast between the words from the printer in ink and Viv's neat handwritten pencil correction made everything clear. Her authorship had been denied. Her work, not her purse, had been stolen.

Not by Dodsley. Dodsley would not have omitted Viv's name from the title page in error, and Lark remembered Viv's words—*Dodsley is not the problem.* Only by Lady Melforth's order could the manuscript have been so altered. Lark turned the pages. The structure and elements of the guide remained what Viv had described, but when he came to the writing, the stories of women woven into the brief walking tours, he saw what Lady Melforth had done. Viv's penciled notes marked those places where Lady Melforth had removed any sign of Viv's liveliness and wit and turned Viv's stories into bland accounts of how to get about London and what to pay for various services. No page remained untouched.

He turned to the story of their meeting. Most of the original story had been omitted and reinstated in Viv's own hand on a page attached to the proofs with a pin. He traced her pencil marks with his fingertips and began to read aloud, hearing Viv as he did so, seeing her eyes flash, catching her joy at the adventure of it all.

> *Women are frequently advised to avoid certain streets in our great metropolis. We are told that danger lurks around unsavory corners, which our sex is ill-prepared to meet. These perilous haunts are not the lonely heaths of highwaymen and footpads nor the dark byways of lawless and predatory cosh-carriers, but streets of commerce and enterprise, politics and publishing.*
>
> *To test the truth of such advice, dear reader, this author took it upon herself to risk a solo perambulation down Babylon Street, notorious for its politics and the prints in its shop windows. The danger, it is presumed,*

is that a woman is likely to fall into a reverie, her gaze caught and bewitched by the spectacle in the windows, so that she becomes the unsuspecting prey of a pickpocket or purse snatcher. I had a great desire to meet just such a type, a master of subtlety.

For the adventure, I took certain precautions. I came by cab and ordered the driver to follow at a distance as I walked the length of the street. I wore a decoy velvet purse on my arm and kept my actual funds secure in a pocket. I carried under my short cape, a serviceable Toby, with the firing of which I am well-acquainted.

For all Babylon Street's evil reputation, I saw little to alarm me. At one end of the street, a kidney-pie man with his portable oven was doing a brisk business with men splashed in the marks of the plasterer's trade. A man in the robes and wig of a barrister, his brief under his arm, hurrying past, indifferent to his surroundings, seemed to me a likelier target for a thief, for the fob of a gold watch stretched across his substantial girth. I took heart from a waif carrying flowers, a shawl around her thin shoulders, showing no fear of her surroundings. A barefoot boy teased a dog. These were my fellow Londoners going about their business undisturbed by the reputation of the street.

There was an air of decay about the shops with their overhanging upper stories above the cobbles. The narrowness of the street admitted little light. But these were merely the signs of great age, of the street's past. I walked on, looking for a likely window to study. One bow window had already attracted a modest crowd while my gaze lighted on a shop advertising schoolbooks. The shop's wares spilled out into the street on trestles and hanging shelves as if the place were bursting with books.

There I paused to study the shop's wares, picking a likely volume from the hanging shelf. In no time I became aware of a ruffian who passed me, close enough to brush the hem of my skirts, and easily identified by the noxious smell that trailed in his wake. I kept my arm at an angle, my little velvet bag, while visible, secured by strings deep in the crook of my arm. I confess I did not expect what happened next.

The ruffian returned. He slammed his body against mine. I fell back against the trestles full of books, the purse slid down my arm and disappeared in his grasp. I righted myself in an instant, drew my Toby, and aimed at the fleeing villain. I called out, intent on stopping him, and seizing the opportunity to talk. Instead, to my surprise, a helpful gentleman addressed me, stepping unwittingly into the path of the bullet.

Mr. Witsworth, like most men, appeared to consider me helpless and unable to deal with the situation. His well-meant but thoughtless interference allowed the villain to escape and cost me an opportunity to understand the workings of the criminal mind. It was he, dear reader, who needed assistance.

She'd enjoyed that line, but it caused Lark a pang. She would no longer think of him as *Witsworth*. The plain room was dark. Lark rose and crossed to stand at the window looking out over London. He rolled his shoulders and shook off the stiffness of sitting so long. In his pocket were the things he and Viv had traded that first day, the spent ball from her Toby and the garnet ring with which he'd proposed. He had to accept that he'd lost her, or he couldn't get his head clear to help her, to figure out what had happened to bring the manuscript to its present state. He closed the book and looked again at the package. Someone had written the street name and number, and then a second writer had scrawled Viv's name in place as the person to receive the proofs. So, Viv had received the proofs, discovered the changes, which could only have been made at her ladyship's orders, and had worked to restore the manuscript. He knew Viv had been to see Dodsley, and that Dodsley had been unwilling to accept her corrections.

He did not know whether Viv had confronted Lady Melforth directly, but Viv's unhappiness meant that Dodsley was going to publish the version sanctioned by Lady Melforth. Dodsley was willing to participate in the theft. His motive would be profit. Viv was an unknown authoress with no following. Lady Melforth was the Traveling Viscountess, a known best seller. It was Lady Melforth whose motive made little sense to Lark.

Across the way a pair of gulls landed on the peak of a roof and did a bit of bird preening before folding their wings and tucking their heads down for the night. Below the birds, the roof sloped down into a hollow behind a low balustrade. The little nook was bordered by a projecting dormer on one side and on the other by the solid bulk of a brick chimney with its red clay pots feeding thin wisps of smoke into a hazy lavender sky. In such hollows, their gang of lost boys had slept until Wenlocke's family found him and claimed him. Then the gang had moved, first into Wenlocke's mother's house, and later into Daventry Hall in the country. They had had beds with sheets, coverlets, and pillows. They had had clothes and shoes and plenty to eat. They had had lessons. But still they had been a gang until Wenlocke had fallen in love.

Lark remembered again with painful clarity the scene of Wenlocke's betrayal, of his walking away from Lark without a backward look. Fragments of memory from that long ago scene and the morning's scene on Henrietta Street tangled together in his mind. He gripped the edge of the window frame. He had walked away from Rook in just such a way. He had saved his old friend from being shot, and he had saved him from being pursued, but Lark could not blame Rook for his anger, or for telling Viv the truth of their partnership. Lark had left their shared life behind. His heart, which had belonged to no one but himself, now belonged to Viv.

Still, he could not see what justified Lady Melforth's betrayal. The woman did not have Dodsley's profit motive. Lark went back in his mind over what Viv had told him and what he had seen of her ladyship. Viv had believed them to be partners, friends. She had been protective of her ladyship in the face of the Strydes and eager to share her daily discoveries of London with her ladyship. All that seemed to have changed. An explanation that made sense was Lady Melforth's illness. Perhaps, her ladyship's immobility, her shaking hand, her falls, had made her more dependent on Viv than she wished to be. He tried to imagine how her ladyship felt seeing two names on a guide where always before there had only been one. He knew what it meant to be in the grip of strong resentment and what one could do in that state. But now that he had renewed his friendship with Wenlocke, he knew the folly of keeping an old injury alive in one's heart for far too long.

Lark turned from the window, lit the candles in the darkened room, and opened a bottle of porter. He needed a strategy for seeing Lady Melforth and convincing her to approve of Viv's corrections.

CHAPTER TWENTY-TWO

VIV HAD WRITTEN to her aunt and to her family and packed all that she thought might be of use to her in Weymouth. Two trunks had been sent ahead. She would never wear her fine London clothes at home, but her mother and sisters might cut up her gowns for new ones for themselves. The letter to her aunt had required several attempts as Viv had dissolved into a watering pot with each early draft.

She had had to take herself to task and list Lark's acts of perfidy before she could manage a clean, un-tear-stained copy. Item: he had deceived her from the first moment of their acquaintance, allowing his rough accomplice to make off with her purse. Item: he had given her a false name and lied about his position in the duke's household. Item: he had prolonged their acquaintance by involving her in a deception of her friends. Item: he had kissed her without meaning anything by it, just as her former suitor in Bath had done. Item: he had stolen the corrected proofs of the book, her only record of the work on which she had placed her hopes.

The trouble with her list was that her heart looked at each of his treacherous acts and saw something different. He had stepped between her pistol and his friend, saving the friend. His spontaneous proposal had saved her for a time from the Strydes. He had ignored whatever real business he was meant to be doing to show her London as she had not seen it. He had challenged her and laughed with her. He had told her the name his friends called him. He had kissed her as if he meant it. He might not be a duke's secretary, but he was clearly a duke's intimate friend.

Her poor heart had been knocked about between the two ways of seeing him, like a sack of potatoes in a farmer's cart jolted and bruised on a rough road. In the end, the theft of the proofs settled it. He was a thief, he stole things, purses, notebooks, pearls, perhaps even the ring he'd offered her. And if he read those proofs, and she knew he would, he would see how Lady Melforth had betrayed Viv. He would think Viv a rare idiot for believing that she, a dead man's unwanted daughter, a girl from nowhere really, from an obscure seaside town long past its moment as a fashionable resort, could take on the great metropolis and tell its stories. It had all been vanity. She truly deserved her fall.

Her letter home had been easier to write as her family had never heard of her false betrothal. A reply came from her mother in Pippa's handwriting saying that she could have her old bed in the room she had shared with Pippa and Charlotte.

Resigning before being sacked was small comfort. Since that day the Strydes had made themselves quite at home in the upper rooms, and Viv had moved like a ghost, nearly invisible as she went about her few tasks, using the servants' stairs, speaking little, and eating her meals in her room. Only Jenny seemed to notice Viv at all. And in the morning, she would leave for home.

Jenny found her in the stillroom, the perfect refuge for a

ghost, where she was in nobody's way.

"Miss, an invitation 'as come for you."

"Thank you, Jenny. Set it on the table, and I'll get to it when I can."

"It's quite posh, miss, with a crest and all."

Viv went on mixing a cordial for Lady Melforth. Now that she was leaving, she wanted to be sure that a good supply of Newberry's headache cordial was on hand. She had no confidence in a nurse of the Strydes' choosing. They would favor someone stern and of their moral leanings, but also cheap, and they would not look for a woman capable of compassion.

Out of the corner of her eye, Viv could see Jenny hovering, looking for a place to put the card. Viv set aside her work, wiped her hands on a towel, and came around the big table. "I'll take it, Jenny, if you're worried about setting it down among the herbs and such."

"Thank you, miss. It's from a duchess."

Viv accepted the card. It was indeed from her grace, the Duchess of Wenlocke. For a moment a flutter of hope stirred in her. Then she recollected herself. The invitation came from her other life, the one she had led before she learned Lark was a pickpocket, before she knew he'd lied, before he'd stolen the proofs. In that life, she would have eagerly torn open the envelope and lost herself in anticipation of what to wear and whom she would meet. She was grateful to the duchess for the distinction of a personal invitation, and not as a lady's companion might expect, a mention of herself as part of the household invitation.

But that life had ended. In her new life, the invitation

meant nothing. Viv would be with her family in Weymouth long before the duchess's dinner party.

"Will you go, miss?" Jenny asked. "Everyone says the duchess has great kindness."

"I'm sure she does," Viv answered, "but I must return to my family."

"Oh miss, must you leave? Nothing will be the same without you."

Viv shook her head. "If I tried to stay, I would be sacked."

"We will all be sacked soon, miss, and whatever will we do? Mr. Haxton may find another situation, but I'm sure no one will want me."

Viv tucked the duchess's card into her apron pocket, took Jenny by the shoulders, and looked into the round, sweet face. "You must go to an agency, Jenny. I'm sure Haxton knows some very good ones."

"But if you leave, miss, the mistress will die, I know she will, and if she dies, 'er 'orrible Stryde cousins will turn us all out at once."

"You are probably right about the Strydes, Jenny, but not about her ladyship. Her low spirits make her case seem desperate, but it's not. She has you and Sarah and Mrs. Brandle and Dr. Newberry to look out for her. She won't die. Once her spirits recover, she'll go along much better. You will see."

"Oh, I hope so, miss. She used to laugh ever so much. Do ye remember?"

"I do, Jenny."

"And, she doesn't anymore."

"It is the shock of learning about her illness, Jenny. You must give her time to discover that she can get along quite well in spite of it. You can help her by being your usual self."

"Me, miss?"

"You, Jenny. You go on doing for her with your quick cheerful ways, and you'll see."

"Thank you, miss, for saying so, and for telling me to find an agency. I won't forget, miss."

NOT AN HOUR later, Viv was summoned to Lady Melforth's room. The closed curtains gave the room a stale and gloomy air. Her ladyship looked small and lost in the great bed, and white as if she had already died. Viv arranged the pillows and set a fresh draught of cordial at her ladyship's side.

"Will you take a drive this afternoon, Lady Melforth?" Viv asked. For days it had fallen to her lot to promote the disagreeable, as she could not be sacked twice.

"I will not. I dislike riding with Eustacia excessively. She stops to introduce me to every horrid acquaintance of hers from the Anti-Vice Society. It's like going about London in a green shoe blacking van with THE TRAVELING VISCOUNTESS writen large on the sides."

Viv sympathized, but she was unmoved by the rebuff of her suggestion. "Nevertheless, those rides lift your spirits. If you won't go with Mrs. Stryde, you must take advantage of my aunt Louisa's offer of her landau. We can easily send to have it brought round, and I'm sure Sarah is willing to go with you. Dr. Newberry particularly encourages those rides to reduce your tremor."

Viv crossed to the window and drew one of the curtains aside, letting in a shaft of brightness.

Lady Melforth held a hand in front of her face, blinking in the light. "Hah. Newberry is as bad as the other fellow. They won't leave me in peace to die."

"You are hardly in peace, ma'am. Nor are you dying. You are simply wallowing and refusing to confront this palsy and deal with it as both Newberry and Dr. Pridmore believe you can."

"I didn't summon you to preach to me, miss," said Lady Melforth. "Your pickpocket has been arrested."

Viv's heart plummeted briefly. She froze, unable to recall what purpose had taken her across the room. In that dreadful moment of understanding who he was and what he'd done, she had wished him arrested. Now that the anger had left her, her heart was undefended against the softer feelings she had for him. She hated to think of him arrested. "Did you bring charges, ma'am?"

"I most certainly did. The fellow denies them, of course, says he never touched any book of mine. It took three constables to subdue the big lout."

"You don't mean Mr. Larkin then?" Viv unfroze and drew aside the second curtain.

"No, not Larkin, the other one, the one Haxton chased away."

"Rook." Oh dear. Viv thought of Rook, the poor man Lark had betrayed. Of course, Rook had not taken the proofs. He'd had no idea they were there on the steps, no notion of their value. He was an easy target for the police because he looked the part of a ruffian.

"Rook? That's the man's name. Suits him, I suppose."

"So, you've not recovered the proofs?" Viv dared to ask. She didn't see how the proofs could matter to Lady Melforth. If Dodsley needed her approval, he would send another copy. "No." Lady Melforth's voice shrank.

The fear in the small voice tugged at Viv, but she refused to bend. "Are you worried that Dodsley won't go ahead with the printing as planned? Surely he has your approval."

"I wanted...to look them over one more time to make sure Dodsley got everything right."

Viv held her breath. Perhaps her ladyship regretted what she'd done. Perhaps she had acted in anger and haste and would change her mind. The trouble with betrayal was that though one should hate and despise one's betrayer, one did not, or not entirely. The betrayer had stopped loving or caring and turned away. Some vital element, which had come from them, had been withdrawn, which one still needed like air, so one gasped for it.

Lady Melforth threw off the coverlet. "No matter. Call Sarah. I will go out. Send for Louisa's landau."

At the door, Viv turned back to say, "You will climb volcanoes again, you know, ma'am."

"Hmmph. You are too bold for your own good, miss."

"If I am, you taught me to be so."

VIV RETURNED TO her work in the stillroom. An hour later, she was finishing up and putting away the bottles of cordial when Newberry walked in.

"I hear you convinced my patient to take a ride today. How did you find her?"

"She looks worse than she is. Her spirits are low. Can you limit the Strydes' visits?"

"Her dear family members?" His voice had a disdainful edge to it.

"You've known for months how her cousins affect her." Viv closed the cupboard door, turned the little key. Newberry stood between her and the hook on the wall where the key belonged.

"If her spirits are low, her disappointment in you is a large part of that."

"Tomorrow I'll be gone. You need no longer worry about my influence on her spirits."

"You could apologize before you go."

"To whom? For what?" Viv could not hold back the sharpness of her tone.

"For your lack of caution and sense in bringing Mr. Larkin here and entering into a betrothal with him. I knew he was hiding something, but really, Viv, to take up with a common pickpocket?"

"I seem to have disappointed your expectations."

"Not mine alone. The expectations of any gentleman of proper feminine behavior. How can a decent man have any regard for you?"

Viv's temper was stirring, flickering to life, and she tried to tamp it down. Newberry said only what the world thought of Lark and of her. "I suppose you're right, and only a pickpocket could care for a woman of my sort."

"I don't understand. Why did you choose him when you—"

He did not say that Viv might have had him. He was very handsome. At one time he had seemed to see her as an equal, and she had thought him the sort of man for whom she might come to feel an attachment, kind, principled, and caring. Maybe Viv was mad, but she thought her common pickpocket had a more generous idea of feminine behavior, and more genuine regard for women as rational creatures and independent beings. "Did you come to quarrel with me?" she asked.

"No. At least I didn't intend to quarrel." He ran a hand through his curls. "I thought we were...partners in our care of her ladyship. She has been good to me, good for my practice. She helped me to establish myself among people who matter. And I know she's been good to you, teaching you how to tell stories and put a guide together."

"I have much to thank her for, and I hoped you and I might part as friends."

"Hoped?"

Viv raised her brows. "It's more difficult to part as friends if you blame me for the effects of her illness and disappointment."

He started to reply, stopped, and gave a rueful laugh. "I don't understand you, Viv, and I don't understand how *I* ended up on the Strydes' side of the aisle, as it were."

"I know." She did. While she had been seeing London through different eyes, the eyes of her betrothed, Newberry had been seeing it more and more from the Strydes' view. She knew London was bigger than he thought and that it was more dependent on people who were not the right sort of people, people on other streets who had other stories to tell. "I've made up some jars of cordial, and trained Jenny to make more. If you rely on Jenny and the staff and don't let the Strydes take over, Lady Melforth will do quite well."

She offered her hand. He took it and looked as if he might say more. Viv gave him no encouragement. He bowed and took his leave.

She was free of everything that kept her in London. She had done the work entrusted to her. She had learned lessons in humility as well as boldness, perhaps not all the lessons she needed to learn. She reflected that her family's household in Weymouth would teach her more. She had had her hopes dashed and her heart broken. Now she had only to pick herself up and go on. She hung the key to the stillroom cabinet on its hook and closed the door.

CHAPTER TWENTY-THREE

Late in Lark's third evening in the Fashion Emporium's upper room, Ezra sat on the edge of the table drinking porter. "You can't stay here indefinitely."

"I won't." Lark took a swig of his porter and went back to his copying. "I'll leave as soon as I finish making a copy of these proofs."

"Remind me. Why do you need a copy?"

"To retain evidence of what the text should say."

"Will you blackmail this writer, the Traveling Viscountess?"

"Not blackmail her. Persuade her to do the right thing by her partner."

"And why do you care about that? You're not in love, are you?"

For a few minutes the room was quiet except for the scratching of Lark's pencil, sounding loud in his ears. He had used up four pencils, dozens of sheets of paper, and quantities of ink, and he wasn't finished. As long as he kept his head down and the pencil moving, he felt nothing. *In* love was an odd phrase when there was no being *in* only being shut *out*.

Around him, the anonymous room had kept a steady vigil, throwing light on his efforts in the morning, collecting heat at midday, and cooling in the evening. The room, which could be any upper room anywhere in London, was unmarked by personal effects, arrangements of books or clothes, favorite chairs or prints. Beyond it, London was a muted rumble, broken by the regular pealing of bells marking time. He had been able to do the most at night when the Emporium below him went quiet for a few hours, and he left the room only when Ezra proudly showed him the Emporium's modern toilet facilities. Another time he would return and show Ezra some proper appreciation for his family's forward-thinking innovations.

"You know," Ezra said, "I could have our printer do up a proof of those corrections. He's fast. It would take him a day, at most two."

Lark stopped copying. He hadn't thought of that. The Emporium had its own printer who prepared a pamphlet of fashion advice each season to hand to customers. "Would you?"

Ezra shrugged. "You haven't tried the Cossack pants yet."

Lark glanced at the trousers hanging from the wardrobe. The striped fabric reminded him forcibly of Mrs. Stryde. "They're a disaster."

"You could wear them to show your gratitude for my help. Having our printer do a set of proofs will be much quicker than what you're doing. He could make a copy for you while you stroll along Bond Street."

Lark shuddered. He didn't care to become a walking advertisement for the appalling trousers. But the suggestion gave him a different idea of how to repay Ezra for his help.

"What if," he said, "the printer puts one of your ads in the book?"

Ezra's eyes gleamed. He jumped down from the desk. "Oh say, I like that. How do you think this book will do?"

"Well enough." Lark lay his pencil down and took another long pull on his drink. A printed proof with Viv's corrections would be a strong weapon to use against Lady Melforth and Dodsley, should either of them refuse to cooperate. He eyed the Cossack trousers again, brown with a vertical green stripe, full and gathered at the waist, tapering to the ankle straps that passed under the wearer's feet. If a Bond Street stroll in the absurd trousers was the price of a copy of the book, he could do it.

IN THE END Lark did the Bond Street stroll for two days. He felt strangely invisible in the garish trousers and coat with its close-fitting waist and flaring skirts. He was a hollow man, neither Edward Larkin, the would-be gentleman, nor Lark, the pickpocket.

Ezra was as good as his word. While Lark strolled, the Emporium's printer did up a proof using Viv's corrections. The copy closely resembled the original in style and layout with Viv's name on the title page, and her words restored, plus there was an ad for the Isaacson Brothers Fashion Emporium.

Early on the following day, Lark paid a visit to Dodsley & Sons. Then, with the proof copies in hand, he went to Wenlocke. He could not risk returning to his rooms, so he was conscious of his drooping tie and stale linen as he waited in the duke's study. When Wenlocke entered, Lark asked, "You got my message?"

Wenlocke's face wore a drily amused expression. "*Don't worry. Not taken up.* Your note did not inspire total confidence."

Lark drew in a breath. "There was no time to elaborate."

"But there is now. Sit. Tell me. You look as if you are in need of refreshment, and coffee." The wry glance passed over Lark's rumpled attire.

Lark shook his head. "My business is urgent, and I have a favor to ask."

Wenlocke shrugged. "Or, don't sit, and don't tell me?"

"I need you to keep something safe for me." Lark placed the original proofs with Viv's penciled corrections on Wenlocke's desk.

Wenlocke crossed to the desk and glanced at the brown package, his gaze narrowing. "How did you come by this?"

Lark straightened and met the sharp, clear-eyed gaze fixed on him. "In the way I've come by many things over the years."

Wenlocke tapped the stolen proofs. "You know Rook was taken up for the theft."

Lark rocked back. "No! Viv knew *I* took them. There could be no mistake about that. You've spoken with Rook?"

"Robin has, in Newgate. The Force has been watching Rook for a list of offenses since last October. A pawnbroker in Grays Inn Lane spoke against him. I suspect that Rook faces transportation."

"A lagging."

"It's a *Ticket of Leave*, a bit like bail, renewed yearly for seven years, and a likely pardon once the sentence is complete. It might be better for him than the path he's on."

Lark was not convinced. Wenlocke must have used his influence, but Rook was a creature of habit. He liked his dark little corner of London with its narrow lanes and decaying grandeur, its beer and bloaters, its girls like Liza, and its easy escape after a click. A journey across vast oceans, a new and unfamiliar world seemed beyond Rook.

"Sit. You look done in." Wenlocke put a hand on Lark's shoulder.

"Some late nights." This time Lark took the offered chair. He should have expected that ending his partnership with Rook would embitter his friend. And he knew how resentment could make a man reckless and indifferent to his fate.

"I see that you blame yourself." Wenlocke took a seat opposite Lark.

"Who else?"

"You must allow Rook his share of the fault. He had quite a lot to say against you. Chief among your many offenses is that you asked him to quit dipping into pockets and enter some legitimate enterprise with you."

For a few moments Lark stared at the pattern in the Turkish carpet, his mind in a haze of sleeplessness and change. The world was strange and different, and he couldn't unravel its pattern. He was not Rook's partner, but surely Lark could do something for him.

"When did you let go of your bitterness?" Wenlocke asked.

Lark looked up. It was awkward to be so well understood, but there was no denying that he had been bitter or that he had let his bitterness go. He had wanted to be done with it. He had realized that it was a resentment against life itself and that it had been holding him back, making him see London as a set of chains binding him. Every click had been a shaking of those chains. But they had been chains of his own forging. He had made those links. The night of the fire he had decided to file them off.

"The night of the fire," he said. He had not expected it, but when the commons and lords were clearly gone, and the call came to save the adjoining hall, Lark had answered. He had manned a pump with other Londoners amid swirling smoke, flying embers, and falling glass, and they had saved the hall. The exhilaration of triumph in a common effort had been like nothing he'd ever felt before. When he'd returned to their rooms, exhausted and tasting soot with every breath, he found Rook grinning with satisfaction over a pile of watches and wallets. And Lark knew he would never feel the satisfaction of a click again. The next day he had begun the search for his mother. And then he'd met Viv.

He shook off the memories and looked at Wenlocke. "What if Rook goes to Sydney as a free man with a stake to start a business?"

"Could he?"

"I know a man who could arrange it. I have...investments in his shipping company."

"I thought you had urgent business."

"I must see Lady Melforth." He didn't know how much Wenlocke already understood, but Lark did not want to expose her ladyship's betrayal if he could avoid it. He simply needed to act because Viv was hurting.

"May I suggest that you bring in reinforcements, to create a distraction. You don't want to be taken up now."

"Reinforcements?" In his head, the word *now* rang oddly.

"The duchess, of course. A morning call from her, coming on the heels of your visit, will keep Lady Melforth pleasantly occupied, not summoning the constables."

Lark nodded. He liked the plan. Maybe he had been wrong about the *now*.

Wenlocke stood and indicated the door. "Let me tell the duchess our plan, and don't worry, I will keep your document safe."

Lark nodded and rose to his feet. "Can you keep Rook from a lagging until I talk to the emigration agent?"

"Robin can. Your place is watched, by the way, so use my dressing room. I'll send for coffee, and my man can help you put yourself to rights. Oh, and when you're ready"—he paused, and Lark halted—"I have news of your mother."

"Alive?"

He read the answer in Wenlocke's eyes. Once again, the haze descended, and Lark fought to clear his head. First, he would help the living, then he would mourn his mother.

LARK USED THE basement entrance to the Henrietta Street house, carrying the Emporium printer's copy of the guide under one arm. In the kitchen he caught the eye of Mrs. Brandle and with her help summoned Jenny. Under the stairs outside the stillroom, they had quick conversation.

"Mr. Larkin, sir, why are ye 'ere? Miss Bradish's gone away to 'er parents' 'ome in Weymouth."

"Was she sacked?" A hot surge of anger welled up in him, tightening his mouth.

"She resigned. She was most particular about it. She told me I shouldn't worry."

"When?" He didn't believe that Viv had simply resigned.

"That day the ruffian came to the 'ouse. It was such a to do with Mrs. Stryde saying 'orrible things, and Mr. Haxton waving a poker about."

Lark almost laughed. Maybe Viv had simply chosen to leave a house gone mad. "Do you want her back?"

Jenny gave a fervent nod. "It's right dismal 'ere now, it is. Nurse Coates 'as more bones than a snake, and not a single kind one."

Lark smiled. "Then you need some help. You need Viv back."

"Can you get her back?" Jenny's eyes grew wide in her smooth, round face.

That was more than he could promise. "Can you get me a chance to speak with her ladyship alone?"

"Oooh, that's a scary thing. She'll be right furious." Jenny clutched two great bunches of her apron in her hands, squeezing pleats into the crisp linen.

"She won't know you were a part of it. It's for Viv."

Lark waited while Jenny crumpled her apron and chewed her lower lip.

"I'll do it. Ye just wait 'ere a bit until I see she's in 'er sitting room. She likes to be alone there in the morning."

"Thank you, Jenny."

Minutes later Jenny returned with a conspiratorial smile. She handed Lark a silver hand bell. "'er ladyship's. She's alone and can't reach the bell pull by the wall."

Jenny led Lark up the servants' stairs and into the great room along the front of the house. From there, through open double doors, he could approach her ladyship unannounced.

He entered the darkened drawing room. Lady Melforth sat staring at nothing, her imperious face pale and blank. Even the red hair had a dull, sullen look, like a dying fire in the grate. When she saw him, she started, and reached for her little bell, the one Jenny had taken. He held it up. "Calm yourself, Lady Melforth. You are in no danger from me."

"You, how dare you come here! You should be taken up. Thief!" She shot a wild glance at the distant bell pull by the door.

"That makes two of us then, ma'am." He crossed the room slowly, his tread lost in the rich carpet underfoot. The silk pillows piled around her ladyship made a faint brightness in the dim room. He stopped as he had done weeks earlier where her ladyship must look up at him, and laid his copy of the proofs on an apricot-colored silk cushion at her side. She seized it at once with a shaky hand.

"What is this?"

"A new proof copy of your book based on Viv's corrections, an honest copy that reflects the work you did together."

With an unruly jerk of her hand, Lady Melforth flipped open the book, her hawkish gray stare fixed on the title page.

Lark watched as the truth of what she was seeing registered on her face. "You haven't permitted Dodsley to publish yet. Your conscience troubling you?"

"You are impertinent." She did not meet his gaze.

"I've spoken with Dodsley and advised him not to publish the original proofs unless he wants to face legal action." Lark pulled up a chair and sat facing her.

"What are you talking about?"

"That copy in your hands, printed up by a friend of mine, is based on Viv's corrections. I retain the original printer's proofs, the ones delivered here, with Viv's handwritten notes."

The sharp gray gaze swung to him. "You dare to threaten me. You! What are you? A common pickpocket...a nobody with no connections. Your ties to the duke a mere fiction..."

Lark met her disdainful gaze while she said what the world had always thought of him. The words were so much empty noise, a blast of fear and resentment that couldn't touch him. He was no hollow man any longer, no picture of a gentleman. He was someone new now, the man who loved Viv Bradish. When her attack faltered, he spoke again.

"Say what you like, you can't change what you did to Viv."

"Viv left me. She resigned." It was a plea for pity, but he wouldn't yield, not yet anyway.

"She stood up to you. She refused to salve your vanity, by pretending that the book was all your work."

"I taught her everything. And she has time to write other books, while I can't hold a...a pen steady." The imperious voice wavered between anger and desperation.

"Viv *will* write other books. In any case you can't stop

her. But you know she was glad to write with you. She admired you. She was eager to learn from you. And you betrayed her, used her."

Her gaze faltered under his. Her voice grew thin. "She was not supposed to fall in love. She was not supposed to leave me. She is well-served for choosing a charming villain. You're no better than that stepfather of hers."

"Do you want her back? Or do you prefer your cousins and Nurse Coates?" His voice was low, and he hoped, not unkind. The suffering brought on by her illness was real, but it couldn't blind him to the suffering of her own making.

"What do you know of Nurse Coates?"

"What does it matter?" Lark stood. "I know Viv. I know the difference between mean and kind, between judgmental and generous. She's a bit rash, our Viv, obstinate, maybe, tenacious, and fearless. She doesn't back down. Do right by her, and she'll think the best of you, as she once did. She might even return to London. If you have Viv in your household, you will laugh, you will pull the curtains back, you will find a way to go on writing. Together you will have adventures and shake up London. But if you let her go, you have nothing. If you publish without acknowledging her, you have a printed lie with your name on it."

From below came sounds of a bustle in the hall. He set the little silver bell on the table at Lady Melforth's side. "You may want to have Jenny or Thomas open the drapery. I believe her grace, the Duchess of Wenlocke means to call upon you this morning."

AN ORNATE IRON gate swung open on a tree-lined path to a red brick house with an air of substantial prosperity and a white pedimented door.

"Ready?" asked Wenlocke at Lark's side.

"Not at all," Lark replied, and passed through the gate. The house, Lark's mother's childhood home, was the end of the journey he'd been on since the great fire, a journey that had taken him to the Penitent Women's Hospital and from there to a private hospital in Surrey and a grave. From the grave he had circled back to a small church in the East End where the vicar remembered marrying Miss Ada Wheatley to Captain Caperton. Now Lark was to meet his great-aunt Beatrice, sister of his deceased grandfather Sir Henry Wheatley, founder of the Old Clock Bank. At every stage of the journey his friends had helped him, Wenlocke and his brothers, and Robin, Finch, and the others, their fellowship restored. Only Rook was no longer part of the gang. Soon Lark would get his old friend out of prison.

A lean, brisk-looking butler with a trim moustache admitted them to the house and led them to a light-filled yellow drawing room, where a tall white-haired woman in a pewter-colored silk gown stood erect and keen-eyed by the mantel.

"Your grace," she said with a slight bow to Wenlocke. Then, turning a warm gaze on Lark, she said, "My dear boy, you have no idea how gratifying it is to welcome you…home."

"Ma'am." Lark bowed. His throat ached, and he did not trust himself to say more.

"Aunt Bea," she corrected.

Lark felt Wenlocke's hand on his shoulder. "I will take myself into the garden while you and your aunt talk."

"Shall we sit?" asked his aunt.

Lark nodded. He should not keep his elderly aunt standing.

"I want you to tell me everything about yourself. Everything, good and bad, with no fear or hesitation. You must consider Wheatley House your home now whenever you wish it. But first, I expect you want to know more of your mother. Do you remember anything of her?"

"I remember watching her hands turn the pages as she read to me. She wore rings."

"Ah, she did like to wear rings, from the time she was a girl." His aunt did not prompt him to say more. She seemed content with what he offered. Maybe it was the place itself that bred a kind of peace, just a short distance from the noise and smoke of London, but above it, surrounded by trees and swathes of heath.

He hesitated over the next memory, the one it had taken so long to recover. But the mystery nagged at him. Everything around him spoke of love and comfort. The great gap in his mother's story was how she had become separated from such a life. "I remember watching her carried into the women's hospital by my father and a man named Sneath."

His aunt's expression sobered. "We do not know what happened in that marriage. My brother was against it from the beginning, distrustful of Captain Caperton and his intentions, but your mother would not be cautious or suspicious. That was not in her nature. She ran off with him and sent word that they were married and living in London.

Your grandfather refused to see her with her husband, and she refused to see him without her husband."

A little breeze came into the room through an open window fluttering the linen curtains. Outside birds sang. His aunt in her unhurried way took up the story again. "For a time, there was little correspondence except for a brief notice of your birth and christening. Then an alarming letter came, unlike the others, written in haste, and promising that everything would soon be well again. That was shortly before her twenty-fifth birthday. On that birthday she came into her full inheritance. The money was sent to her account, but no further letter came. Within a few weeks, your grandfather received notice that the account had been emptied and closed by Captain Caperton.

"Your grandfather went to the house they had taken in Chelsea, but the place was leased to new tenants, and none of the neighbors seemed to know what had become of the previous family. With your mother's disappearance and the failure of his efforts to find her, your grandfather became distraught. He ceased to care about himself. He became a figure of curiosity hereabouts, wandering, speaking only to himself, picking up whatever fell in the roadway, falling into more and more decay. He could not bear not knowing your mother's fate."

Lark understood.

"But it is not a day for sad tales. You are here now. You will have your own much happier story to write, soon. Come, there is a portrait of her in the music room, if you would care to see it."

"Yes, thank you."

His aunt rang for a footman. "We'll have refreshments in the garden, Matthew," she said.

Then she and Lark passed into a pale green room with a piano against one wall. The nameboard with brass inlays declared it to be a Broadwood. Above the piano was a portrait of a girl in white muslin gown bent over the keys of the instrument. She leaned forward slightly, her back straight, her dark hair gathered in a knot from which a few curls dangled, her eyes cast down upon the instrument, her cheeks round and rosy, and the ringed fingers of her right hand spread to play some chord. There was no mistaking his mother's hand or the garnet ring she wore. Lark could not resist touching his finger to the painted one. It was after all just a dab of pigment from an artist's brush, but he felt that by touching it, he touched the past.

"I'll leave you here, shall I?" his aunt said. "I will be in the garden with your duke when you are ready to join us."

He heard the gentle swish of her skirts and the closing of the door. He sat at the bench and opened the instrument, laid his hands on it, stretching his fingers apart in imitation of his mother's hand, and let the long-denied memories come. He had no explanation for why memories that had lain hidden in his mind should at last stir and parade before him.

He waited to see whether the memories would change him again. He had a name now and a lineage, not so grand a one as duke, but not a mean one, either. He would not take the name of Caperton. He thought briefly that he could take his mother's family name, but he realized that the name he wanted was the one he'd given Viv that first day. He was

Edward Larkin, the man who loved Viv Bradish. In the end it was the only name that suited him. He was impatient to go to her, but first he would free himself from all past claims.

Voices and laughter from the garden roused him from his thoughts. He closed the instrument and went to join the others.

They sat at a white iron table on a flagstone terrace above a sunken expanse of green lawn. He joined them, and his aunt poured him a cup of tea. "Now that you're here, I wonder if you might stay a fortnight or so."

Lark accepted the tea and glanced at Wenlocke.

"I can arrange for anything you need to be sent here," Wenlocke said.

"Then it is settled?" asked his aunt.

"You know," Lark said. "When I had no family, I invented an aunt for myself."

"Did you? You must tell me what expectations you had for this imagined aunt. Was she to dote on you?"

"Absolutely."

"Cake then?" said Aunt Bea, her eyes alight with merriment.

IN THE COOLNESS of a May morning, three groups of passengers waited dockside to board the *Arcadia*. A stiff breeze blew off the Thames carrying the scent of the ocean, straightening the ensign and jacks flying from the stern and bow, and rattling lines and blocks on the masts and spars. Clouds tore by above the crisscrossed shrouds and rat lines.

Crewmen moved about the deck while shoremen rolled barrels up a ramp and swung crane arms to lower dangling bundles into the hold. An officer on the upper deck oversaw the activity, while another officer and a clerk stood by at the ready to see the passengers on board.

Rook stood, stony-faced, among a group of single male passengers, easily a head taller than the others, wearing sturdy, serviceable clothes from the Fashion Emporium, which, Lark had learned, did a business outfitting those bound for the colonies. A bold woman or two from the raucous group of single women passengers called out, asking Rook his name. With laughter and shoving, the women pushed a freckled redhead in a blue bonnet to the front of their group. "Kitty wants ter meet ya, luv," was the cry. Families traveling with children made up the third group of passengers, talking quietly among themselves and watching the necessary preparations for such a voyage. The *Arcadia* would stop at Plymouth and Tobay for water, and then on to Sydney. If they were not required to quarantine before landing, they'd make it by September.

Lark waited with Robin and a copper from the Force to see Rook safely aboard. The constabulary were taking no chances on letting Rook slip away. Rook steadfastly refused to look at Lark or speak to him, though from time to time, he mumbled in reply to Robin. Lark did not expect forgiveness. A betrayal was a betrayal. He had kept his arrangements on Rook's behalf quiet. Rook knew only that he had a trunk full of gear and a place in Sydney with a wool dealer if he wanted it. Lark would do one more thing for his old friend and let him go.

THE LADY AND THE THIEF

The crane arm swung away from the ship, and the shoremen left her. Pipes sounded, and the crew scrambled into position, ready to cast off lines. The ship's agent signaled to begin boarding, and passengers shuffled up the ramp to the deck, Rook's group trailing behind the others. Lark removed his hat, slipped a borrowed cap on his head, and adopted a shambling gait to keep pace with the others. Where a little knot of men formed at the base of the ramp, Lark made his move, a quick dip into one of Rook's outer pockets. He shuffled to the end of the line, doffed the borrowed cap, and faded into a small crowd of onlookers.

Rook reached the top of the ramp before he stuck a hand in that pocket. He jerked the hand out, drawing with it a wad of notes, which he returned as quickly to his pocket. He spun around, his astonished and uncomprehending gaze wildly searching the faces on the dock.

CHAPTER TWENTY-FOUR

VIV HAD LITTLE time to be heartbroken. She did not think of her brief, false engagement above once or twice in the quarter hour. It did take a bit of resolution at night when the house at last grew quiet not to wonder who Lark, her mysterious lover truly was, and why he had made such a game of her. If she could only write, she believed she would forget him.

By her count, Viv had not written a word in nearly a month, not since a week after she'd returned. Somehow a regular writing schedule eluded her in her mother's house. Today she would begin again. A thin shaft of morning light fell on the bare wood floor as she reached under her bed to draw out her box of pencils and paper. For a moment the room she shared with Charlotte and Pippa was blessedly quiet. She realized how spoiled she had been in Lady Melforth's house with a room of her own and a desk and endless supplies of paper, ink, and candles. And, a thing she never had at home, time alone.

She had little to show for her London sojourn, but her fashionable gowns. As she had predicted, they had already been remade for her sisters. London's wide skirts had no place in their cramped Lennox Street rooms. Tonight, Charlotte and Pippa would wear real silks to the local assembly celebrating the twentieth anniversary of Waterloo. In a few hours there would be a parade along the Esplanade past a viewing stand erected near the old king's statue, later the tea shops would open, the assembly would begin, and the evening would end in a fireworks display over the bay. With luck her family would be out on the town for hours and Viv could work on her latest project, the idea that had come to her in front of the Penitent Women's Hospital. It was near enough to midsummer that the sky would stay light, and she would not have to borrow a candle from her mother's supply.

Below a door banged open, and the latch to the girls' shared room gave. The mingled scents of coffee and porridge and the sound of her stepfather's half-joking grumble carried up the stairs. He complained that Waterloo, the army's triumph, and not Trafalgar, the navy's grand victory, always got the parades and fireworks. Then the twins, Anne and Eliza, began one of their usual quarrels. No one seemed to notice that it was Viv's birthday. She knew that her mother had not forgotten, but she could detect no sign that the event would be mentioned.

"Well, we shouldn't celebrate Waterloo at all if there are to be fireworks," Anne said. "They disturb the gulls."

"No fireworks because of gulls! Whoever heard of such a daft idea! When did gulls ever save the nation!" replied Eliza. "Gulls are a pure nuisance. They interfere with the economy and drive visitors away."

"If the visitors had any sense, they'd not feed the gulls. Then the gulls would not dive at their hats and snatch food from their hands. The gulls would eat fish instead."

"They'd still be useless. Visitors spend money. Gulls only scavenge and leave droppings. I say, bring on the fireworks!"

The quarrel was escalating as it usually did between the twins.

"Girls," said their mother. "Your father is trying to read his paper."

Viv heard the rustle of her stepfather's newspaper and the snap of it closing. "This house has too many damned females. I'm going out."

There was a flurry of apologies, cut off by the slamming of the front door.

"Sorry, Mama," said Anne.

"Sorry," murmured Eliza.

"Eat your breakfast, girls," said their mother.

The front door opened again, and Viv heard Charlotte and Pippa enter. "You should see the Esplanade, Mama," said Charlotte. "It's very festive with bunting and flags, and the Assembly Rooms are nicely done up with flowers."

"And so many gentlemen and ladies," added Pippa.

Viv felt the happy energy return to the room below. She set aside her box and began straightening the sisters' shared room until a light knock on the door interrupted her. "Viv," her mother said.

"Yes, Mother."

"You aren't dressed for the festivities?" Her mother frowned at Viv's writing box.

"Surely, the nation's grand celebrations can happen without my presence."

"Perhaps," said her mother. "But this family needs you to find a husband. We really can't afford your keep. You must see how on edge everyone is when there is less to go around."

Viv started to say that Pippa and Charlotte would soon find husbands, but checked her words. Her mother's helplessness was as immovable as iron. Her coppery hair had grown thin and wispy. Her pretty face had a dogged, settled look of resignation. The once white kerchief around her shoulders was gray and limp with repeated washings.

"You cannot languish at home spinning daydreams. You must make a push to be noticed. You must dress in your finest frock and attend the assembly tonight."

"Yes, Mother." The idea that Viv would meet a suitor there was laughable.

"And put that box away. I can't have you taking candles from my cupboard."

"Yes, Mother."

Her mother stood frowning at her a moment longer, as if puzzled to have such a daughter.

"The girls will wait for you, but be quick." Her mother turned away, and Viv heard her light footfall on the stairs.

Viv tucked away the box. From the wardrobe she chose an old lilac gown with a white lace collar, a bit out of fashion, but suited to the warm day. When she had dressed, she pulled her hair into a loose knot at her nape. She was reaching for a straw bonnet of Charlotte's when Eliza and Pippa burst into the room.

"There's a gentleman here to see you," Eliza whispered in a voice Viv was sure could be heard below.

"Oh Viv," said Pippa. "You look like a charwoman. Let me do something with your hair." She took Viv by the shoulders, pressed her down on the bed, and took up a brush.

"And hurry," said Eliza, "because I swear Mama is struck dumb, and Charlotte is trying to flirt with him, and she's very bad at it." Eliza dashed off.

Two minutes later when Viv descended the stairs, she had to stop and grip the banister tight while her heart careened wildly between pain and senseless joy.

Lark, the object of five pairs of dazzled female eyes, stood in the dark, wood-paneled room where her family ate at a plain deal table, even now untidy with empty porridge bowls. Viv's gaze took in the rich chestnut hair, the deep blue eyes, the stark symmetry of his face with its sensuous mouth, and the wayward bend of his once-broken nose, his broad shoulders in a plain buff-colored linen coat, over a white waistcoat, and gray trousers that could not conceal muscular legs above the gleam of his boots. If she thought she'd forgotten him, she had been wrong.

"Why are you here?" Viv asked.

"To wish you a happy birthday," he said.

"We don't celebrate Viv's birthday," said Eliza.

Anne nudged her hard.

"No? I've come a long way." He turned to Viv's mother. "Mrs. Pennington, if it does not violate your family prohibition against celebrating, may I take Viv on a birthday walk?"

Viv's mother seemed to wake from her trance then. "Yes, Mr…"

"Edward Larkin. Viv and I met in London at Lady Melforth's. I meant to call upon her earlier, but business in town delayed me."

"And now?"

"I've taken a house in Brunswick Terrace."

Her mother rose shakily to her feet. "Brunswick Terrace."

"Are you rich, then?" asked the irrepressible Eliza.

This time their mother quelled Eliza with a hand on her shoulder. Their mother addressed Lark. "Yes, you may take Viv on a walk. And you are welcome to call any time while you are here in Weymouth, Mr. Larkin."

He turned to Viv, with that same cheeky, challenging gaze that had met hers in the drawing room of the Henrietta Street house. He offered escape and maybe something more, but she wanted no games. She would walk with him and find out his true purpose. She came swiftly down the stairs, swept past her sisters and Lark, and out the door.

Viv strode rapidly along Lennox Street toward the Esplanade. She didn't let herself look at him. "Who are you now? A fine gentleman or a pickpocket?"

"I am who I have always been." His voice was sober, sure, not teasing.

"A deceiver, an actor?"

"I think you've had enough of deception, haven't you?"

"And games." She stopped and faced him in the middle of Lennox Street with its shops and shabby lodging places. "Why are you really here?"

"To court you properly. You may have to help me, or we may have to figure it out together, as I've never courted anyone before."

"Court me? You can't mean it. You see me as I am. You saw my family's house. You see the neighborhood. As Lady Melforth told you, my parents can do nothing for me. I am nothing but a burden to them." Hot tears welled up in her eyes, and she dashed them away.

He took her by the shoulders in the dingy street. "I don't need you to come to me with anything more than yourself."

She closed her eyes against the tears. She wanted to believe him. When she opened her eyes again, there was no denying the warmth of his gaze. She had to laugh.

"Will you pick pockets to feather our nest?"

He turned her toward the sea, and took her arm through his. "It turns out that I won't need to, but why shouldn't *you* support *me*?"

"And how would I do that?"

"By writing."

"Hah, I haven't written a word in weeks."

"But you will. I will insist. I will bring you coffee every morning and demand a thousand words before you are permitted to leave our bed."

"*Our* bed? You do get ahead of yourself."

"We will be married first. In London, I think, from your aunt Louisa's house."

Viv was speechless. He spoke with such certainty and confidence as if he had arranged everything while her mind was struggling to catch up, consumed with questions and doubts. They reached the Esplanade with its grand hotels draped in England's colors. The wide bay spread out before them, the ocean gray green, with little peaks glinting in the sun and waves lapping the shingle. To their right along the shore stood a long line of tall white-painted bathing machines waiting for swimmers. To the east the shore curved out to sea and rose to a grassy headland.

He pointed. "This morning I found a knoll with a nice prospect in that direction. What do you think? A birthday stroll?"

"Very well," she said. "I have questions, you know."

"Ask," he said.

"How did you find me?"

"Lady Louisa was most helpful and encouraging."

"And what did you do with those proofs?"

"I read them."

"Oh, then you know." She stopped.

He tugged her along. "I know what Lady Melforth did, if that's what you mean. Is that why you resigned? Jenny insisted that you were not sacked."

"I hoped that she would change her mind. That she had only given into her fear that she'll never write again, or travel again. She's always been the Traveling Viscountess. She's climbed volcanoes, you know. I could not blame her for being afraid. We all make bad choices when we're afraid and there seems to be no other way, but I hoped, *hoped* she would change her mind. I hoped we could talk, and I could convince her that I wasn't trying to take anything from her."

"Then I took the proofs."

"Why did you? It made, makes, no sense to me."

He stopped and turned her to face him. The breeze off the bay ruffled her skirts, brushing them against his boots.

"I did not do it to hurt you, Viv. You were already hurt. I wanted to know what had caused your distress."

Viv nodded. That unwavering gaze made her pulse kick up. She began walking again, wanting to finish her own explanation. "There was a moment when it seemed that Lady

Melforth might change her mind, but it passed, and I knew I couldn't stay and pretend that the work was all hers and not mine. So, I came home."

"Have you heard from her?"

"No." She wondered that he would ask.

They came to the end of the last row of cottages along the beach front where a path led upward through tall grass into open fields. He gestured for Viv to take the path.

"Wait," she said, taking hold of his sleeve. "What did you do with the proofs when you read them? Why did you speak with Jenny?"

"Let's find a place to sit."

She looked at him in his exquisite coat. "You must not get grass stains on that coat. My mother would never forgive me."

She took his hand and dragged him along the beach to a line of boulders making a natural jetty. She scrambled up, and waited while he shed his boots, and came up after her, nimble as if he climbed rocks daily. A large boulder with a rough, sun-warmed surface accommodated them both.

"I don't understand how you could see Jenny. Lady Melforth meant to have you arrested. Your partner Rook was arrested, wasn't he?"

"My former partner. For other crimes. He is now on a ship bound for Sydney and a new life."

Viv stole a glance at him. He was perfect, exquisite, and seemed to have answers for all her questions. She wanted to undo him, to ruffle him the way the breeze dared to ruffle his hair. She was a mess in an old muslin gown and a borrowed straw hat, the wind pulling strands from her barely contained hair. She had accused him of deception, but that first day, she had been equally false, dressed in borrowed plumage, her purse full of pebbles.

"Did you ever love me?" she asked.

"From the first moment I saw you, like a piece of sky fallen to earth." He was staring out to sea.

"You could not have. I shot you."

He turned to her, and his mouth quirked up in a grin. "And changed my idea of who and what a woman could be. Will you marry me?"

"Madness! You are a pickpocket, and I am the dowerless daughter of people who cannot manage their pennies."

"Actually," he said. "I am a banker's grandson, and you are a published author, Viv. I brought you a birthday gift to prove it."

"What do you mean a banker?"

"Remind me," he said, "to tell you the true story of my life someday, but first, I want you to open this." He handed her a brown paper package.

Viv took it into her lap.

"Go on," he said.

She unknotted the string and unfolded the wrapping. There was the lady's guide to London. She shot him a worried glance.

"Open it. Look at the title page."

She did as he bid. There was her name, right where she had dreamed it would be. She turned to him astonished. Tears came and rolled down her cheeks unchecked. "You did this?"

"Happy birthday, Viv. Lady Melforth chose to do right

by you."

A plaintive cry interrupted him. Viv turned to locate the sound. Below them on the sand was a gull chick, with the dark gray plumage of a young bird. It limped toward the water, crying its sad cry, dragging one wing that didn't fold properly, leaving an odd trail in the wet sand. At the water's edge a white gull hovered briefly above the chick, then landed, bustled to the sad one's side and offered a morsel of food. The desolate cry ceased. The two birds nestled into the sand, facing out to sea.

Viv turned away from the birds to find Lark watching her. She wiped the tears from her wet cheeks. He reached into a pocket and pulled out something that flashed briefly in the sun as he held it out to her in his open palm, a gold chain run through a small lead ball. Her gaze flashed up to his. "You kept it."

"Do you love me, Viv?"

She reached out and took hold of his perfect silk tie and tugged it loose, exposing the column of his throat. "I didn't want to love you," she said. She flattened her palm against his chest. "I didn't think I did." She pushed against him. His arms came around her and held, but she kept pushing until they keeled over, coming to rest against the warm rock. Looking down into his face, she said, "I couldn't explain to myself why I was so out of reason sad without you. Now, I know. I love you, Lark."

"I love you, Viv." His arms tightened around her, and his mouth met hers, and she did not think she would ever stop kissing him, until she stopped thinking at all.

EPILOGUE

LATE ON A mellow September day Viv stopped in front of Number 36, Babylon Street. Lark had asked her to meet him there. He now spent his days at the Old Clock Bank founded by his grandfather and most recently run by his great-aunt Bea. The irony of a reformed pickpocket working for a bank made him laugh, but he refused to let his aunt down. Viv discovered that he was as quick at numbers as he was at picking pockets. He showed her some rudimentary ploys for lifting items from the unsuspecting, but she would never match him in that.

At the peal of a nearby church bell, she looked up to the narrow strip of sky above the gables and chimney pots and smiled at the direction of her thoughts. Everything reminded her of Lark. He had explained how the duke, as a boy, had named their gang of lost boys for birds because they lived free as birds on the rooftops of London. Since the duke's restoration to his title, he had attempted one by one to find the true parentage of his childhood companions. With the finding of Lark's family, the two men had renewed the friendship of those days when Lark, Viv learned, had been the duke's second in command.

She turned back to the books on the hanging shelf outside Number 36. Lark might be late, but Viv had no fear of

Babylon Street now. Behind its seedy shop fronts, book sellers kept their daring wares, the scurrilous pamphlets that the Strydes meant to stop. For the new book she was writing, Viv found the pamphlets useful, giving her a map of places in London where women lived other lives and told different stories. Viv was learning to prompt those women to speak their thoughts, and most of all she was learning to listen. She had begun by listening to Liza, a woman who complained that Rook's lagging cost her desperately needed pennies to feed her children.

Through Liza, Viv had met more women willing to talk about their stratagems for keeping their families fed and avoiding the workhouse. And through Viv, Liza had gone to work for the modiste Adele St. Claire, while Liza's children attended a school supported by the duke. Liza's new employment gave her a glimpse into the world of fashion, and she amused her friends with tales of that world's excesses. Liza and her friends joked that Viv must start a trend for colors that didn't show dirt. In their view if the fine ladies of London made it fashionable to wear clothes the color of potatoes or bricks, tree bark or beer, rust or mud, ladies like themselves would reap the benefit when those gowns landed in the slops dealers' shops in a year.

Viv was smiling at the thought when a hand snagged her arm and tugged her into the neighboring doorway to Number 36. A pair of strong arms came around her, pulling her into a close embrace. She looked up into the eyes of her love and laughed. She leaned back in his hold, studying his face, reading his expression. If she had to give it a name, she would call the look in those deep blue eyes...*delight*. He was happy.

She reached up, intent on giving him a quick kiss, but his lips clung to hers, his arms tightened around her, and for several minutes, she was lost in that place that was theirs alone. When he had kissed her nearly witless and released her, she guessed that he was up to something. She looked up a little breathless. "What?"

"I've brought you something."

"Something that couldn't wait for tonight?" Viv was staying with her aunt Louisa and uncle Oswald, and later they were hosting a dinner for Lark's great-aunt Bea, Lady Melforth, and the duke and duchess. The dinner was part of Viv and Lark's plan to connect their friends before their October wedding. With a new nurse and regular outings with Louisa, Lady Melforth's health and spirits had improved. The publication of the London guidebook, with both their names on it, had happily revived interest in Lady Melforth's earlier books.

"Close your eyes," he said.

Viv gave him a skeptical look but complied.

He took her hands in his and spread them palms up. Then he placed something light and square on her palms. "Open," he said.

Viv opened her eyes and found a small blue pamphlet.

FURTHER WALKS IN LONDON
A WOMAN'S GUIDE TO THE HIDDEN
METROPOLIS
WITH VIVIAN BRADISH
THE FOOTLOOSE LADY SCRIBE

She hugged the little pamphlet to her chest and reached up to lay her palm against Lark's cheek. He turned his head and placed a kiss in her palm.

"It is the first copy. Your publisher let me have it straight from the printer."

"Thank you." She said it solemnly, thanking him not merely for this moment of bringing her the pamphlet, but for believing in her, for changing the way she found stories, and the way she told them.

"Remember," he said, grinning down at her. "A thousand words a day."

"But only if you bring me coffee in bed every morning," she replied. A flash of awareness lit up the blue of his eyes at her meaning.

He offered his arm, and they stepped out of the doorway into the street. They had become adept at finding nooks and alcoves and even a secluded corner in the far reaches of Aunt Bea's garden, but Viv was impatient to begin their life together with all that it would bring them.

About the Author

Kate taught English Literature to generations of high school students, who are now her Facebook friends, while she not-so-secretly penned Romances. In Kate's stories an undeniable mutual attraction brings honorable, edgy loners and warm, practical women into a circle of love in Regency England or contemporary California. A Golden Heart, Golden Crown, and Book Buyers Best award winner and three-time RITA finalist, Kate lives north of San Francisco with her surfer husband, their yellow Lab, toys for visiting grandkids, and miles of crowded bookshelves.

Thank you for reading

The Lady and the Thief

If you enjoyed this book, you can find more from all our great authors at TulePublishing.com, or from your favorite online retailer.

Made in the USA
Middletown, DE
09 May 2024

53968063R00189